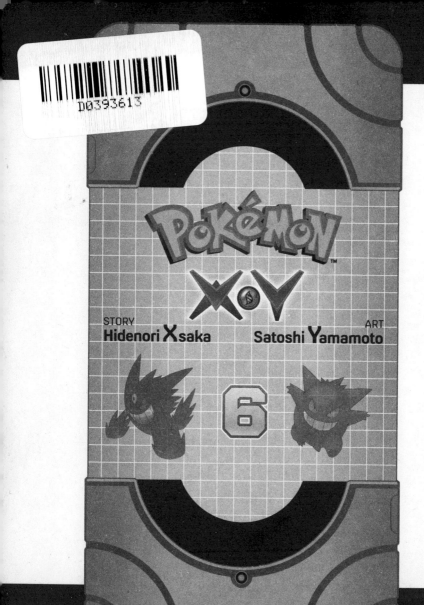

POKÉMON™ X•Y

STORY
Hidenori Xsaka

ART
Satoshi Yamamoto

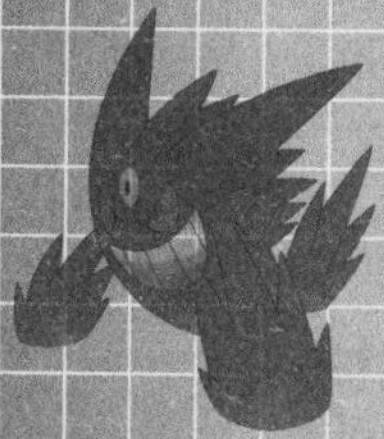

6

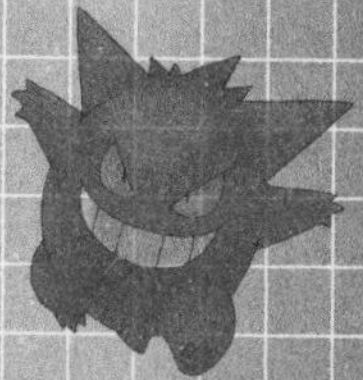

CHARACTERS

MARISSO

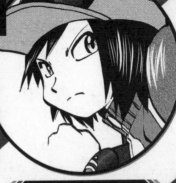

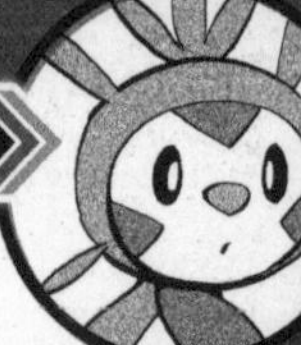

SALAMÈ

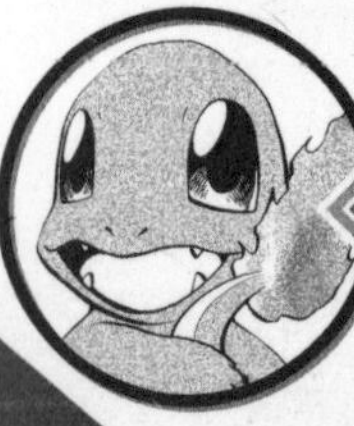

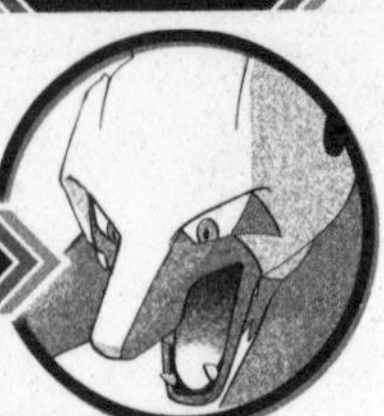

ÉLEC

X

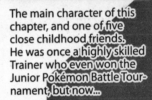

The main character of this chapter, and one of five close childhood friends. He was once a highly skilled Trainer who even won the Junior Pokémon Battle Tournament, but now...

KANGA & LI'L KANGA

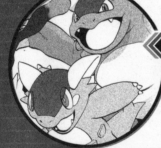

X's longtime Pokémon partners with whom he won the Junior Tournament.

OUR STORY THUS FAR...

In Vaniville Town in the Kalos Region, X is a Pokémon Trainer child prodigy. But then he falls into a depression and hides in his room avoiding everyone. A sudden attack by Legendary Pokémon Xerneas and Yveltal, controlled by Team Flare, forces X outside. Now he and his closest childhood friends—Y, Trevor, Tierno and Shauna—are on the run. X has a ring that Mega Evolves Pokémon, and Team Flare wants to steal it! On their journey through Lumiose City, Route 5, and Camphrier Town, X adds a Chespin (Marisso) to his official team, as well as a Charmander (Salamè) and a Manectric (Élec) who Mega Evolves. With the help of a computer technician named Cassius, our friends continue on their way...! En route, they are attacked by Y's former classmates from the Sky Trainer Training School! But then Y gets separated from the others and overhears Team Flare's plans...

MEET THE

Y

X's best friend, a Sky Trainer trainee. Her full name is Yvonne Gabena.

TREVOR

One of the five friends. A quiet boy who hopes to become a fine Pokémon Researcher one day.

SHAUNA

One of the five friends. Her dream is to become a Furfrou Groomer. She is quick to speak her mind.

TIERNO

One of the five friends. A big boy with an even bigger heart. He is currently training to become a dancer.

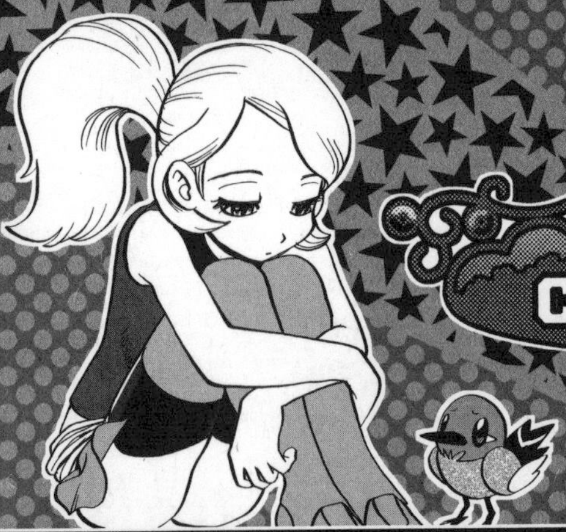

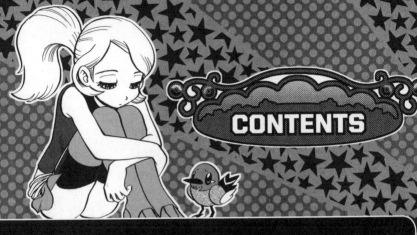

CONTENTS

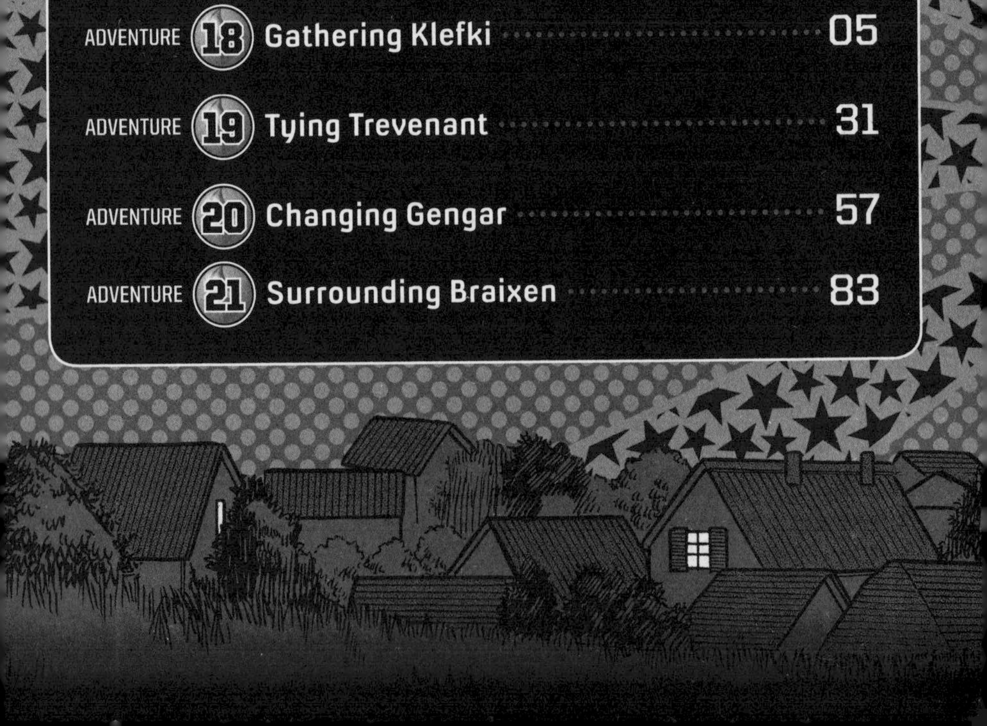

Adventure 18 Gathering Klefki

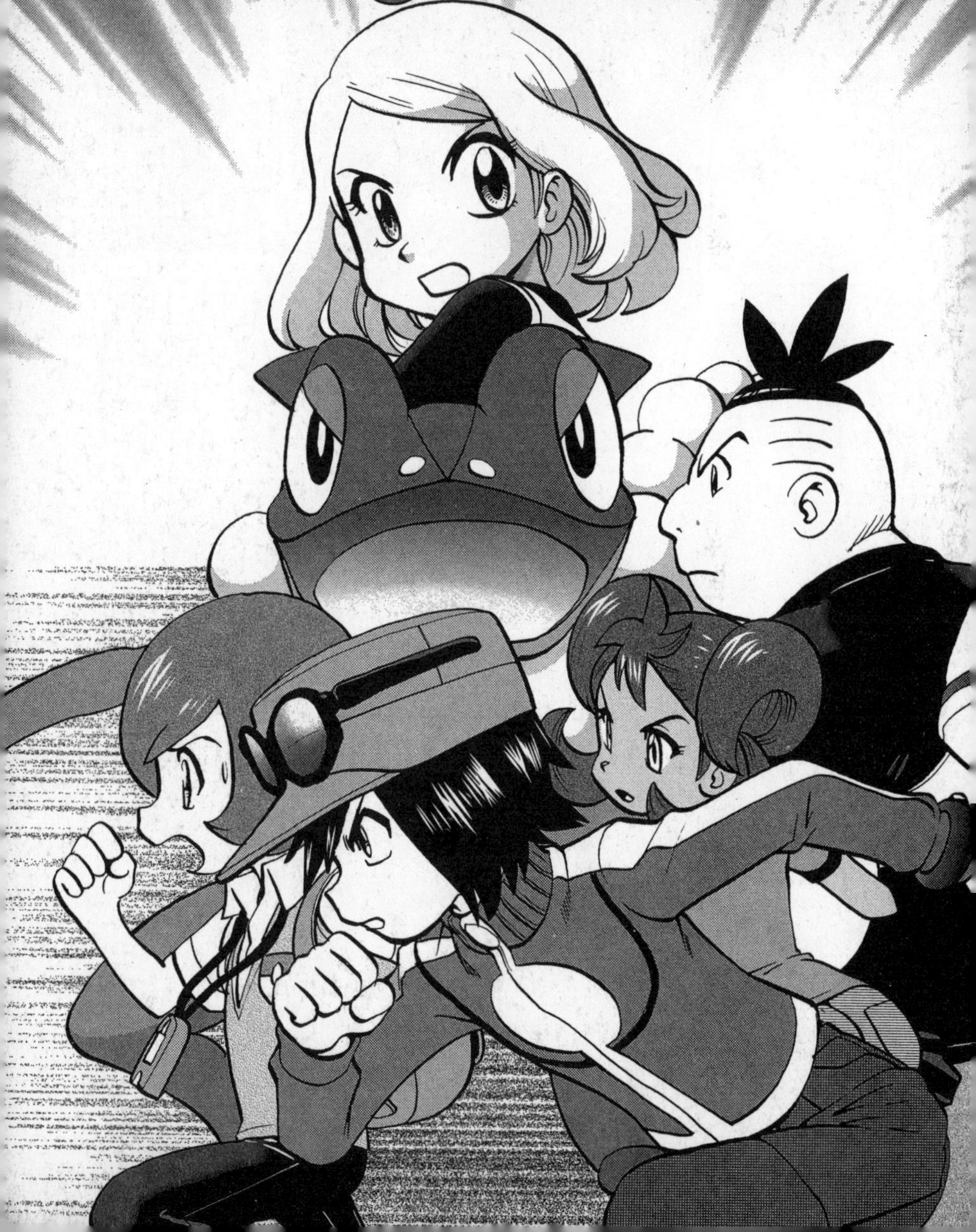

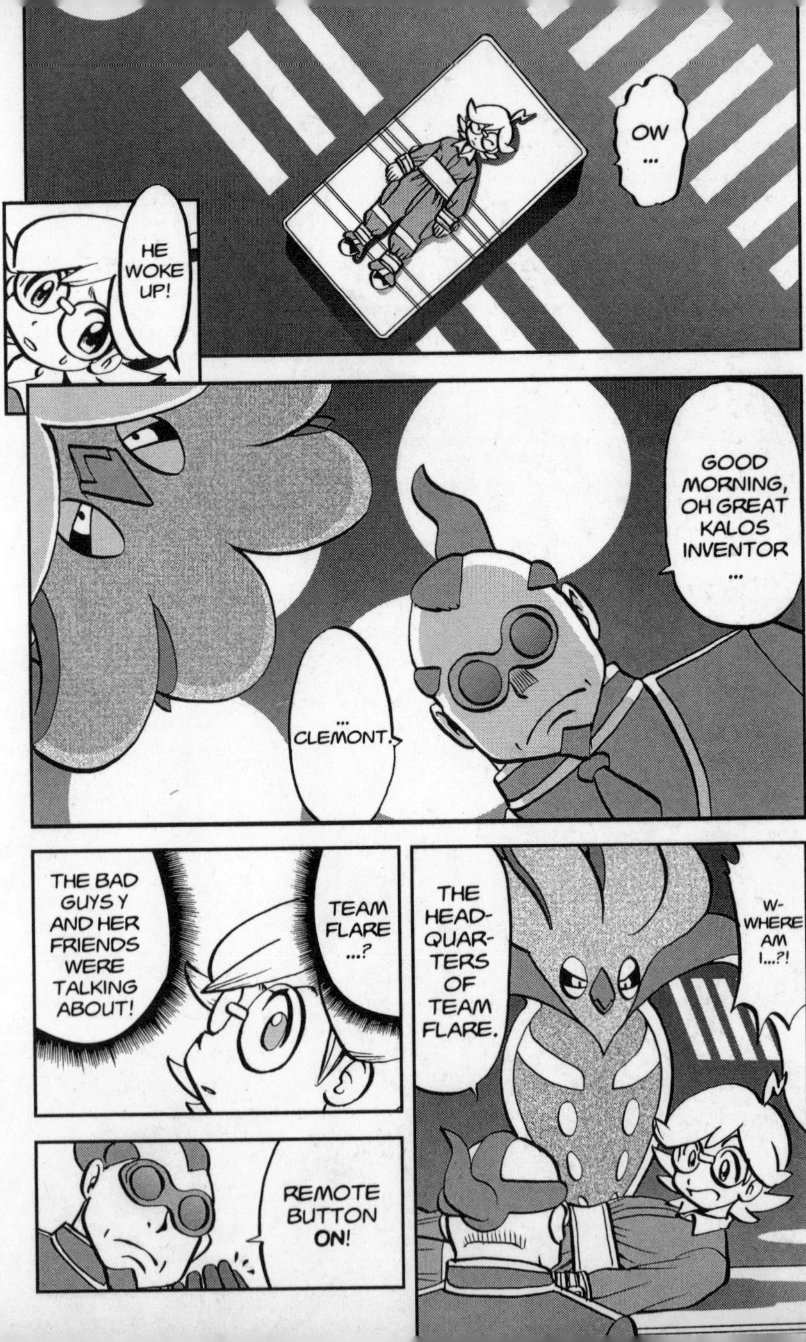
OW ...
HE WOKE UP!
GOOD MORNING, OH GREAT KALOS INVENTOR ...
... CLEMONT.
W-WHERE AM I...?!
THE HEAD-QUAR-TERS OF TEAM FLARE.
TEAM FLARE ...?
THE BAD GUYS Y AND HER FRIENDS WERE TALKING ABOUT!
REMOTE BUTTON ON!

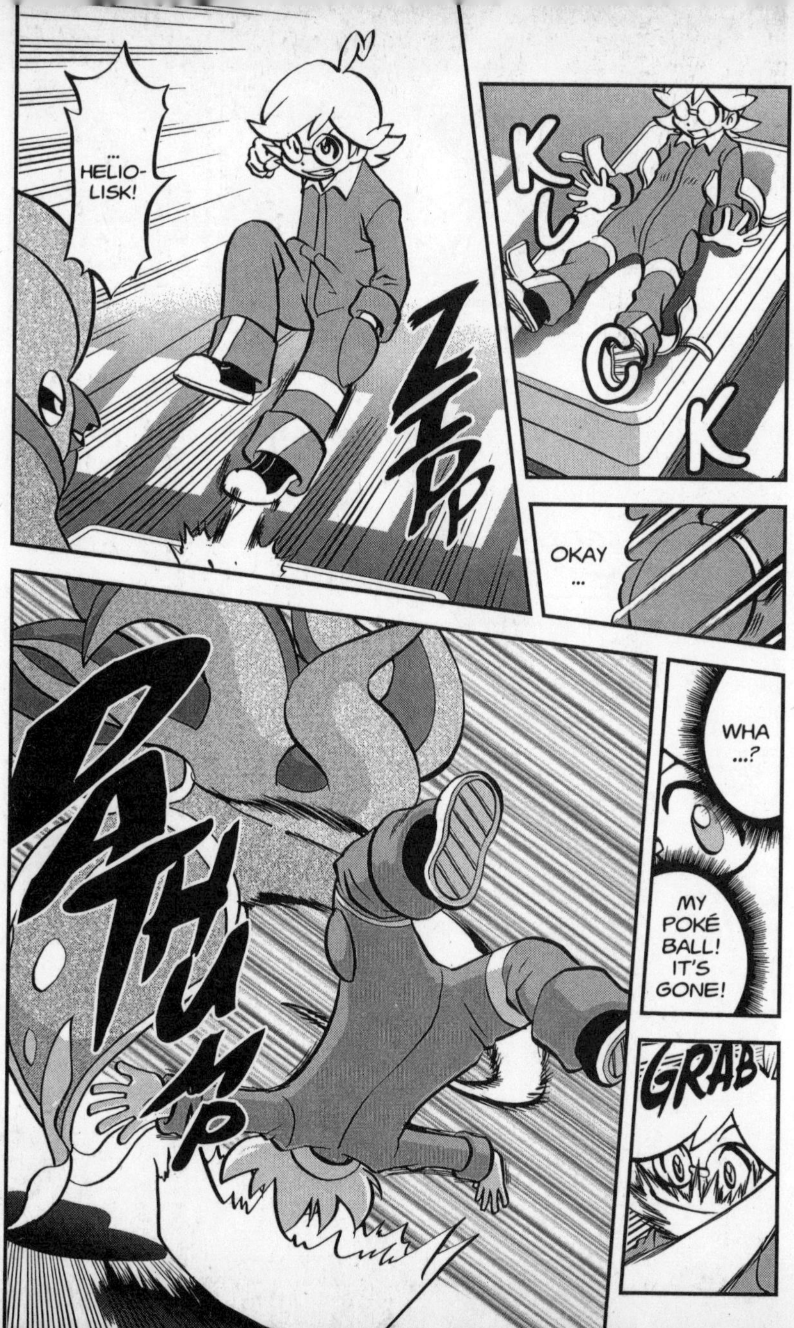
KLCK
OKAY ...
... HELIO-LISK!
ZIPP
WHA ...?
MY POKÉ BALL! IT'S GONE!
GRAB
THUMP

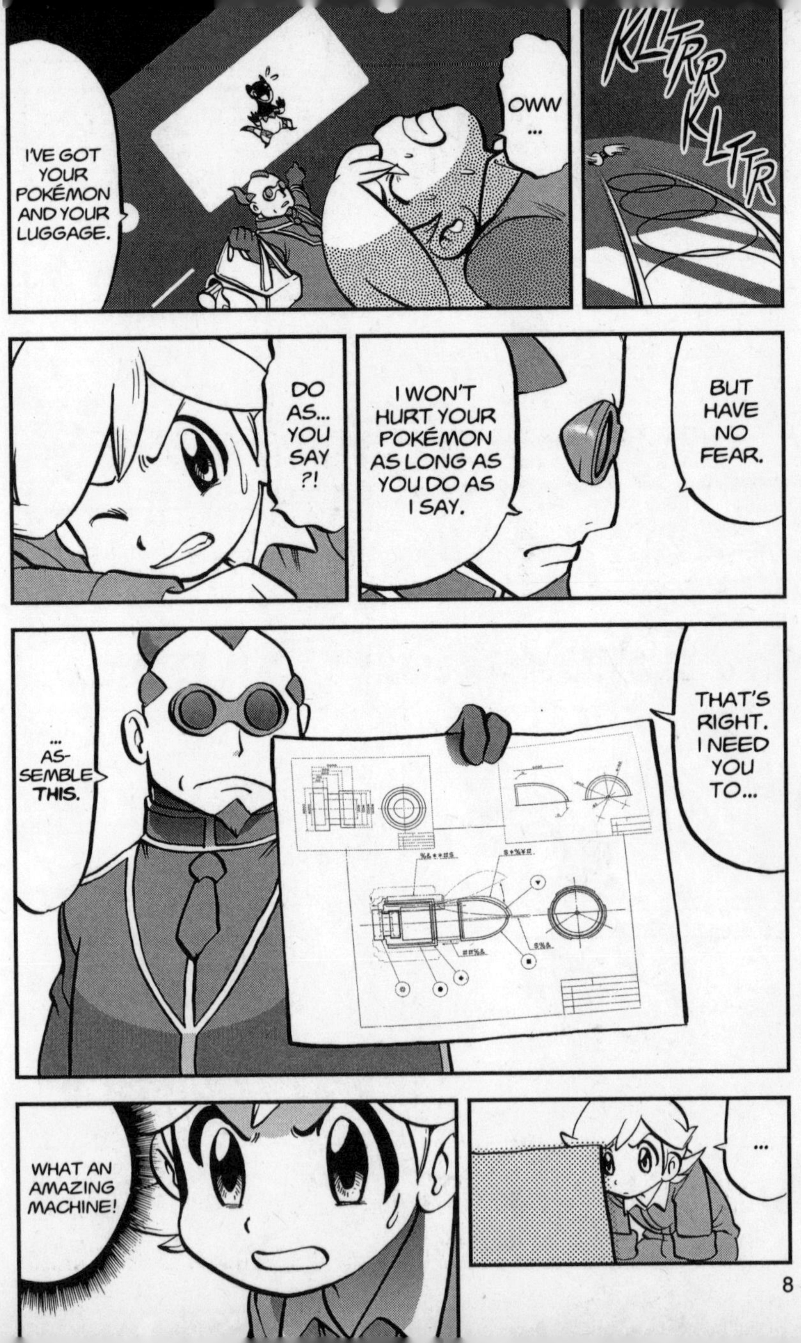
KLTRR KLTTR
OWW ...
I'VE GOT YOUR POKÉMON AND YOUR LUGGAGE.
BUT HAVE NO FEAR.
I WON'T HURT YOUR POKÉMON AS LONG AS YOU DO AS I SAY.
DO AS... YOU SAY ?!
THAT'S RIGHT. I NEED YOU TO...
... AS- SEMBLE THIS.
...
WHAT AN AMAZING MACHINE!

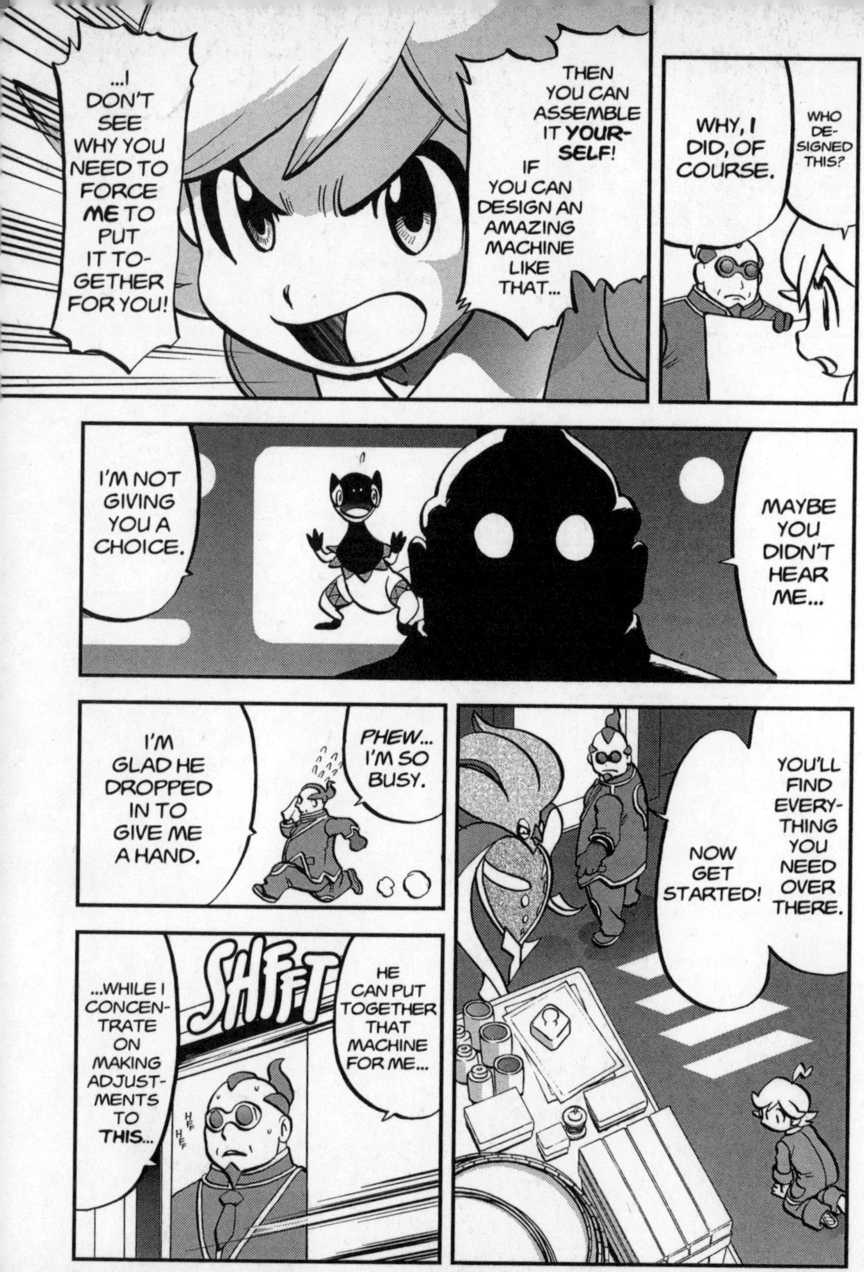
WHO DESIGNED THIS?
WHY, I DID, OF COURSE.
THEN YOU CAN ASSEMBLE IT **YOURSELF**!
IF YOU CAN DESIGN AN AMAZING MACHINE LIKE THAT...
...I DON'T SEE WHY YOU NEED TO FORCE **ME** TO PUT IT TOGETHER FOR YOU!
MAYBE YOU DIDN'T HEAR ME...
I'M NOT GIVING YOU A CHOICE.
YOU'LL FIND EVERYTHING YOU NEED OVER THERE.
NOW GET STARTED!
PHEW... I'M SO BUSY.
I'M GLAD HE DROPPED IN TO GIVE ME A HAND.
HE CAN PUT TOGETHER THAT MACHINE FOR ME...
SHFFT
...WHILE I CONCENTRATE ON MAKING ADJUSTMENTS TO **THIS**...
HEF HEF

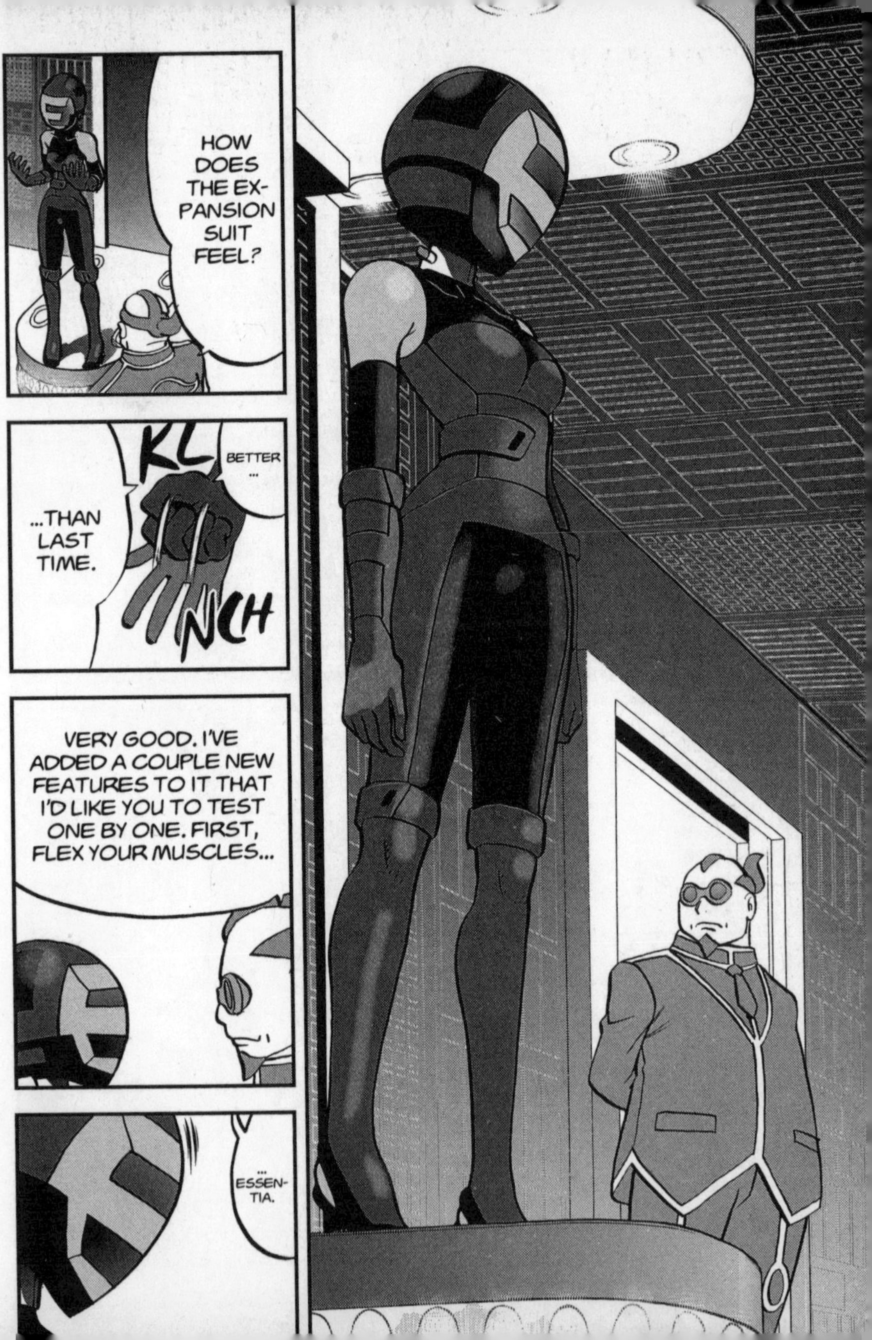
HOW DOES THE EX-PANSION SUIT FEEL?
BETTER ...
...THAN LAST TIME.
KLNCH
VERY GOOD. I'VE ADDED A COUPLE NEW FEATURES TO IT THAT I'D LIKE YOU TO TEST ONE BY ONE. FIRST, FLEX YOUR MUSCLES...
... ESSEN-TIA.

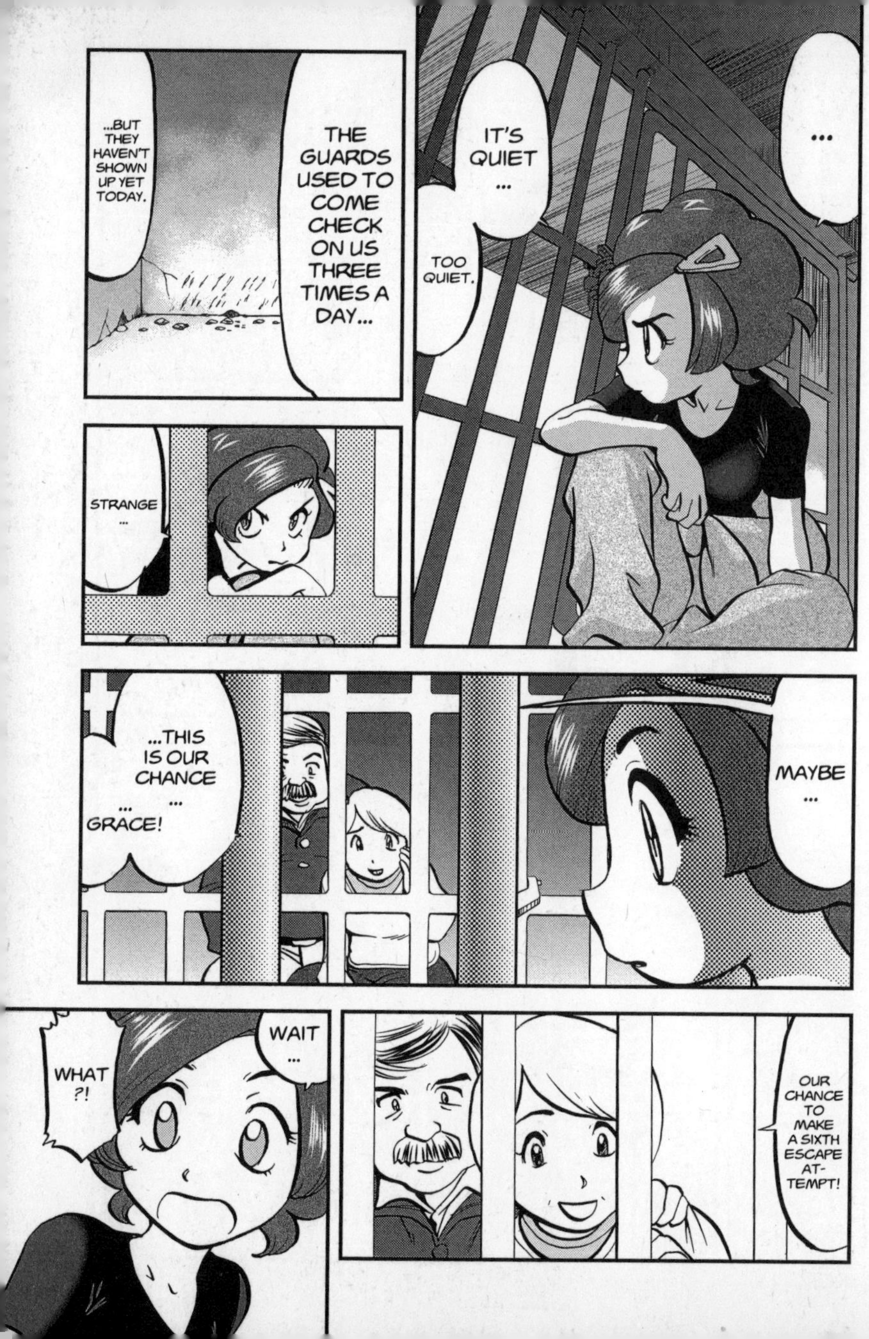
...
IT'S QUIET ...
TOO QUIET.
THE GUARDS USED TO COME CHECK ON US THREE TIMES A DAY...
...BUT THEY HAVEN'T SHOWN UP YET TODAY.
STRANGE ...
MAYBE ...
...THIS IS OUR CHANCE ... ... GRACE!
OUR CHANCE TO MAKE A SIXTH ESCAPE AT-TEMPT!
WAIT ...
WHAT ?!

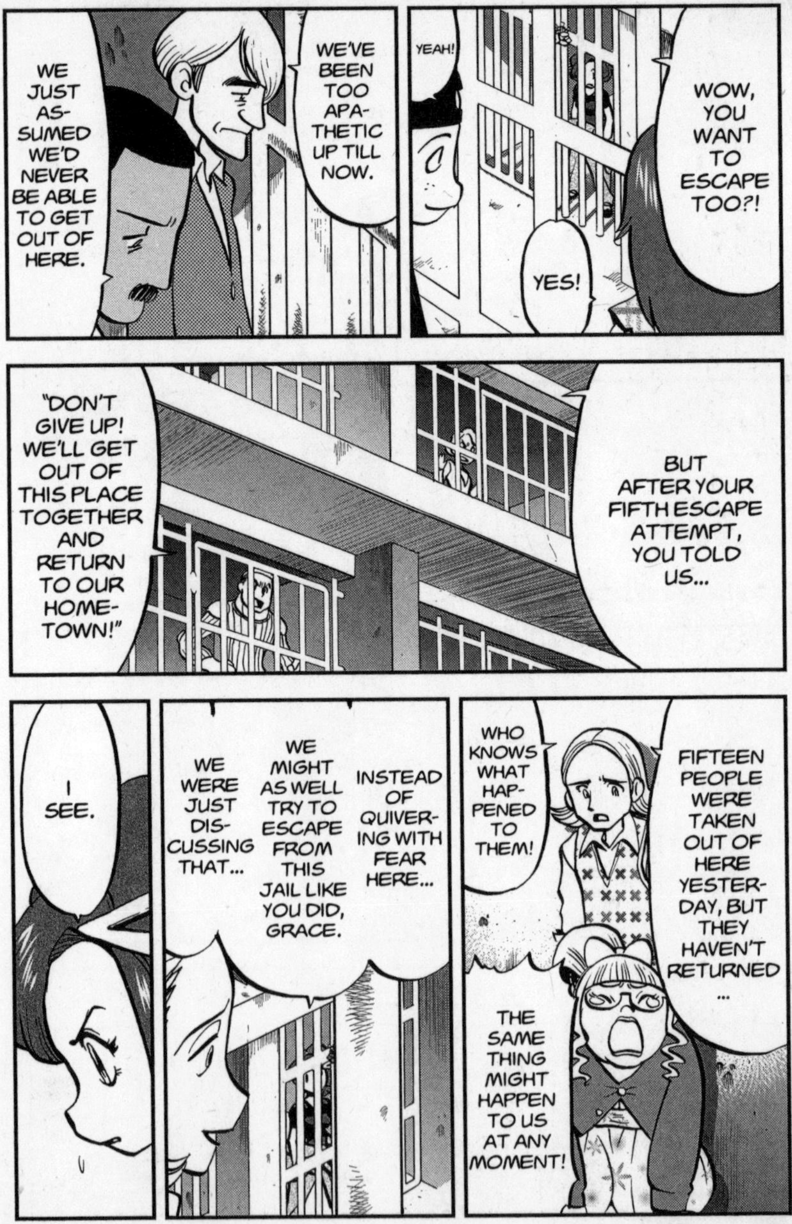
WOW, YOU WANT TO ESCAPE TOO?!
YEAH!
YES!
WE'VE BEEN TOO APATHETIC UP TILL NOW.
WE JUST ASSUMED WE'D NEVER BE ABLE TO GET OUT OF HERE.
BUT AFTER YOUR FIFTH ESCAPE ATTEMPT, YOU TOLD US...
"DON'T GIVE UP! WE'LL GET OUT OF THIS PLACE TOGETHER AND RETURN TO OUR HOMETOWN!"
FIFTEEN PEOPLE WERE TAKEN OUT OF HERE YESTERDAY, BUT THEY HAVEN'T RETURNED...
WHO KNOWS WHAT HAPPENED TO THEM!
THE SAME THING MIGHT HAPPEN TO US AT ANY MOMENT!
INSTEAD OF QUIVERING WITH FEAR HERE...
WE MIGHT AS WELL TRY TO ESCAPE FROM THIS JAIL LIKE YOU DID, GRACE.
WE WERE JUST DISCUSSING THAT...
I SEE.

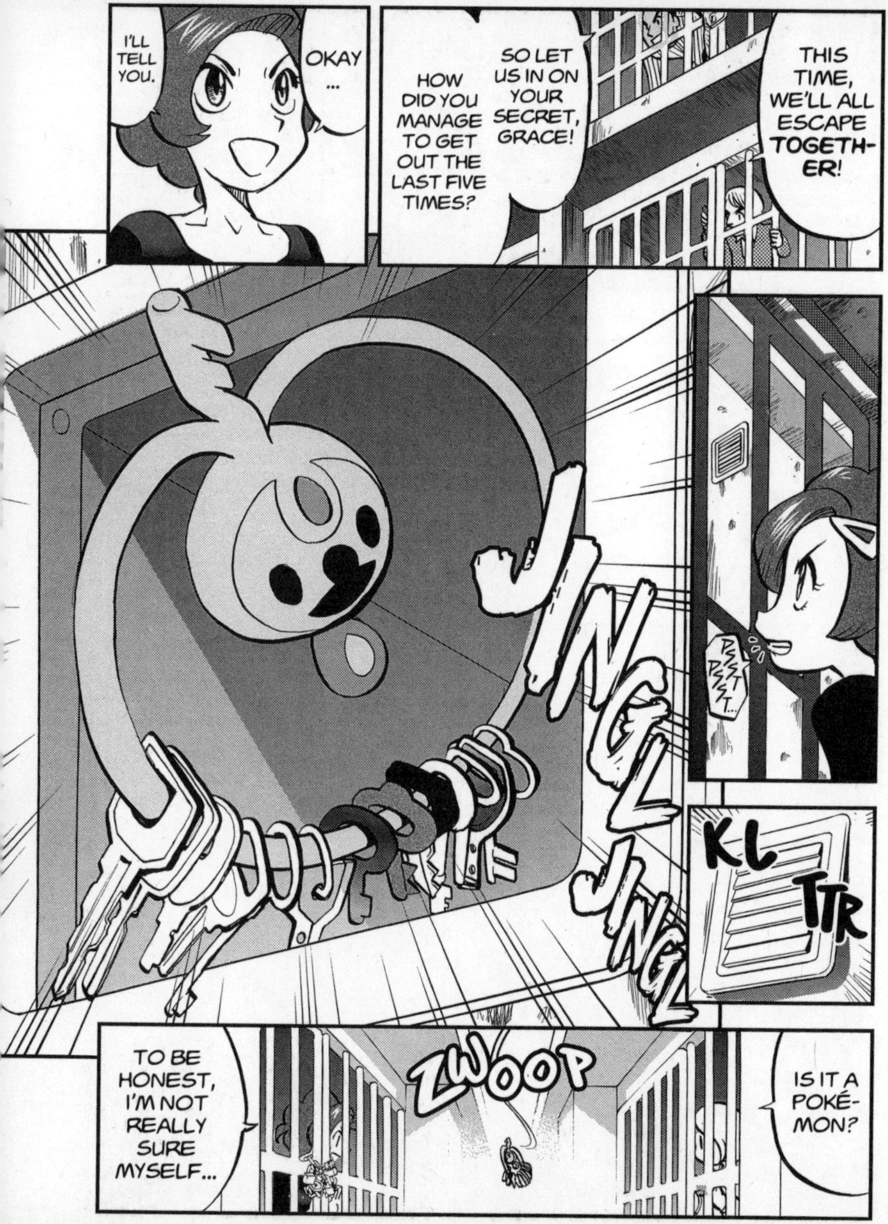
THIS TIME, WE'LL ALL ESCAPE TOGETH-ER!
SO LET US IN ON YOUR SECRET, GRACE!
HOW DID YOU MANAGE TO GET OUT THE LAST FIVE TIMES?
OKAY...
I'LL TELL YOU.
PSST PSST...
KL TTR
JINGL JINGL
IS IT A POKÉ-MON?
ZWOOP
TO BE HONEST, I'M NOT REALLY SURE MYSELF...

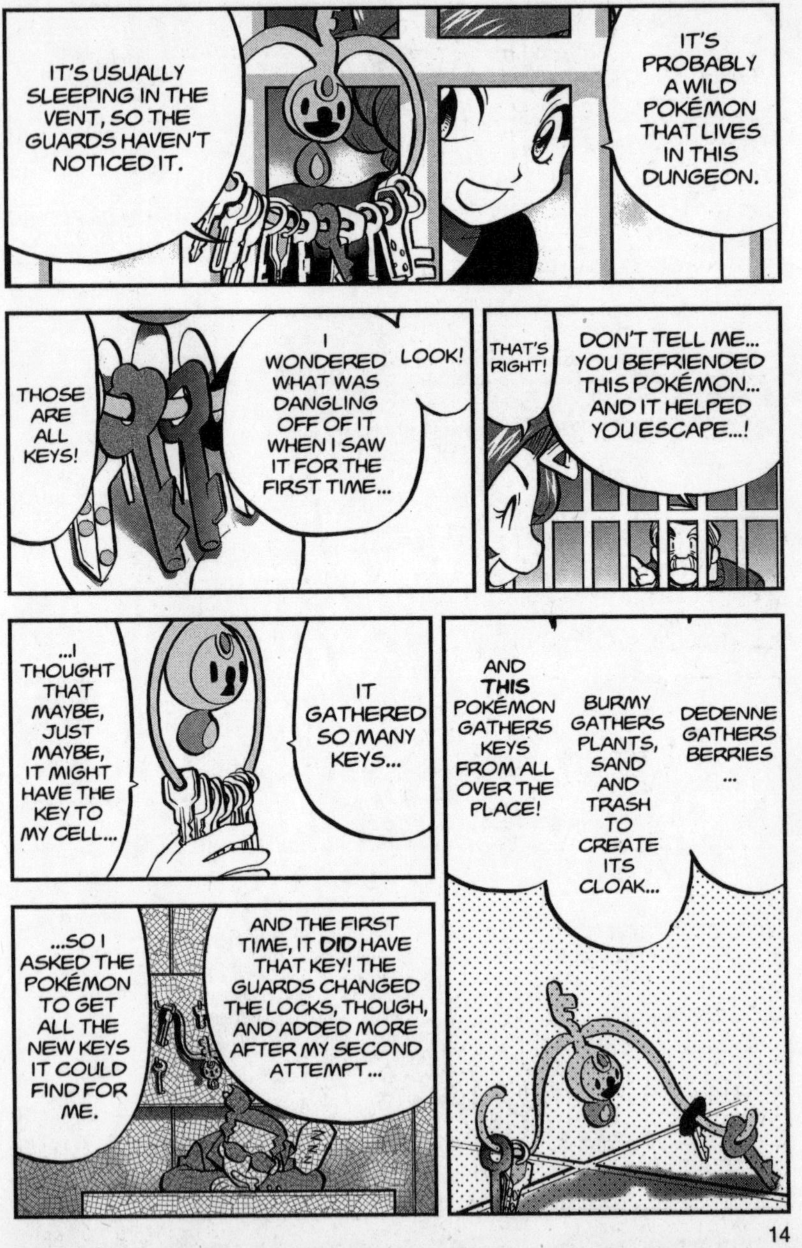
IT'S PROBABLY A WILD POKÉMON THAT LIVES IN THIS DUNGEON.
IT'S USUALLY SLEEPING IN THE VENT, SO THE GUARDS HAVEN'T NOTICED IT.
DON'T TELL ME... YOU BEFRIENDED THIS POKÉMON... AND IT HELPED YOU ESCAPE...!
THAT'S RIGHT!
LOOK!
I WONDERED WHAT WAS DANGLING OFF OF IT WHEN I SAW IT FOR THE FIRST TIME...
THOSE ARE ALL KEYS!
DEDENNE GATHERS BERRIES ...
BURMY GATHERS PLANTS, SAND AND TRASH TO CREATE ITS CLOAK...
AND THIS POKÉMON GATHERS KEYS FROM ALL OVER THE PLACE!
IT GATHERED SO MANY KEYS...
...I THOUGHT THAT MAYBE, JUST MAYBE, IT MIGHT HAVE THE KEY TO MY CELL...
AND THE FIRST TIME, IT DID HAVE THAT KEY! THE GUARDS CHANGED THE LOCKS, THOUGH, AND ADDED MORE AFTER MY SECOND ATTEMPT...
...SO I ASKED THE POKÉMON TO GET ALL THE NEW KEYS IT COULD FIND FOR ME.

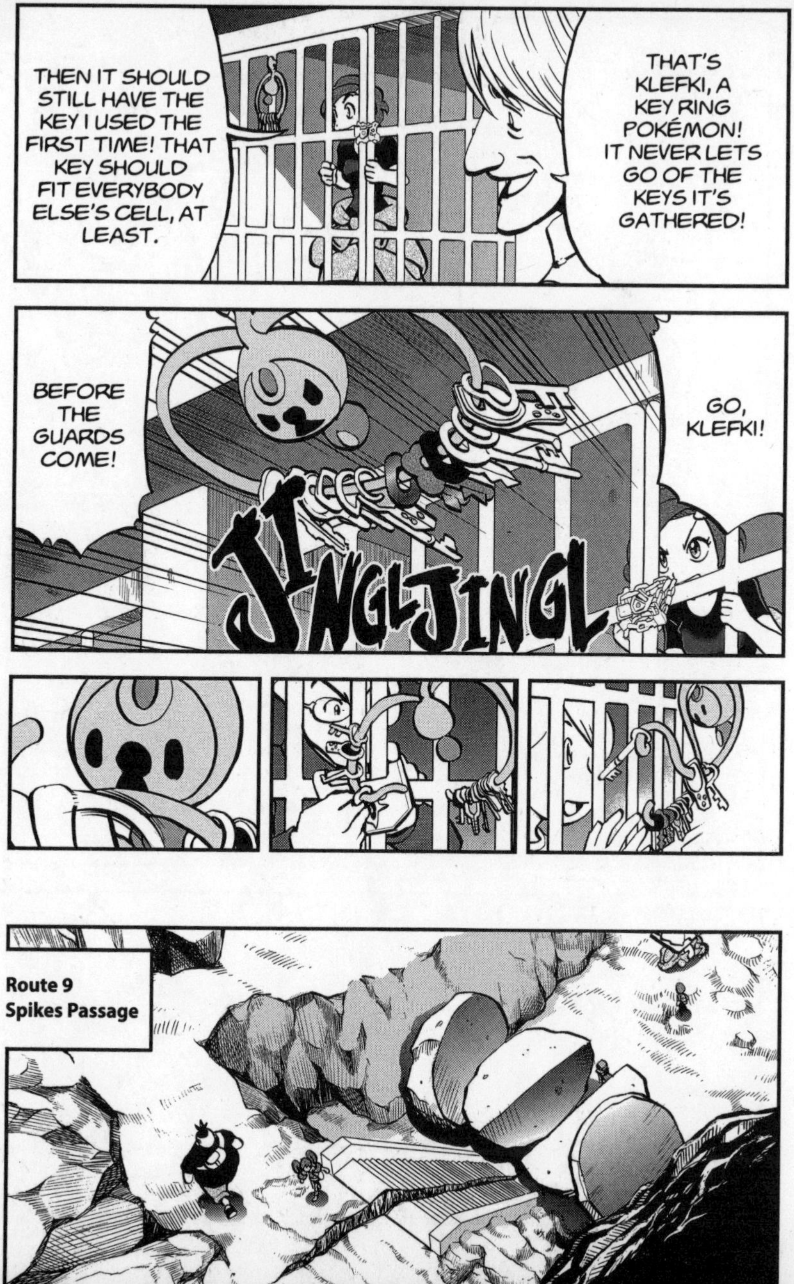
THAT'S KLEFKI, A KEY RING POKÉMON! IT NEVER LETS GO OF THE KEYS IT'S GATHERED!
THEN IT SHOULD STILL HAVE THE KEY I USED THE FIRST TIME! THAT KEY SHOULD FIT EVERYBODY ELSE'S CELL, AT LEAST.
GO, KLEFKI!
BEFORE THE GUARDS COME!
JINGLJINGL
Route 9
Spikes Passage

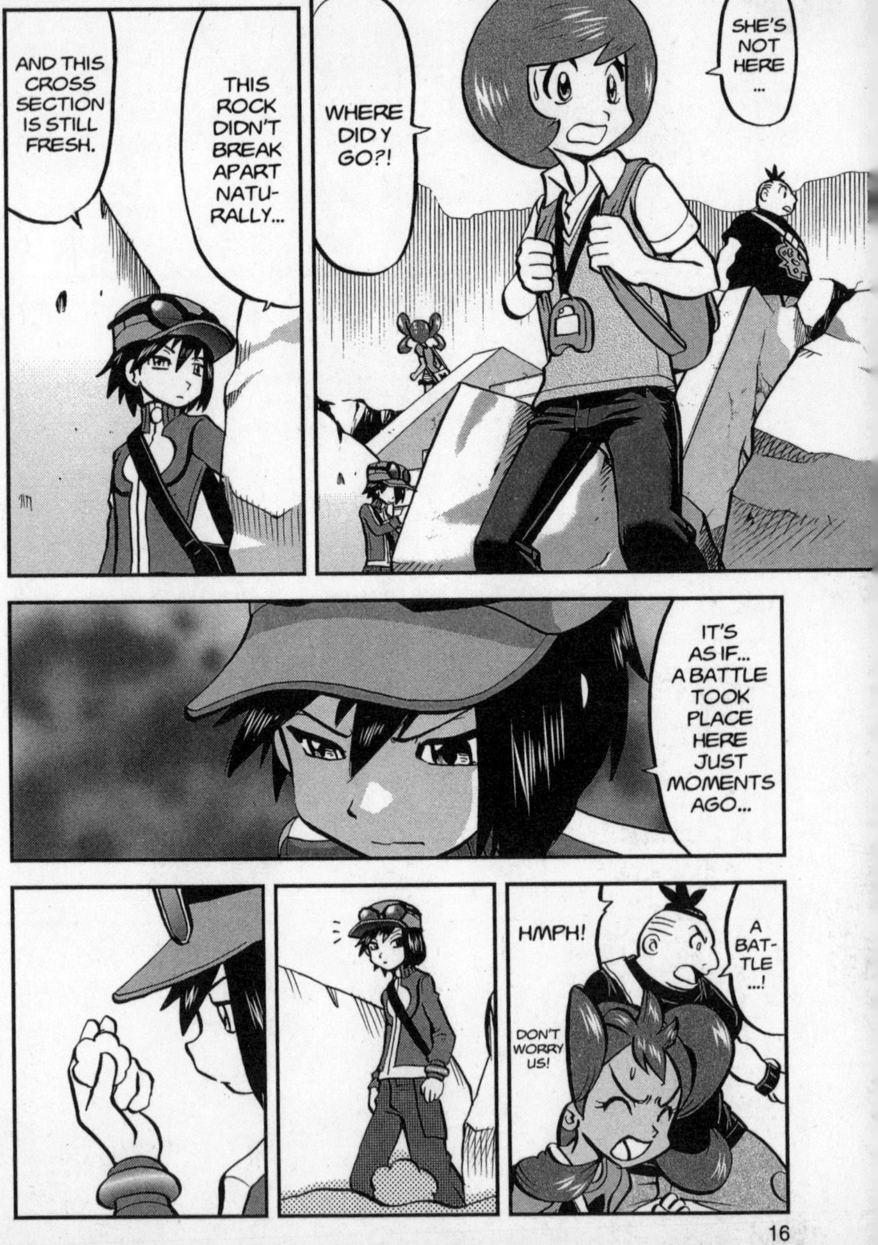
SHE'S NOT HERE ...
WHERE DID Y GO?!
THIS ROCK DIDN'T BREAK APART NATU-RALLY...
AND THIS CROSS SECTION IS STILL FRESH.
IT'S AS IF... A BATTLE TOOK PLACE HERE JUST MOMENTS AGO...
A BAT-TLE ...!
HMPH!
DON'T WORRY US!

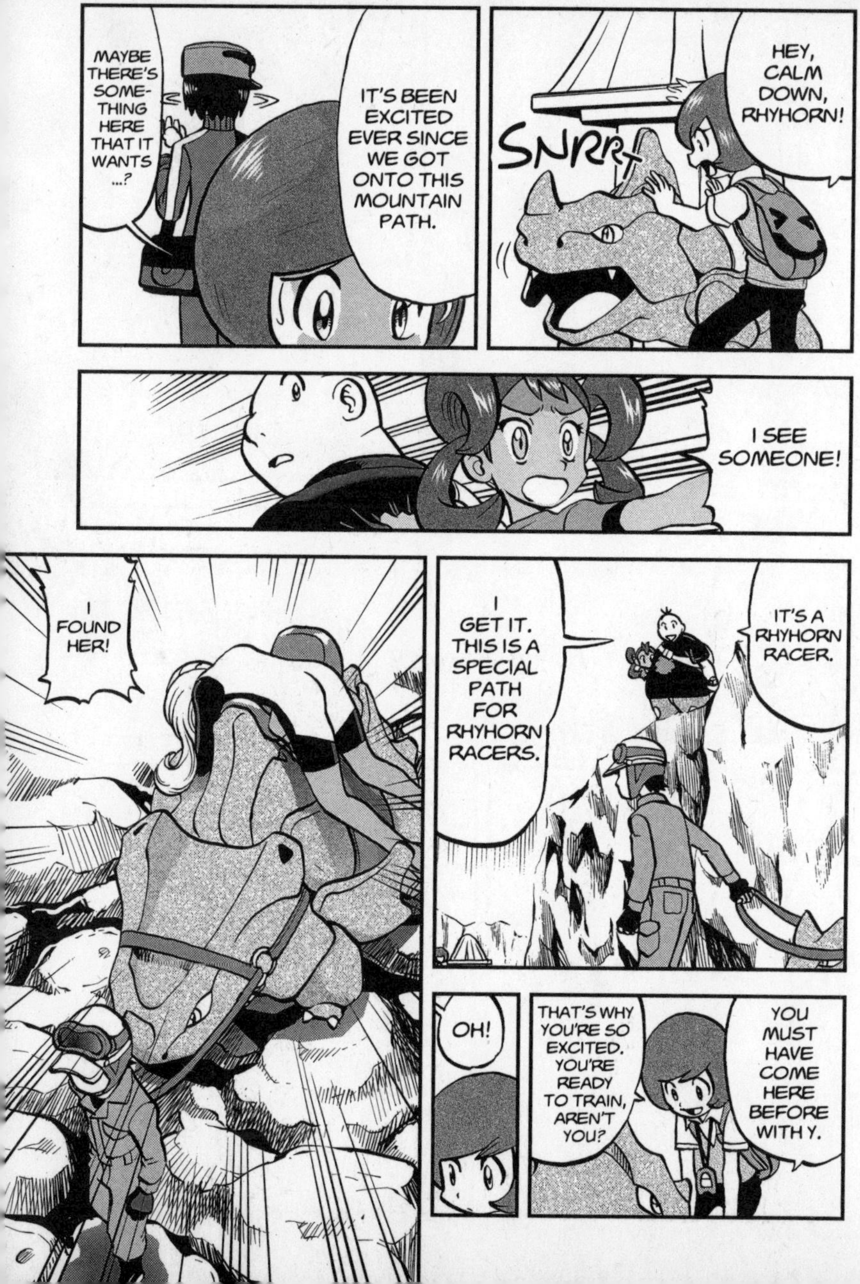
HEY, CALM DOWN, RHYHORN!
SNRRT
IT'S BEEN EXCITED EVER SINCE WE GOT ONTO THIS MOUNTAIN PATH.
MAYBE THERE'S SOME-THING HERE THAT IT WANTS ...?
I SEE SOMEONE!
IT'S A RHYHORN RACER.
I GET IT. THIS IS A SPECIAL PATH FOR RHYHORN RACERS.
YOU MUST HAVE COME HERE BEFORE WITH Y.
THAT'S WHY YOU'RE SO EXCITED. YOU'RE READY TO TRAIN, AREN'T YOU?
OH!
I FOUND HER!

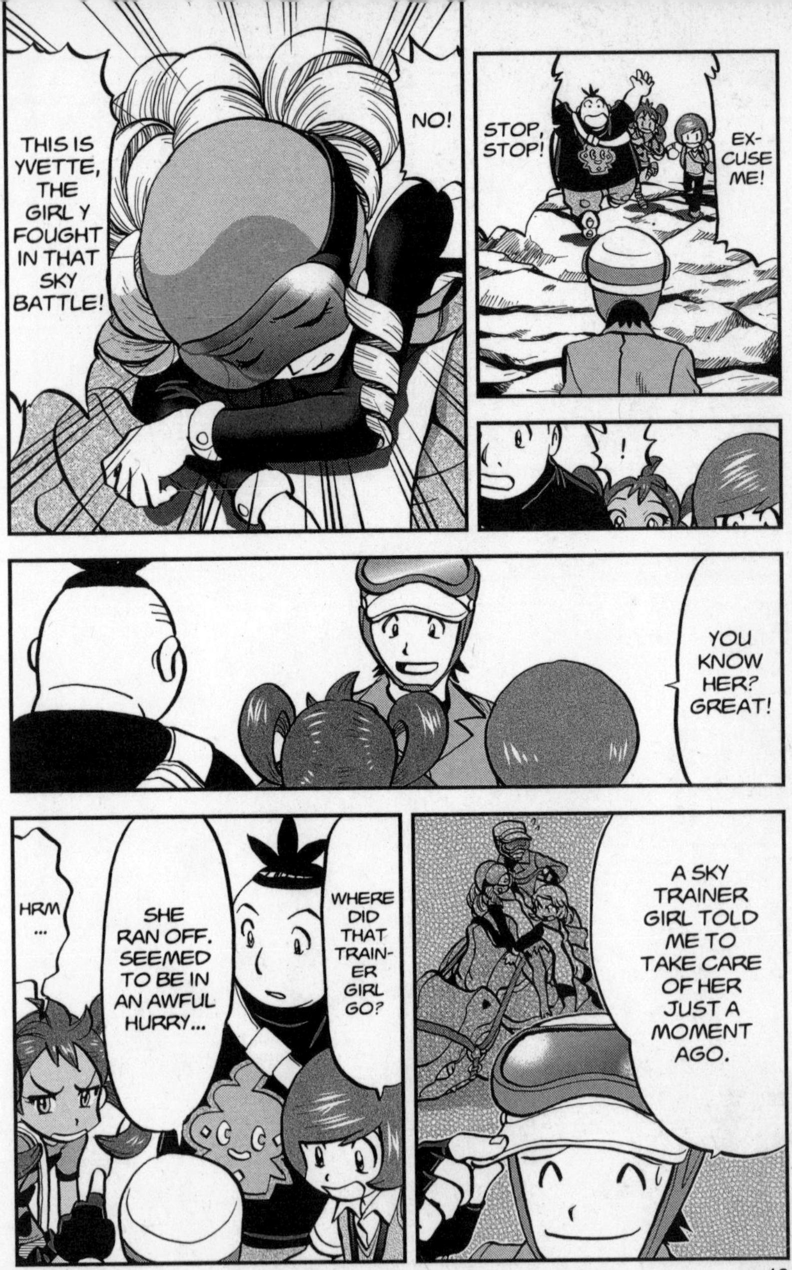
EX-CUSE ME!
STOP, STOP!
!
NO!
THIS IS YVETTE, THE GIRL Y FOUGHT IN THAT SKY BATTLE!
YOU KNOW HER? GREAT!
A SKY TRAINER GIRL TOLD ME TO TAKE CARE OF HER JUST A MOMENT AGO.
WHERE DID THAT TRAIN-ER GIRL GO?
SHE RAN OFF. SEEMED TO BE IN AN AWFUL HURRY...
HRM ...

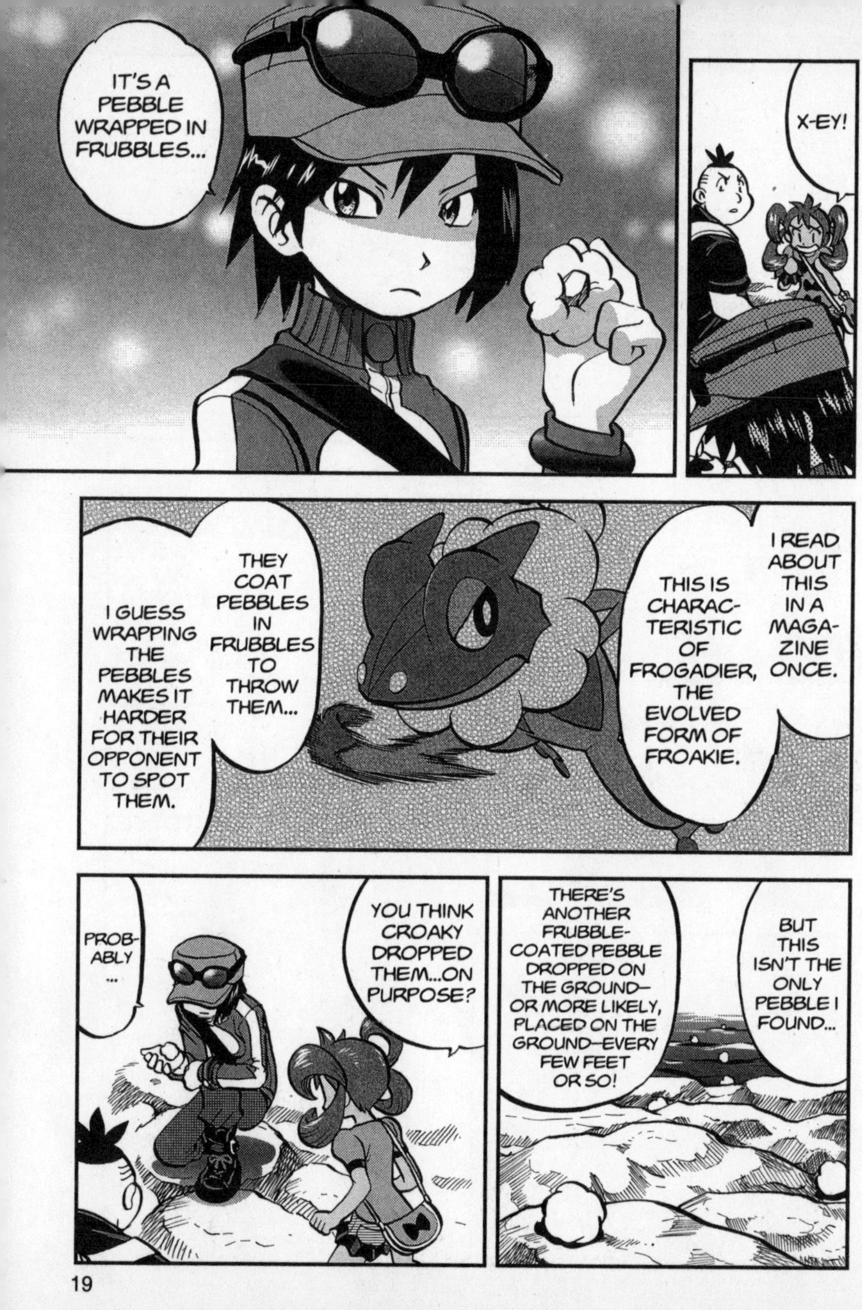
X-EY!
IT'S A PEBBLE WRAPPED IN FRUBBLES...
I READ ABOUT THIS IN A MAGAZINE ONCE.
THIS IS CHARACTERISTIC OF FROGADIER, THE EVOLVED FORM OF FROAKIE.
THEY COAT PEBBLES IN FRUBBLES TO THROW THEM...
I GUESS WRAPPING THE PEBBLES MAKES IT HARDER FOR THEIR OPPONENT TO SPOT THEM.
BUT THIS ISN'T THE ONLY PEBBLE I FOUND...
THERE'S ANOTHER FRUBBLE-COATED PEBBLE DROPPED ON THE GROUND—OR MORE LIKELY, PLACED ON THE GROUND—EVERY FEW FEET OR SO!
YOU THINK CROAKY DROPPED THEM...ON PURPOSE?
PROBABLY...

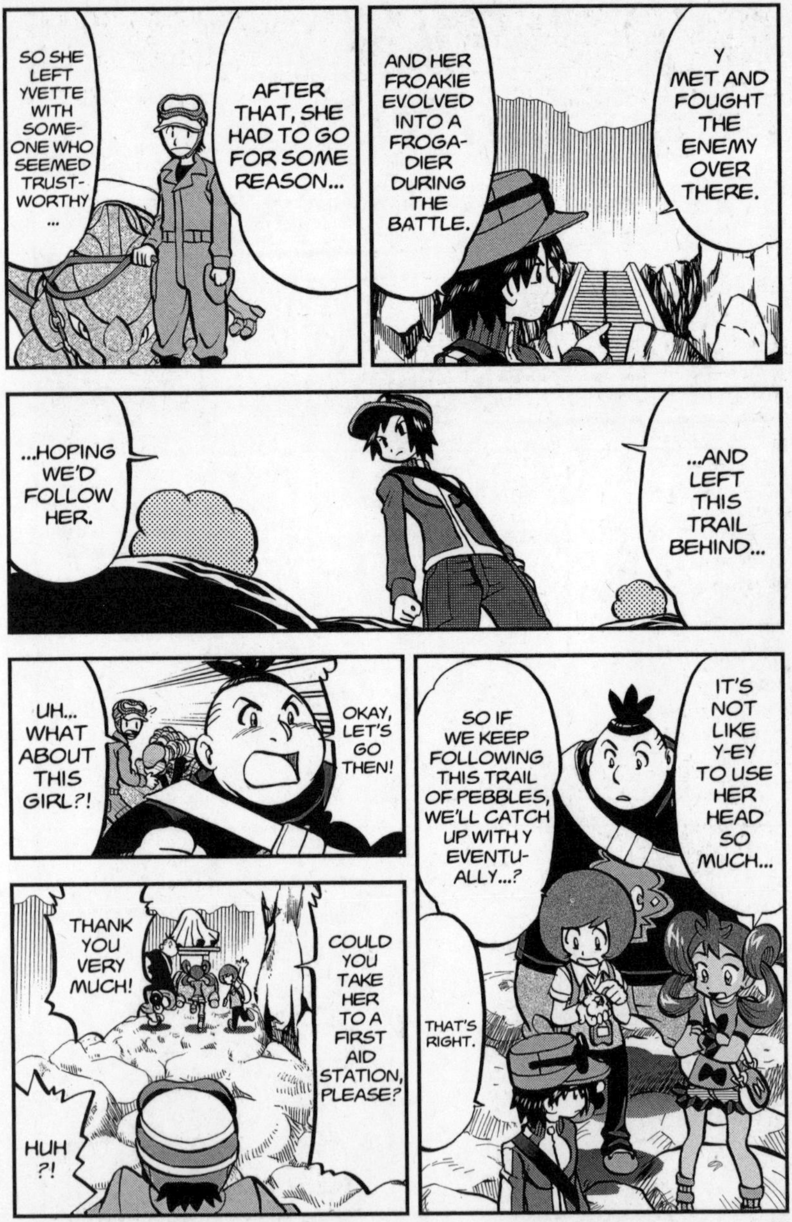
Y MET AND FOUGHT THE ENEMY OVER THERE.
AND HER FROAKIE EVOLVED INTO A FROGADIER DURING THE BATTLE.
AFTER THAT, SHE HAD TO GO FOR SOME REASON...
SO SHE LEFT YVETTE WITH SOMEONE WHO SEEMED TRUSTWORTHY...
...AND LEFT THIS TRAIL BEHIND...
...HOPING WE'D FOLLOW HER.
IT'S NOT LIKE Y-EY TO USE HER HEAD SO MUCH...
SO IF WE KEEP FOLLOWING THIS TRAIL OF PEBBLES, WE'LL CATCH UP WITH Y EVENTUALLY...?
THAT'S RIGHT.
OKAY, LET'S GO THEN!
UH... WHAT ABOUT THIS GIRL?!
COULD YOU TAKE HER TO A FIRST AID STATION, PLEASE?
THANK YOU VERY MUCH!
HUH?!

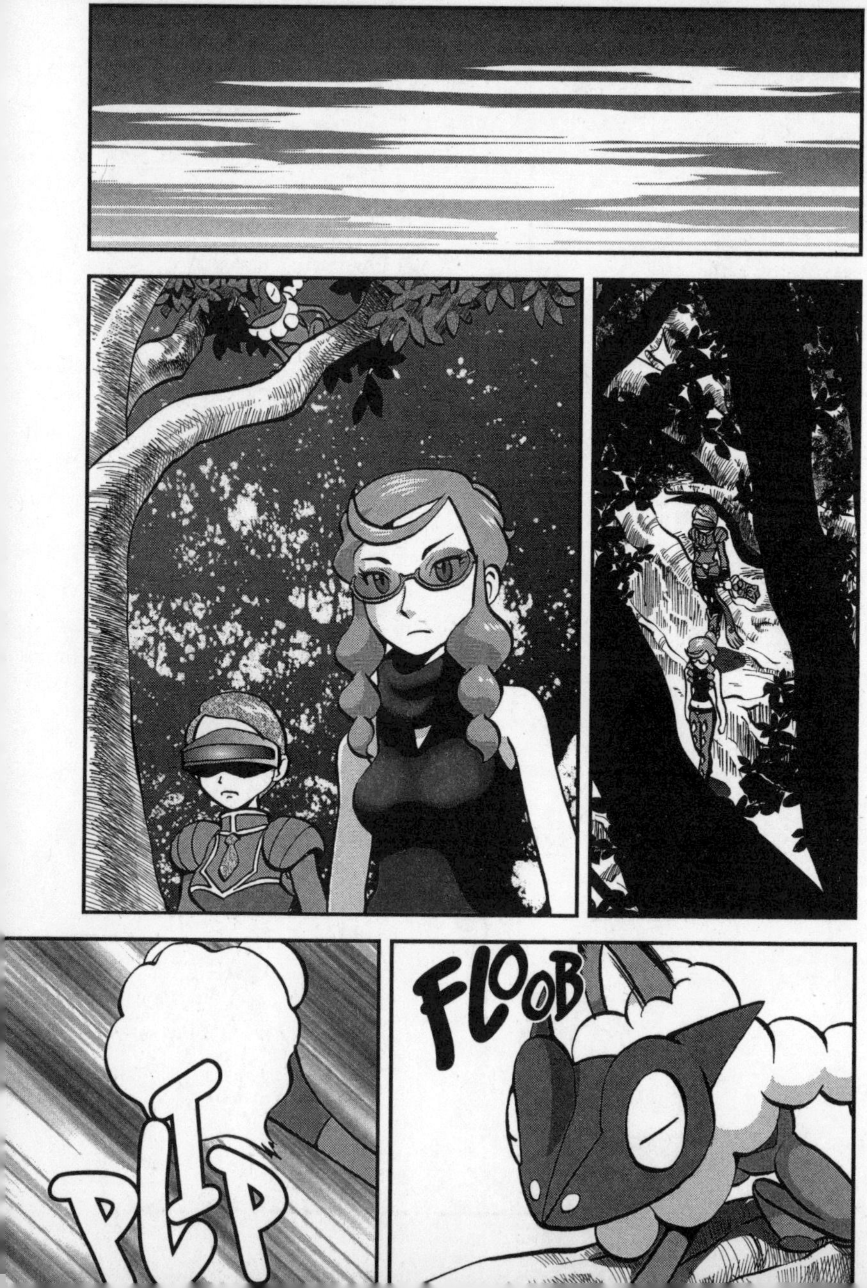
FLOOB
PLIP

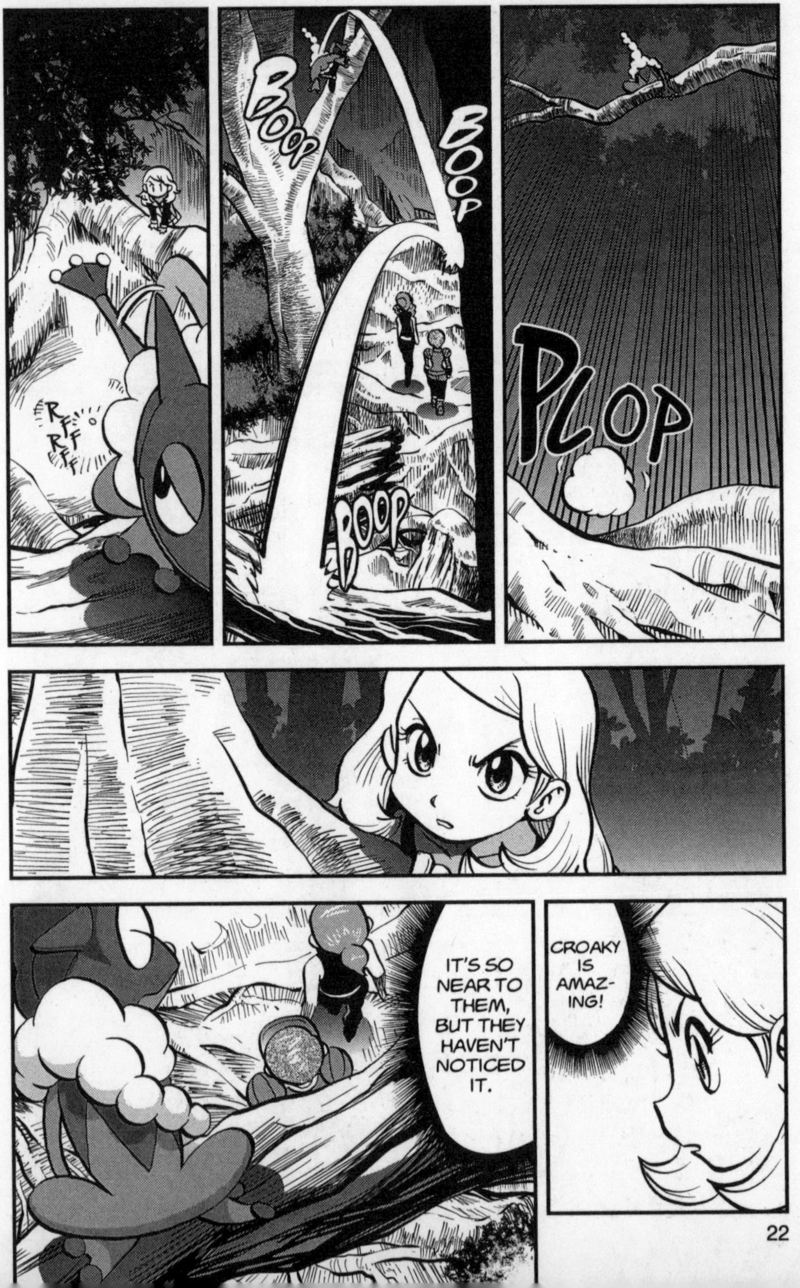
PLOP
BOOP
BOOP
BOOP
RFF RFF RFF
CROAKY IS AMAZ-ING!
IT'S SO NEAR TO THEM, BUT THEY HAVEN'T NOTICED IT.

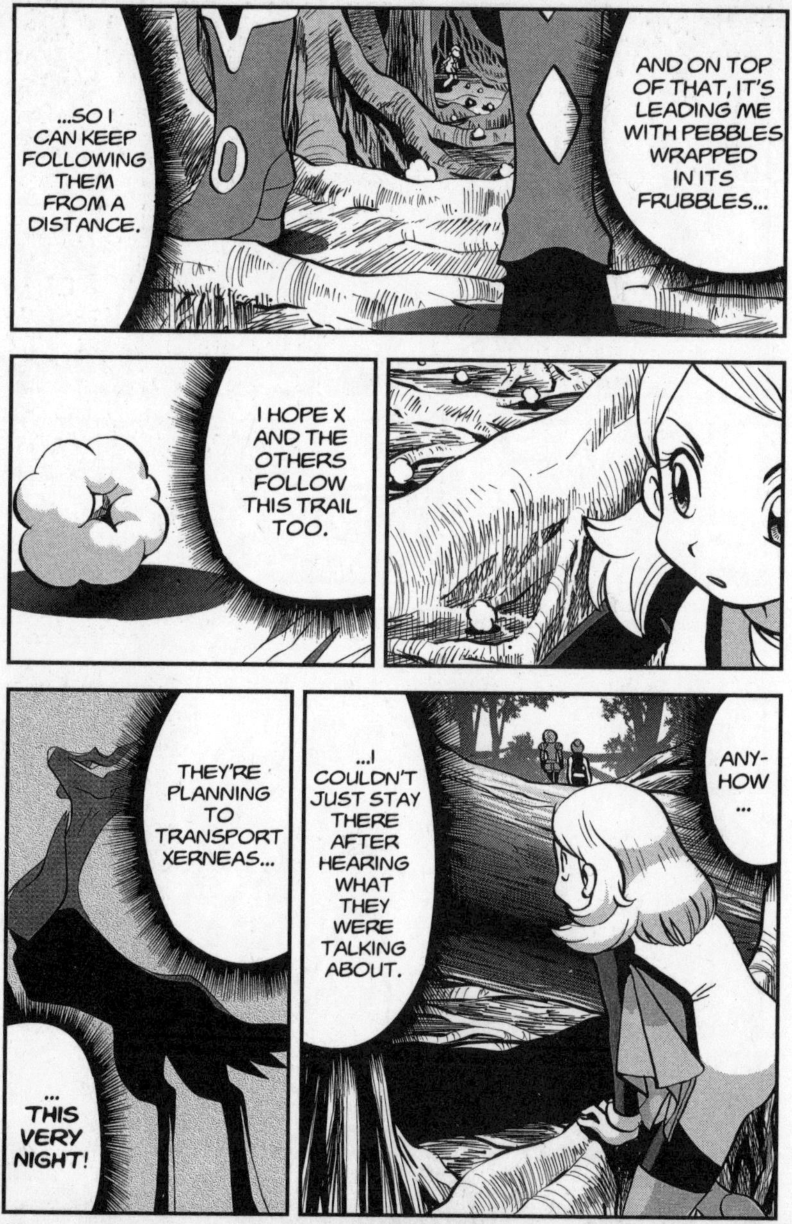
AND ON TOP OF THAT, IT'S LEADING ME WITH PEBBLES WRAPPED IN ITS FRUBBLES...
...SO I CAN KEEP FOLLOWING THEM FROM A DISTANCE.
I HOPE X AND THE OTHERS FOLLOW THIS TRAIL TOO.
ANY-HOW ...
...I COULDN'T JUST STAY THERE AFTER HEARING WHAT THEY WERE TALKING ABOUT.
THEY'RE PLANNING TO TRANSPORT XERNEAS...
... THIS VERY NIGHT!

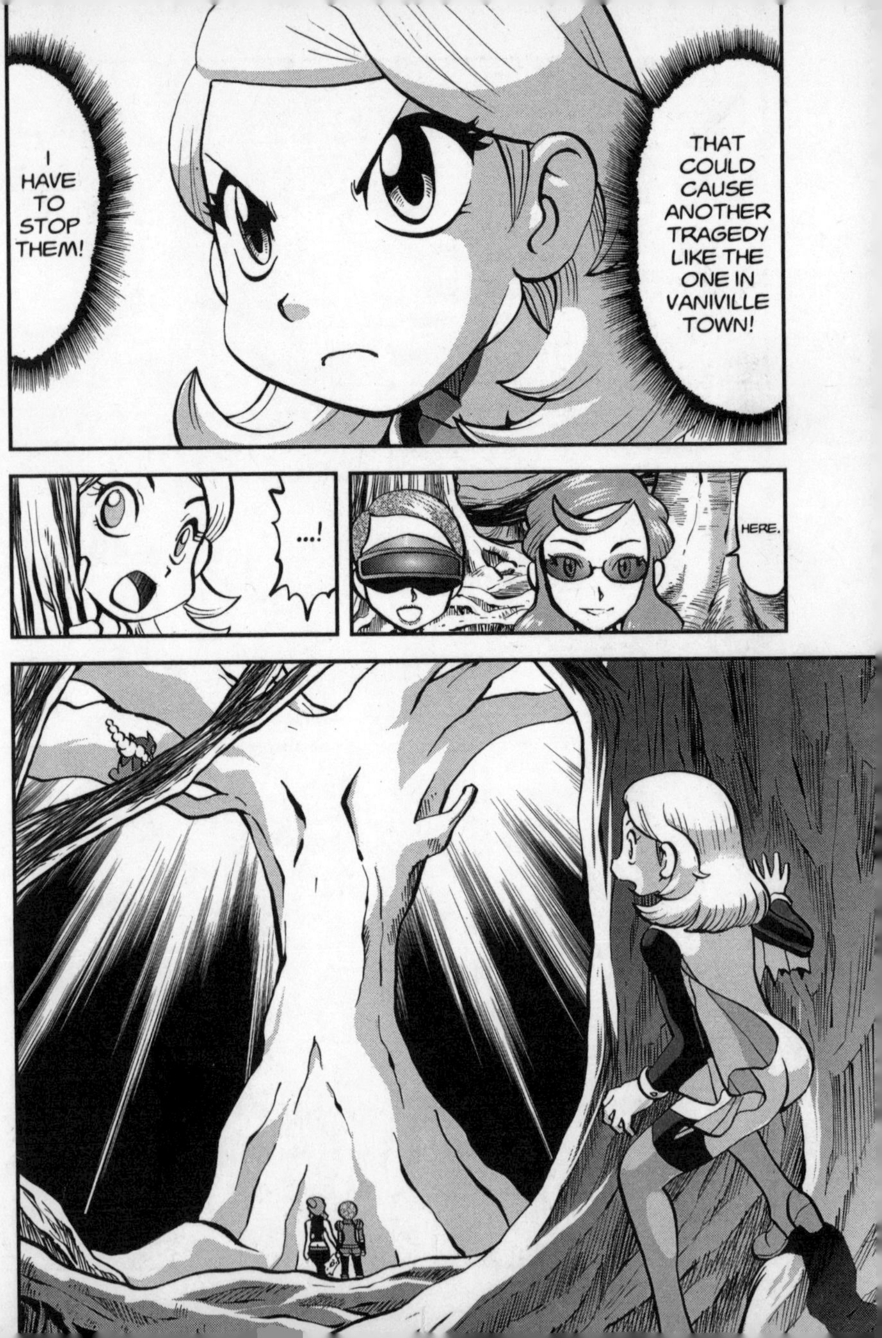
THAT COULD CAUSE ANOTHER TRAGEDY LIKE THE ONE IN VANIVILLE TOWN!
I HAVE TO STOP THEM!
HERE.
...!

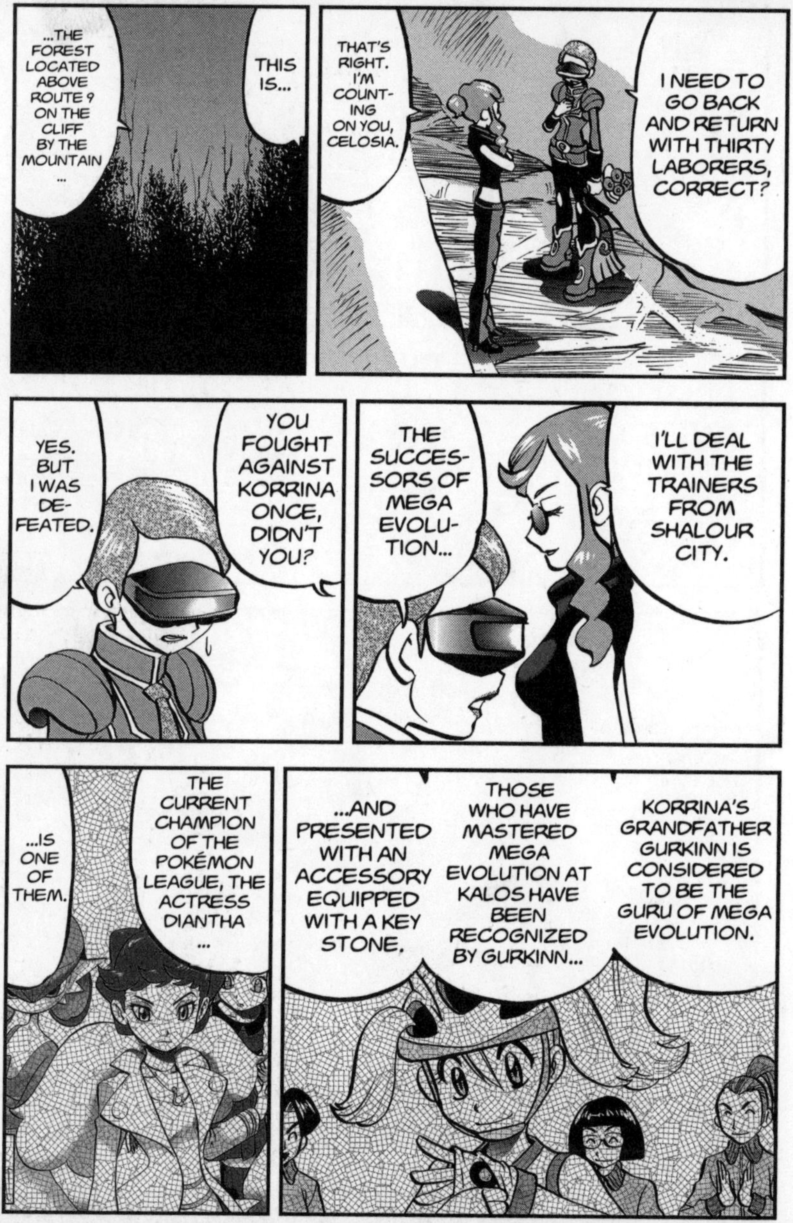
I NEED TO GO BACK AND RETURN WITH THIRTY LABORERS, CORRECT?
THAT'S RIGHT. I'M COUNTING ON YOU, CELOSIA.
THIS IS...
...THE FOREST LOCATED ABOVE ROUTE 9 ON THE CLIFF BY THE MOUNTAIN ...
I'LL DEAL WITH THE TRAINERS FROM SHALOUR CITY.
THE SUCCESSORS OF MEGA EVOLUTION...
YOU FOUGHT AGAINST KORRINA ONCE, DIDN'T YOU?
YES. BUT I WAS DEFEATED.
KORRINA'S GRANDFATHER GURKINN IS CONSIDERED TO BE THE GURU OF MEGA EVOLUTION.
THOSE WHO HAVE MASTERED MEGA EVOLUTION AT KALOS HAVE BEEN RECOGNIZED BY GURKINN...
...AND PRESENTED WITH AN ACCESSORY EQUIPPED WITH A KEY STONE.
THE CURRENT CHAMPION OF THE POKÉMON LEAGUE, THE ACTRESS DIANTHA ...
...IS ONE OF THEM.

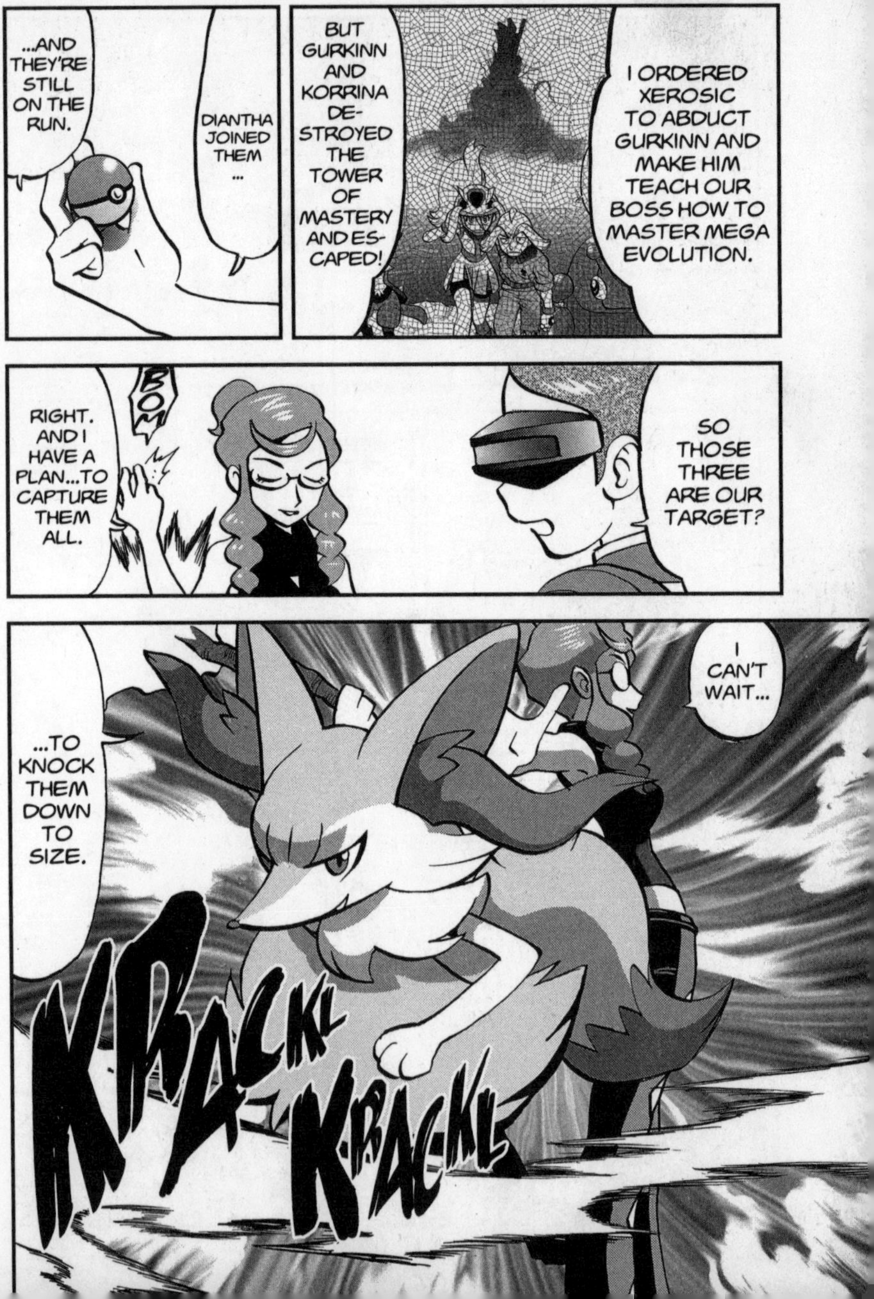
I ORDERED XEROSIC TO ABDUCT GURKINN AND MAKE HIM TEACH OUR BOSS HOW TO MASTER MEGA EVOLUTION.
BUT GURKINN AND KORRINA DE-STROYED THE TOWER OF MASTERY AND ES-CAPED!
DIANTHA JOINED THEM ...
...AND THEY'RE STILL ON THE RUN.
SO THOSE THREE ARE OUR TARGET?
BOM
RIGHT. AND I HAVE A PLAN...TO CAPTURE THEM ALL.
I CAN'T WAIT...
...TO KNOCK THEM DOWN TO SIZE.
K-RACKL
K-RACKL

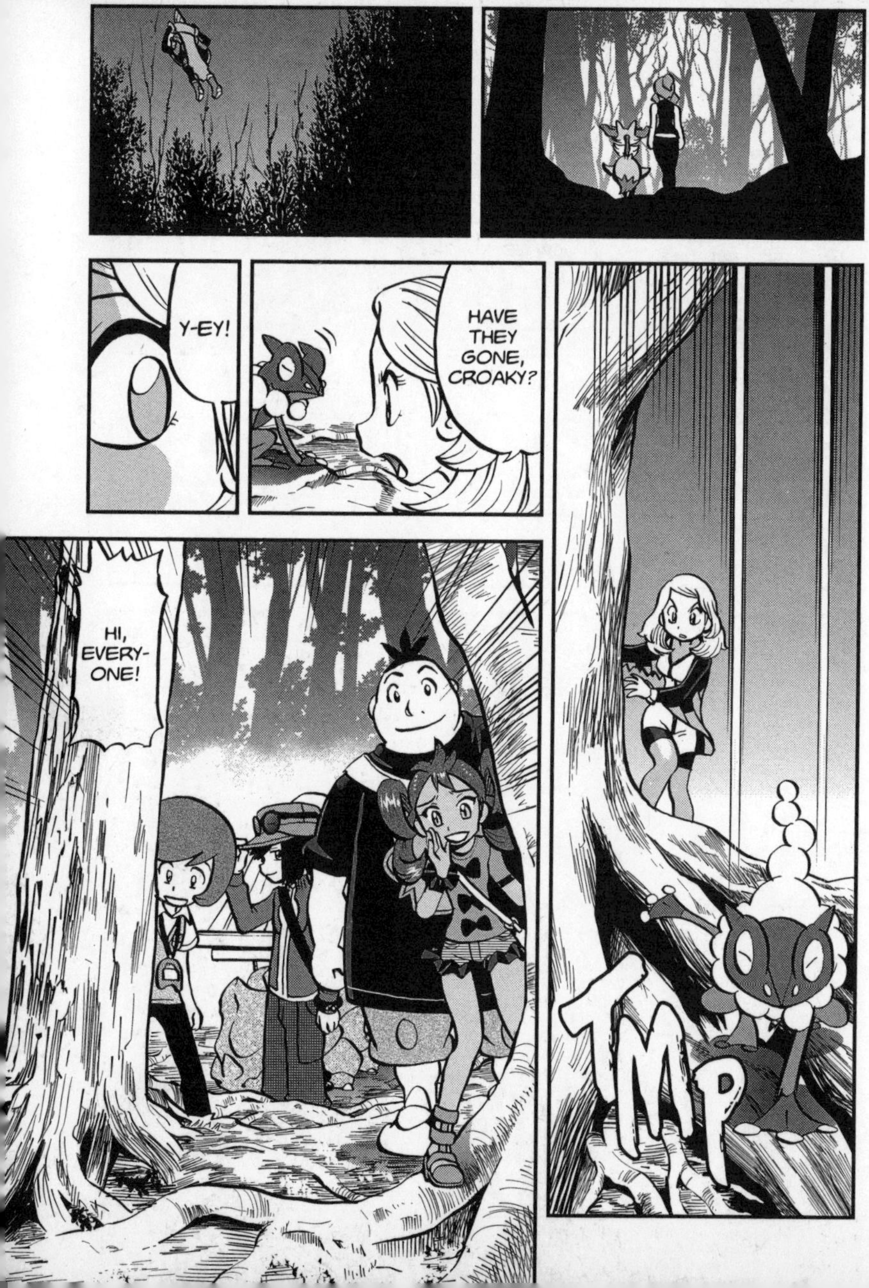
TMP
HAVE THEY GONE, CROAKY?
Y-EY!
HI, EVERY-ONE!

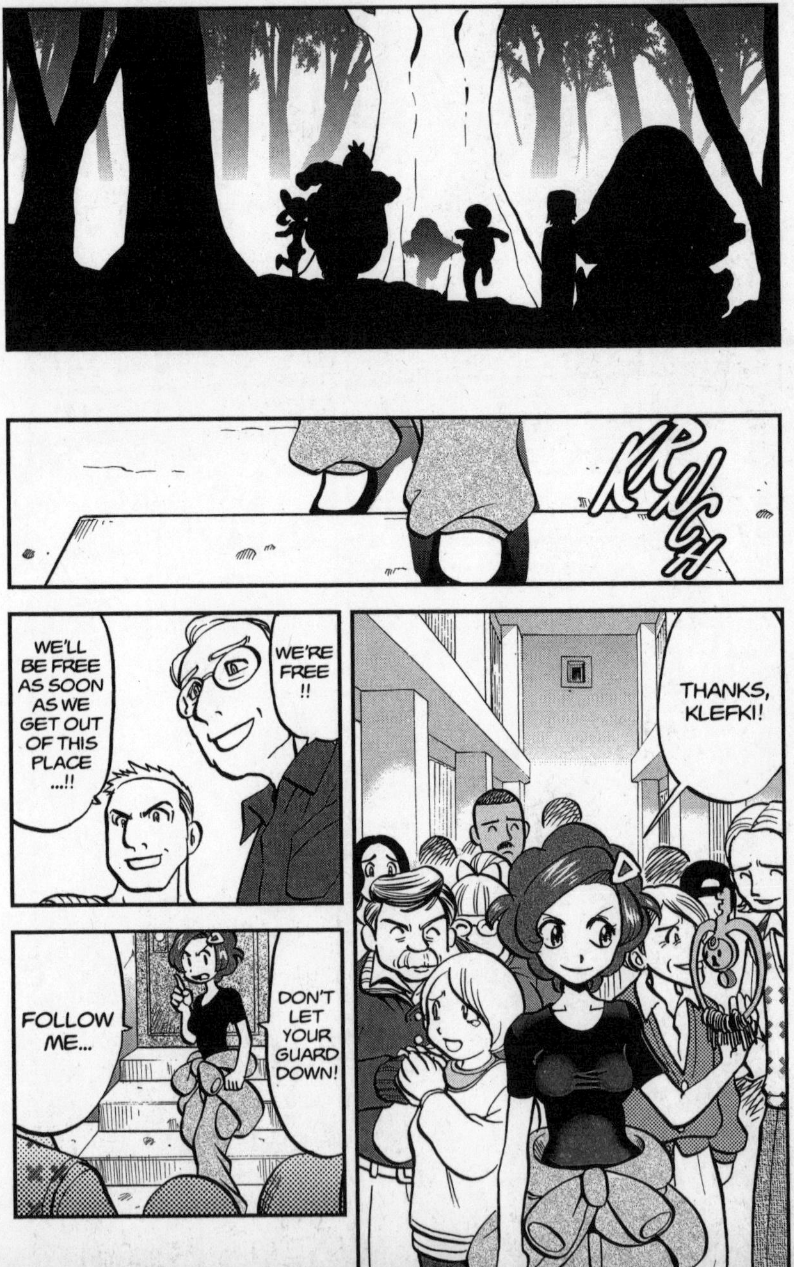
KRNCH
THANKS, KLEFKI!
WE'RE FREE!!
WE'LL BE FREE AS SOON AS WE GET OUT OF THIS PLACE ...!!
DON'T LET YOUR GUARD DOWN!
FOLLOW ME...

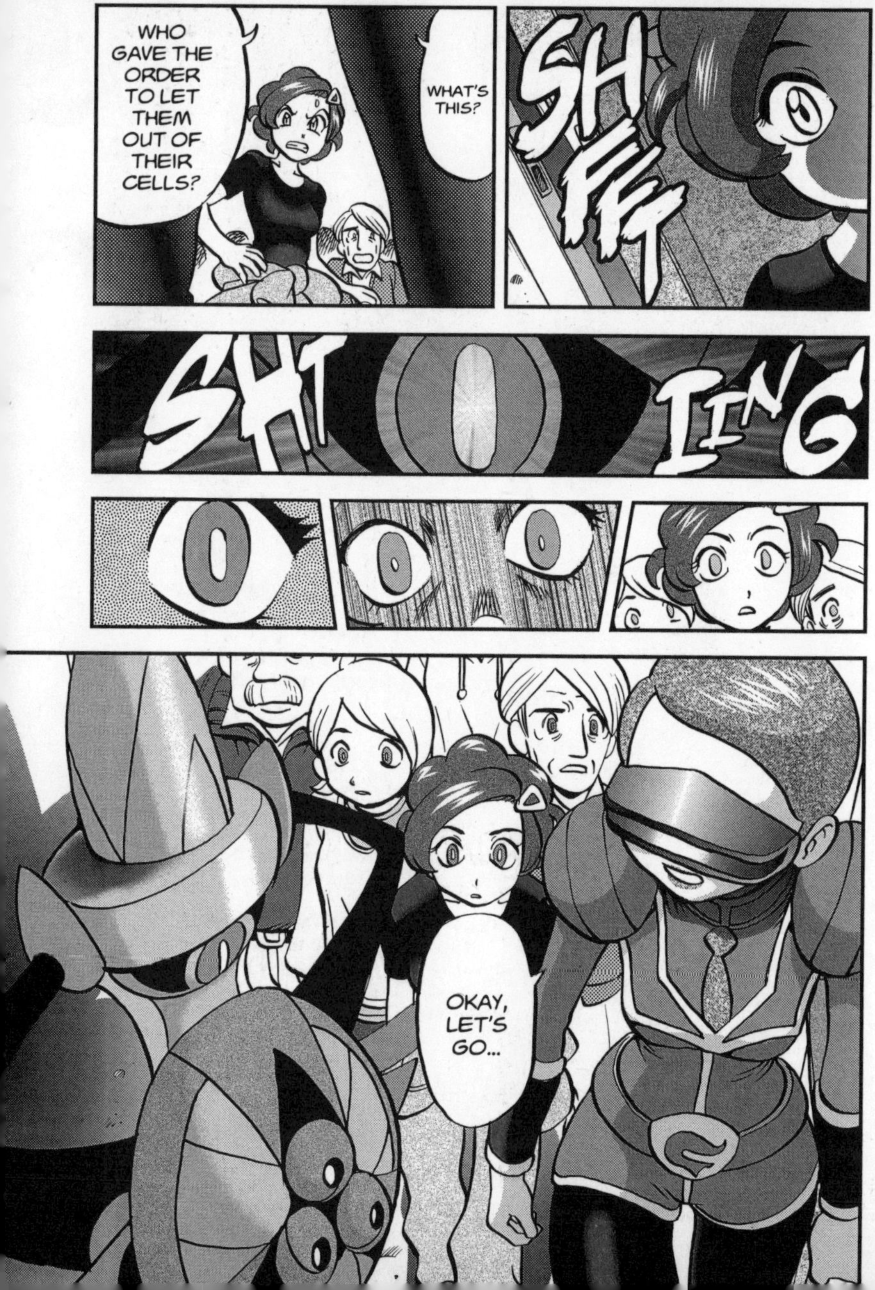
SHFFT
WHAT'S THIS?
WHO GAVE THE ORDER TO LET THEM OUT OF THEIR CELLS?
SHT IING
OKAY, LET'S GO...

Current Location

Route 8
Muraille Coast

This is a road of great contrasts,
from the harsh rock of the cliffs
to the soft sands of the beach.

▼

Ambrette Town

This town was known only for its
aquarium until the discovery of rare
Fossils really put it on the map.

▼

Route 9
Spikes Passage

This rocky passage was created by
retired Rhyhorn racers who forged a
path where there was none.

▼

Route 8
Muraille Coast

This is a road of great contrasts,
from the harsh rock of the cliffs
to the soft sands of the beach.

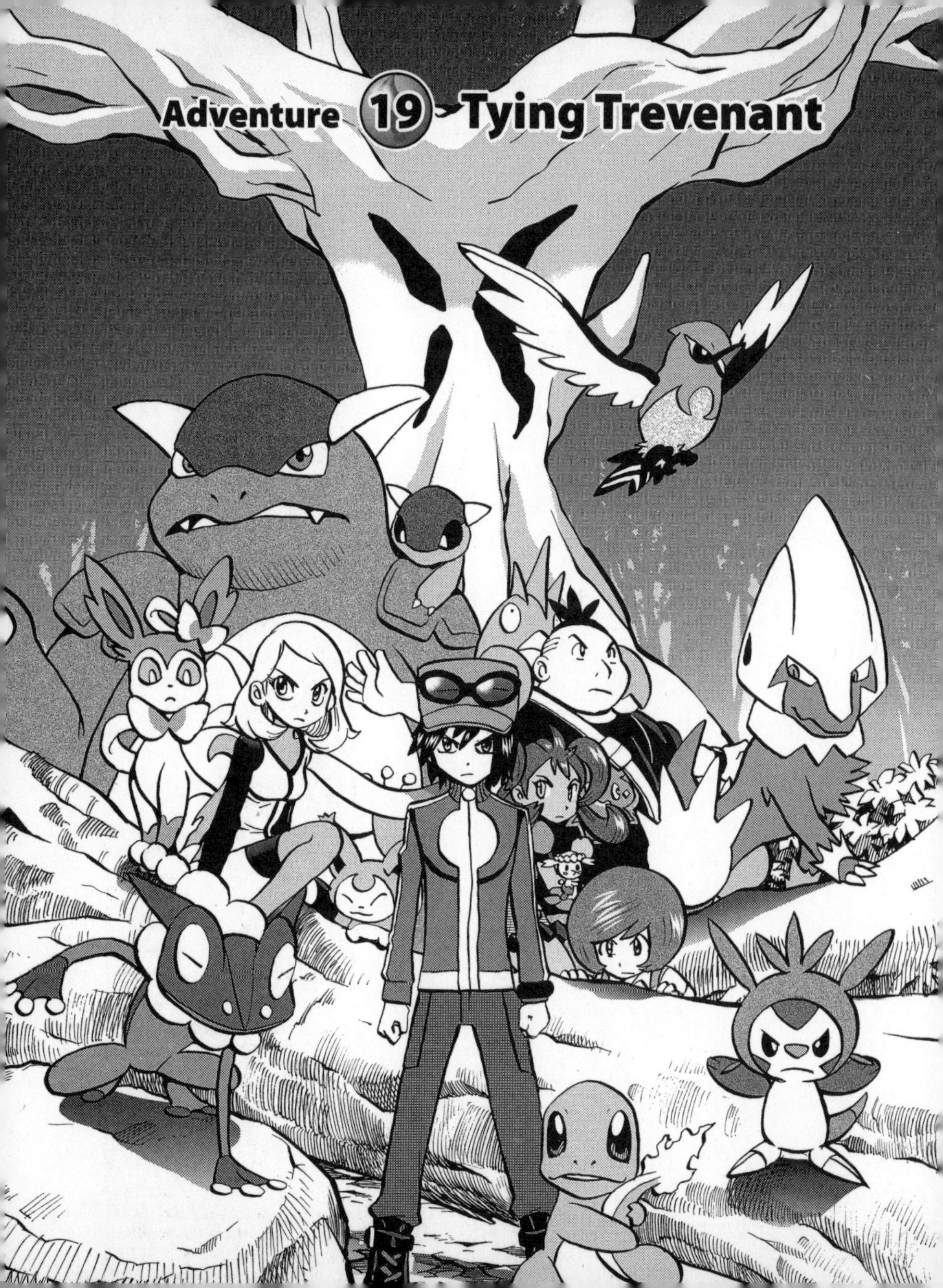
Adventure 19 Tying Trevenant

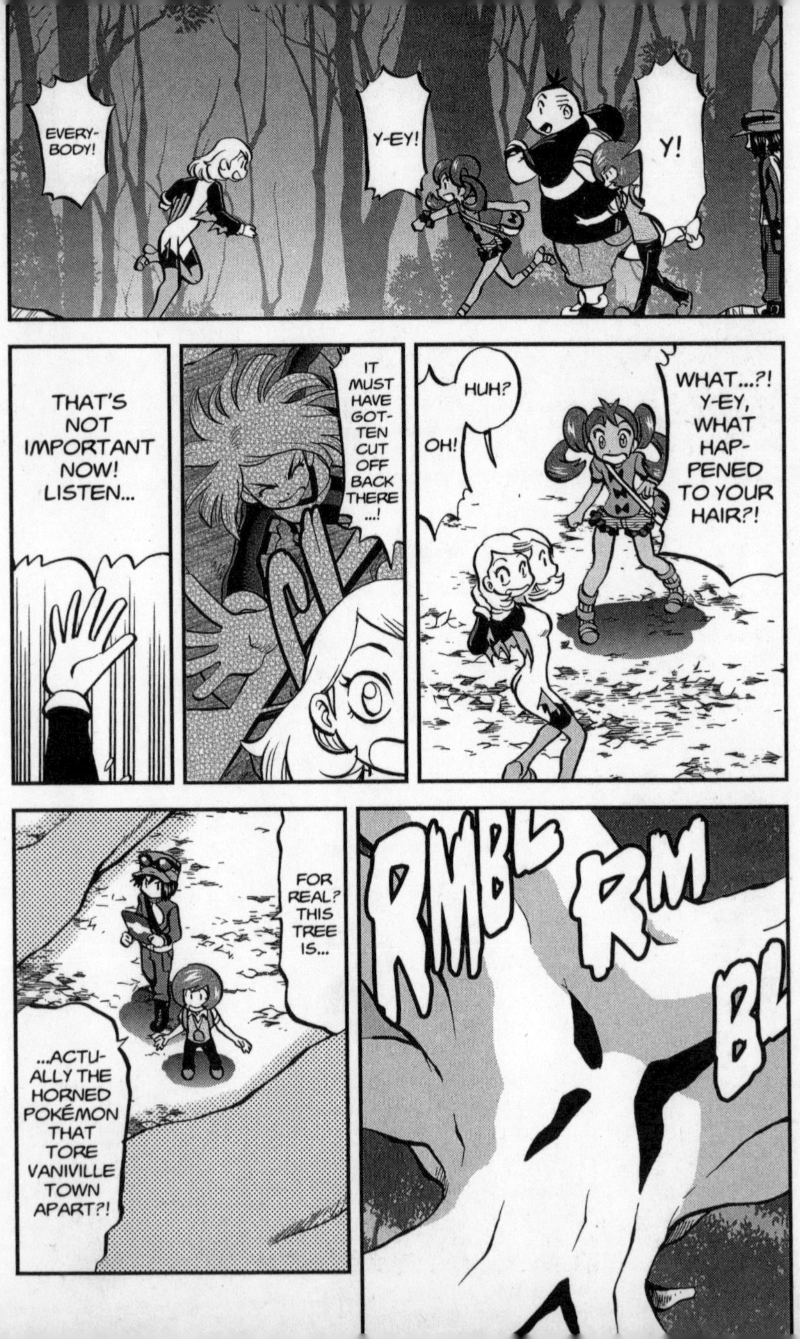
Y!
Y-EY!
EVERY-BODY!
WHAT...?! Y-EY, WHAT HAP-PENED TO YOUR HAIR?!
HUH?
OH!
IT MUST HAVE GOT-TEN CUT OFF BACK THERE...!
THAT'S NOT IMPORTANT NOW! LISTEN...
RMBL
RM
BL
FOR REAL? THIS TREE IS...
...ACTU-ALLY THE HORNED POKéMON THAT TORE VANIVILLE TOWN APART?!

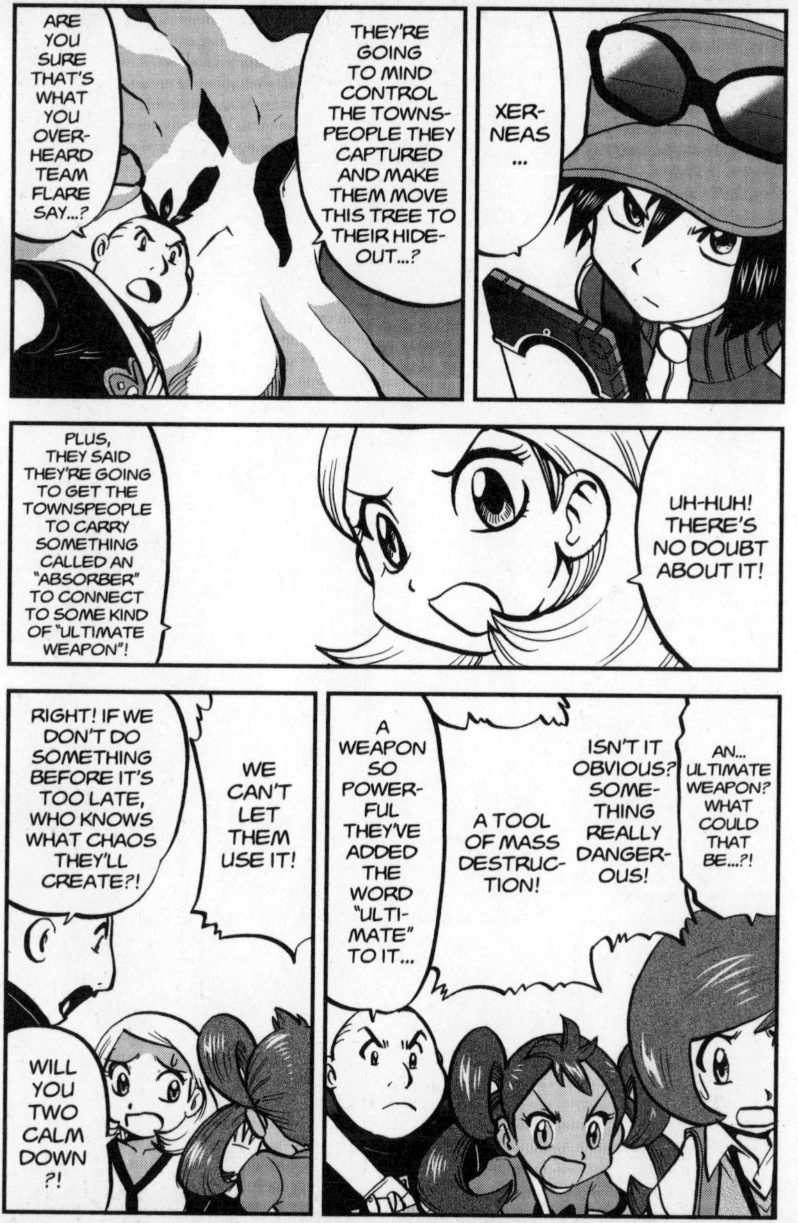
XER-NEAS...
THEY'RE GOING TO MIND CONTROL THE TOWNS-PEOPLE THEY CAPTURED AND MAKE THEM MOVE THIS TREE TO THEIR HIDE-OUT...?
ARE YOU SURE THAT'S WHAT YOU OVER-HEARD TEAM FLARE SAY...?
UH-HUH! THERE'S NO DOUBT ABOUT IT!
PLUS, THEY SAID THEY'RE GOING TO GET THE TOWNSPEOPLE TO CARRY SOMETHING CALLED AN "ABSORBER" TO CONNECT TO SOME KIND OF "ULTIMATE WEAPON"!
AN... ULTIMATE WEAPON? WHAT COULD THAT BE...?!
ISN'T IT OBVIOUS? SOME-THING REALLY DANGER-OUS!
A TOOL OF MASS DESTRUC-TION!
A WEAPON SO POWER-FUL THEY'VE ADDED THE WORD "ULTI-MATE" TO IT...
WE CAN'T LET THEM USE IT!
RIGHT! IF WE DON'T DO SOMETHING BEFORE IT'S TOO LATE, WHO KNOWS WHAT CHAOS THEY'LL CREATE?!
WILL YOU TWO CALM DOWN?!

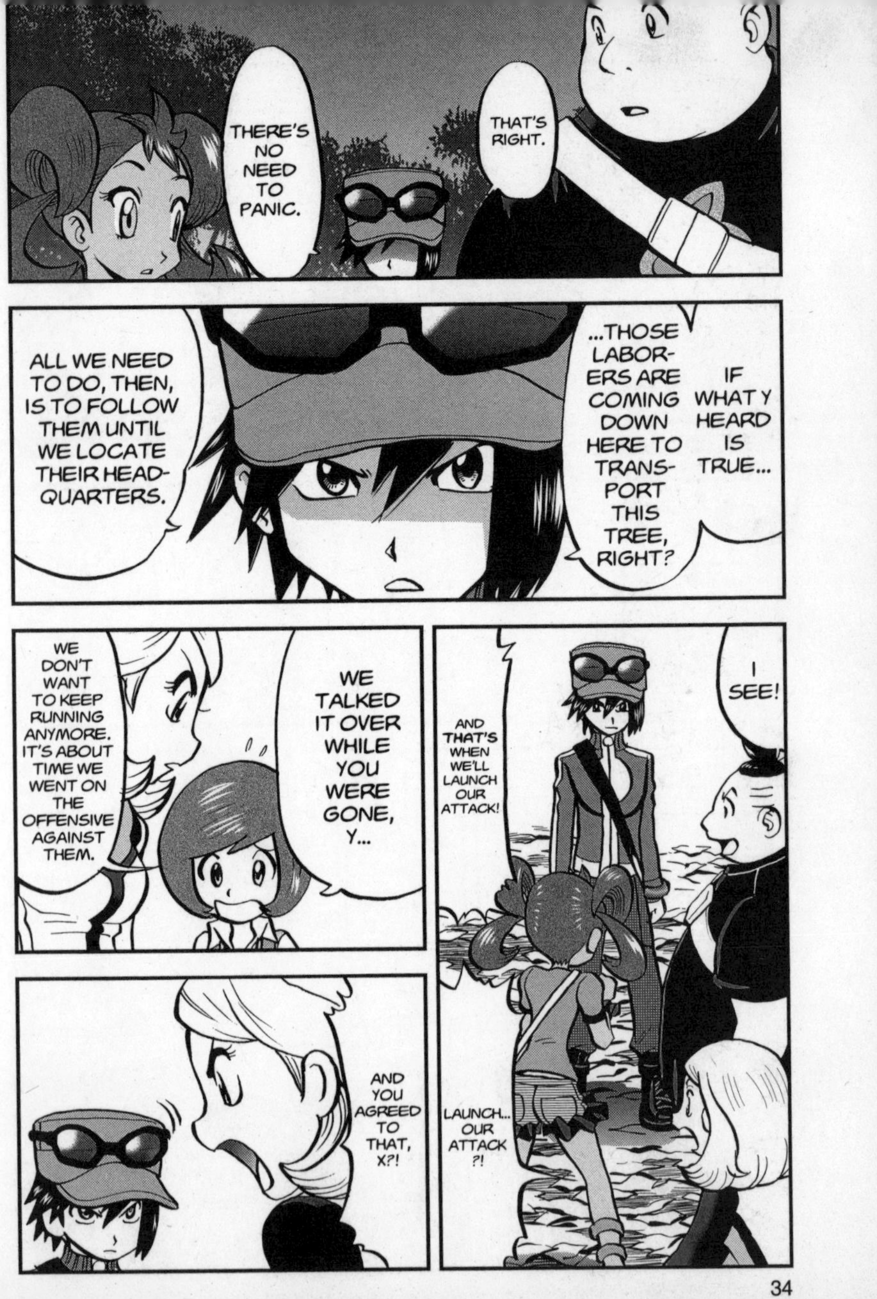
THAT'S RIGHT.
THERE'S NO NEED TO PANIC.
IF WHAT Y HEARD IS TRUE...
...THOSE LABORERS ARE COMING DOWN HERE TO TRANSPORT THIS TREE, RIGHT?
ALL WE NEED TO DO, THEN, IS TO FOLLOW THEM UNTIL WE LOCATE THEIR HEADQUARTERS.
I SEE!
AND THAT'S WHEN WE'LL LAUNCH OUR ATTACK!
LAUNCH... OUR ATTACK?!
WE TALKED IT OVER WHILE YOU WERE GONE, Y...
WE DON'T WANT TO KEEP RUNNING ANYMORE. IT'S ABOUT TIME WE WENT ON THE OFFENSIVE AGAINST THEM.
AND YOU AGREED TO THAT, X?!

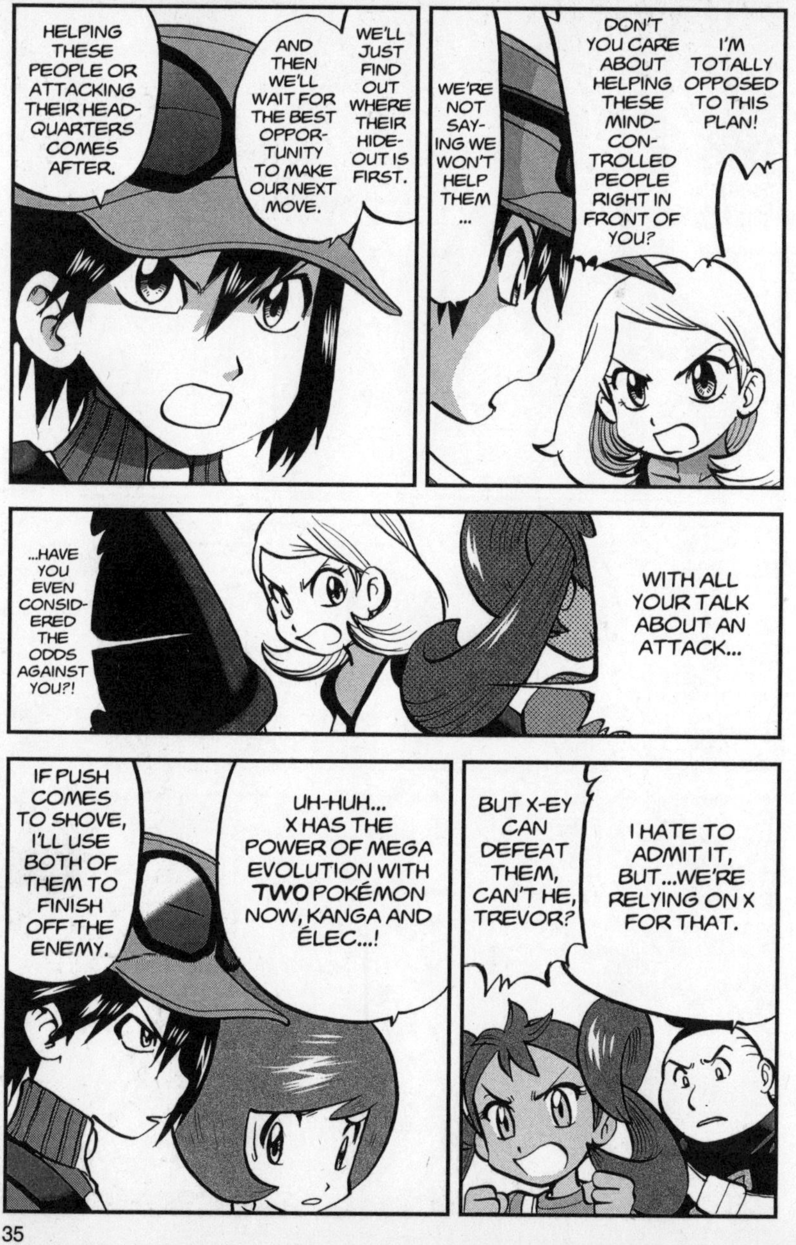
I'M TOTALLY OPPOSED TO THIS PLAN!
DON'T YOU CARE ABOUT HELPING THESE MIND-CONTROLLED PEOPLE RIGHT IN FRONT OF YOU?
WE'RE NOT SAYING WE WON'T HELP THEM...
WE'LL JUST FIND OUT WHERE THEIR HIDEOUT IS FIRST.
AND THEN WE'LL WAIT FOR THE BEST OPPORTUNITY TO MAKE OUR NEXT MOVE.
HELPING THESE PEOPLE OR ATTACKING THEIR HEADQUARTERS COMES AFTER.
WITH ALL YOUR TALK ABOUT AN ATTACK...
...HAVE YOU EVEN CONSIDERED THE ODDS AGAINST YOU?!
I HATE TO ADMIT IT, BUT...WE'RE RELYING ON X FOR THAT.
BUT X-EY CAN DEFEAT THEM, CAN'T HE, TREVOR?
UH-HUH... X HAS THE POWER OF MEGA EVOLUTION WITH **TWO** POKÉMON NOW, KANGA AND ÉLEC...!
IF PUSH COMES TO SHOVE, I'LL USE BOTH OF THEM TO FINISH OFF THE ENEMY.

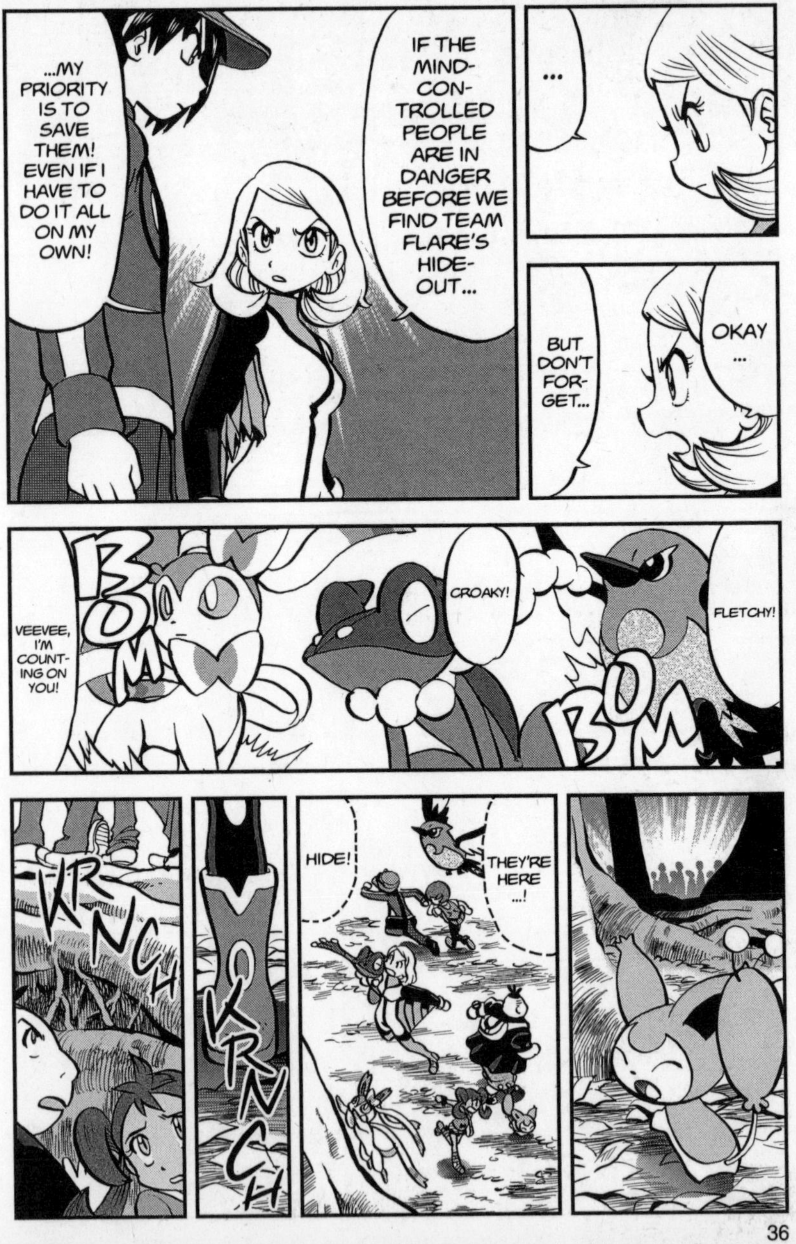
...
OKAY ...
BUT DON'T FORGET...
IF THE MIND-CONTROLLED PEOPLE ARE IN DANGER BEFORE WE FIND TEAM FLARE'S HIDE-OUT...
...MY PRIORITY IS TO SAVE THEM! EVEN IF I HAVE TO DO IT ALL ON MY OWN!
FLETCHY!
BOOM
CROAKY!
BOOM
VEEVEE, I'M COUNTING ON YOU!
THEY'RE HERE ...!
HIDE!
KRNCH
KRNCH

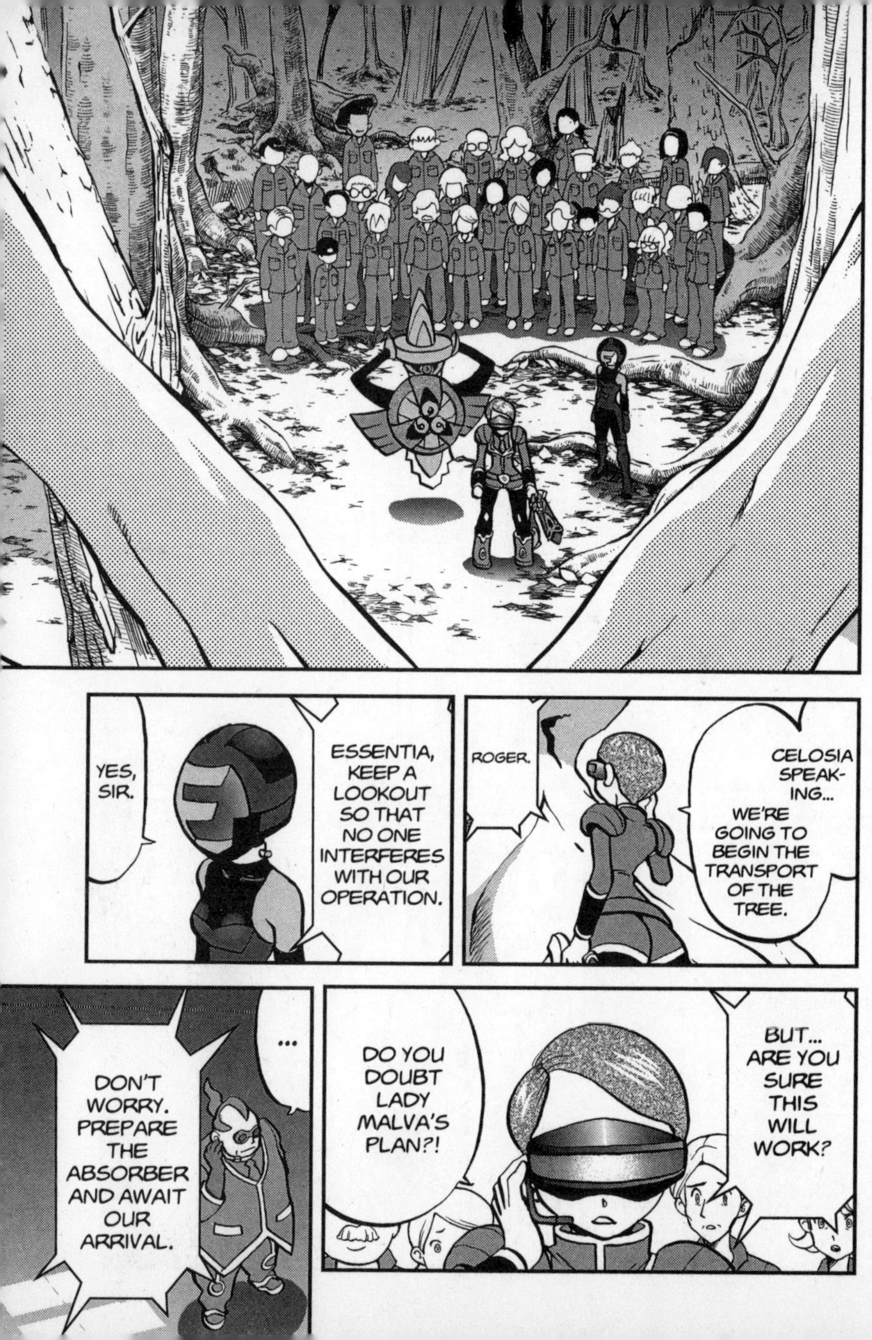
CELOSIA SPEAKING... WE'RE GOING TO BEGIN THE TRANSPORT OF THE TREE.
ROGER.
ESSENTIA, KEEP A LOOKOUT SO THAT NO ONE INTERFERES WITH OUR OPERATION.
YES, SIR.
BUT... ARE YOU SURE THIS WILL WORK?
DO YOU DOUBT LADY MALVA'S PLAN?!
...
DON'T WORRY. PREPARE THE ABSORBER AND AWAIT OUR ARRIVAL.

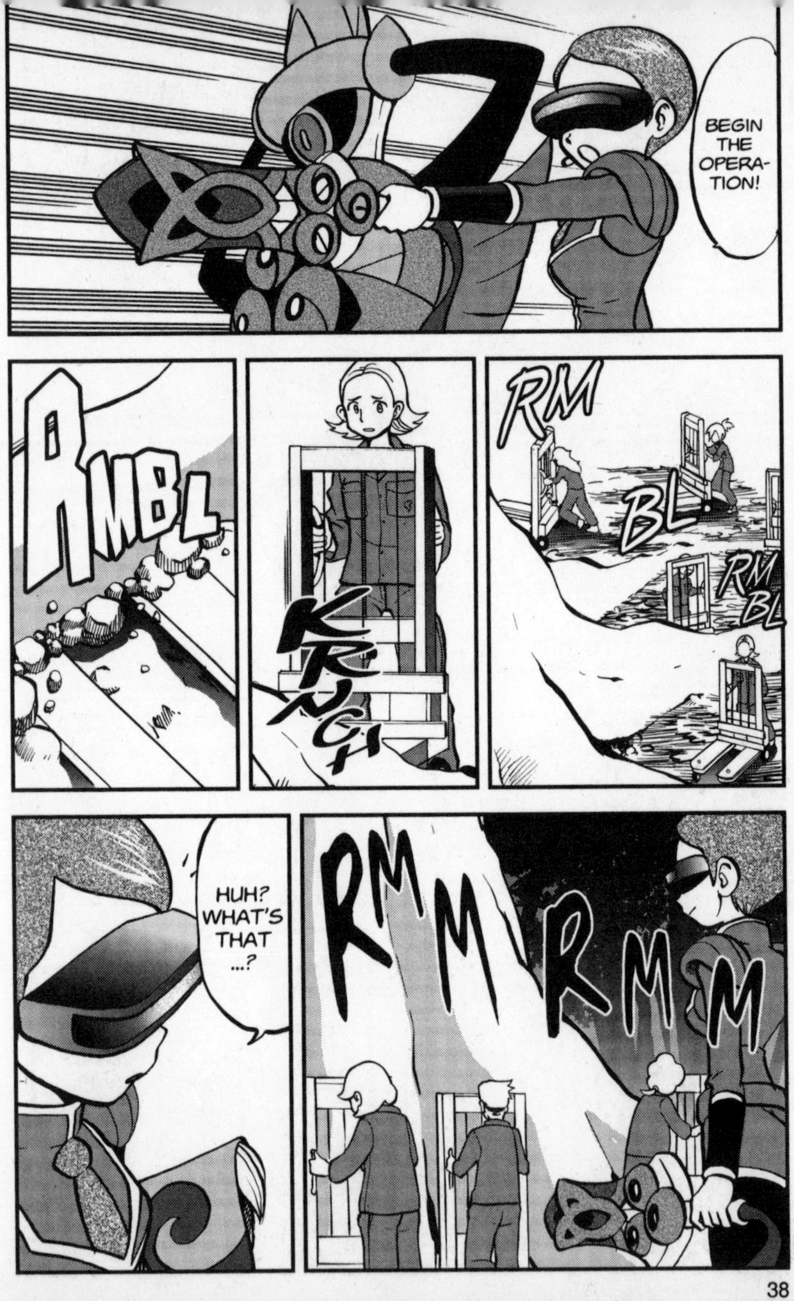
BEGIN THE OPERA-TION!
RM
BL
RM
BL
KRNCH
AMBL
RMM
RMMM
HUH? WHAT'S THAT ...?

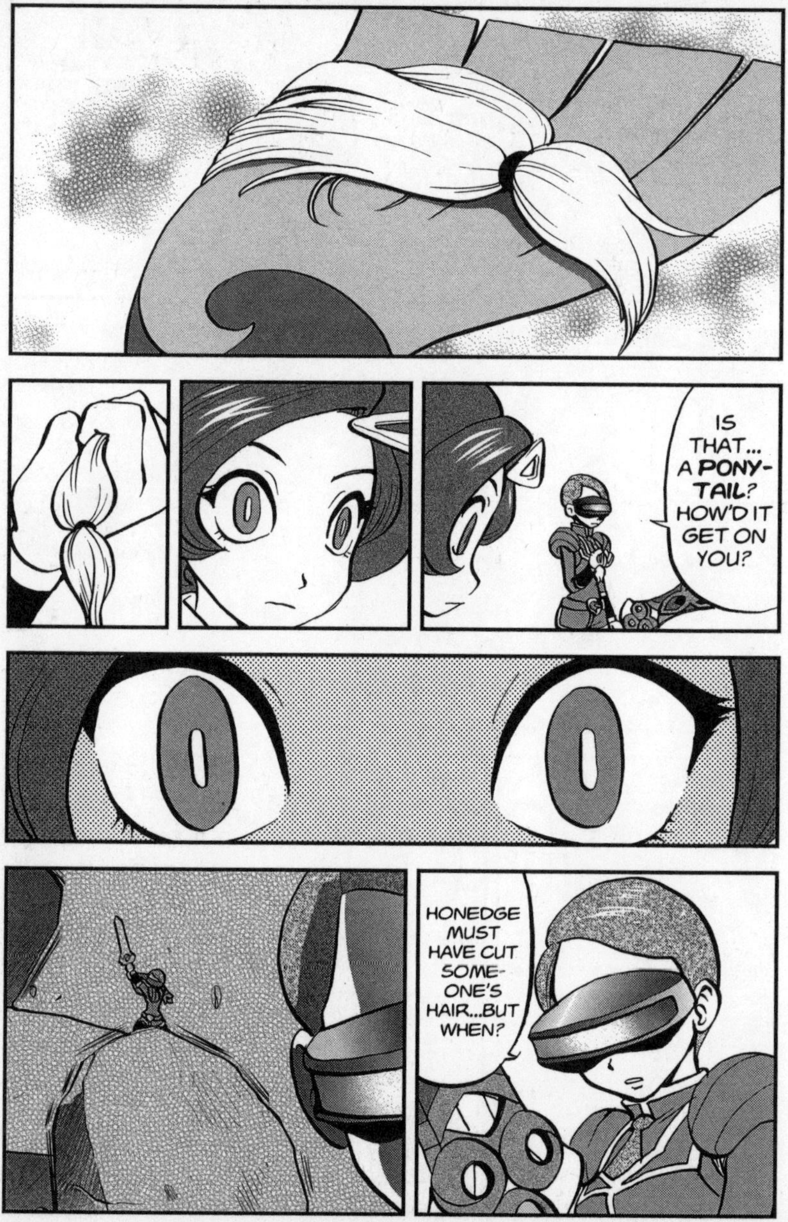
IS THAT... A PONY-TAIL? HOW'D IT GET ON YOU?
HONEDGE MUST HAVE CUT SOME-ONE'S HAIR...BUT WHEN?

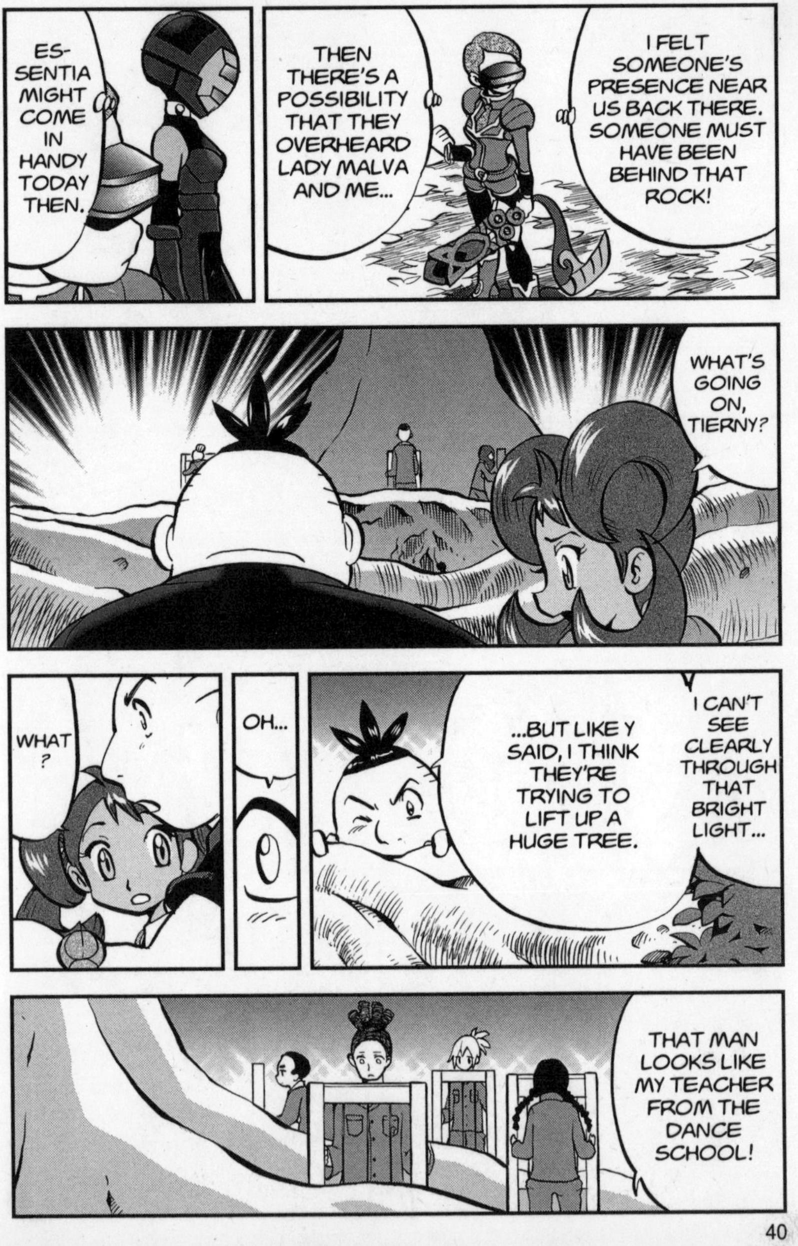
I FELT SOMEONE'S PRESENCE NEAR US BACK THERE. SOMEONE MUST HAVE BEEN BEHIND THAT ROCK!
THEN THERE'S A POSSIBILITY THAT THEY OVERHEARD LADY MALVA AND ME...
ES-SENTIA MIGHT COME IN HANDY TODAY THEN.
WHAT'S GOING ON, TIERNY?
I CAN'T SEE CLEARLY THROUGH THAT BRIGHT LIGHT...
...BUT LIKE Y SAID, I THINK THEY'RE TRYING TO LIFT UP A HUGE TREE.
OH...
WHAT?
THAT MAN LOOKS LIKE MY TEACHER FROM THE DANCE SCHOOL!

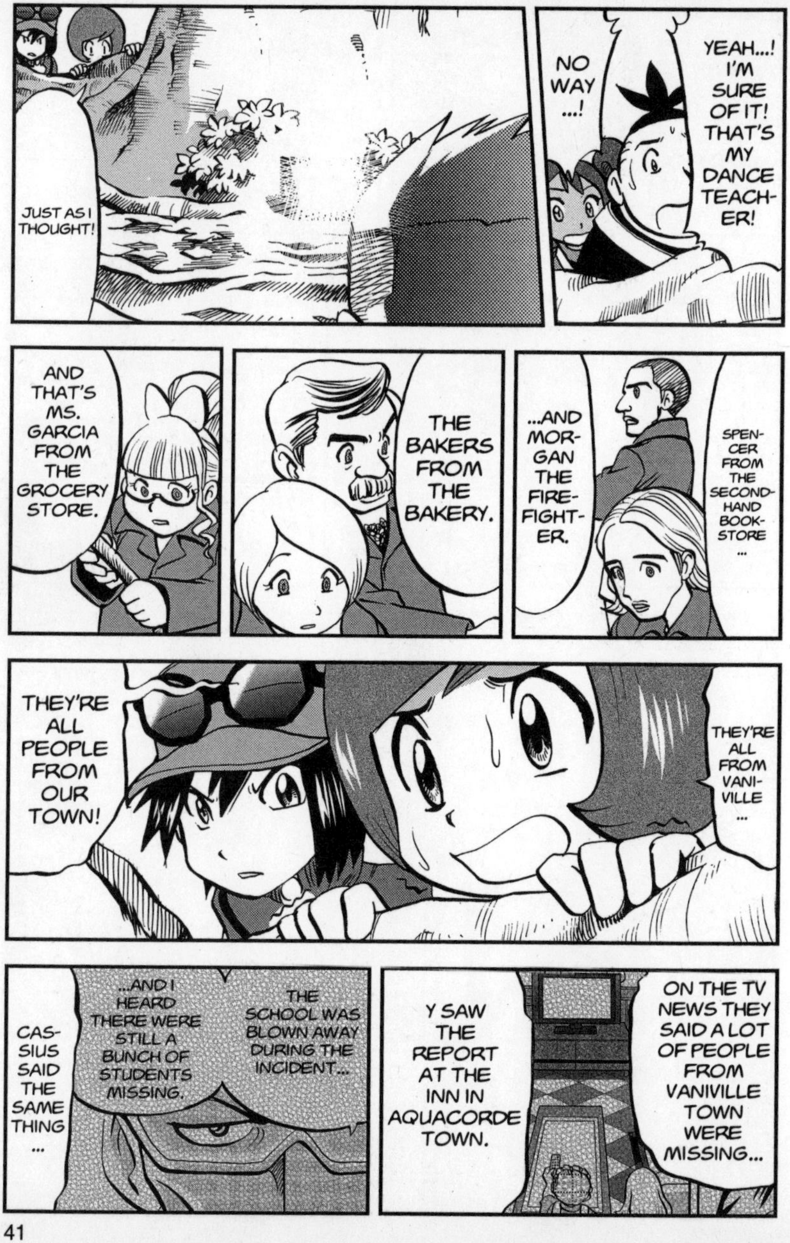
YEAH...! I'M SURE OF IT! THAT'S MY DANCE TEACHER!
NO WAY ...!
JUST AS I THOUGHT!
SPENCER FROM THE SECOND-HAND BOOKSTORE ...
...AND MORGAN THE FIREFIGHTER.
THE BAKERS FROM THE BAKERY.
AND THAT'S MS. GARCIA FROM THE GROCERY STORE.
THEY'RE ALL FROM VANIVILLE ...
THEY'RE ALL PEOPLE FROM OUR TOWN!
ON THE TV NEWS THEY SAID A LOT OF PEOPLE FROM VANIVILLE TOWN WERE MISSING...
Y SAW THE REPORT AT THE INN IN AQUACORDE TOWN.
THE SCHOOL WAS BLOWN AWAY DURING THE INCIDENT...
...AND I HEARD THERE WERE STILL A BUNCH OF STUDENTS MISSING.
CASSIUS SAID THE SAME THING ...

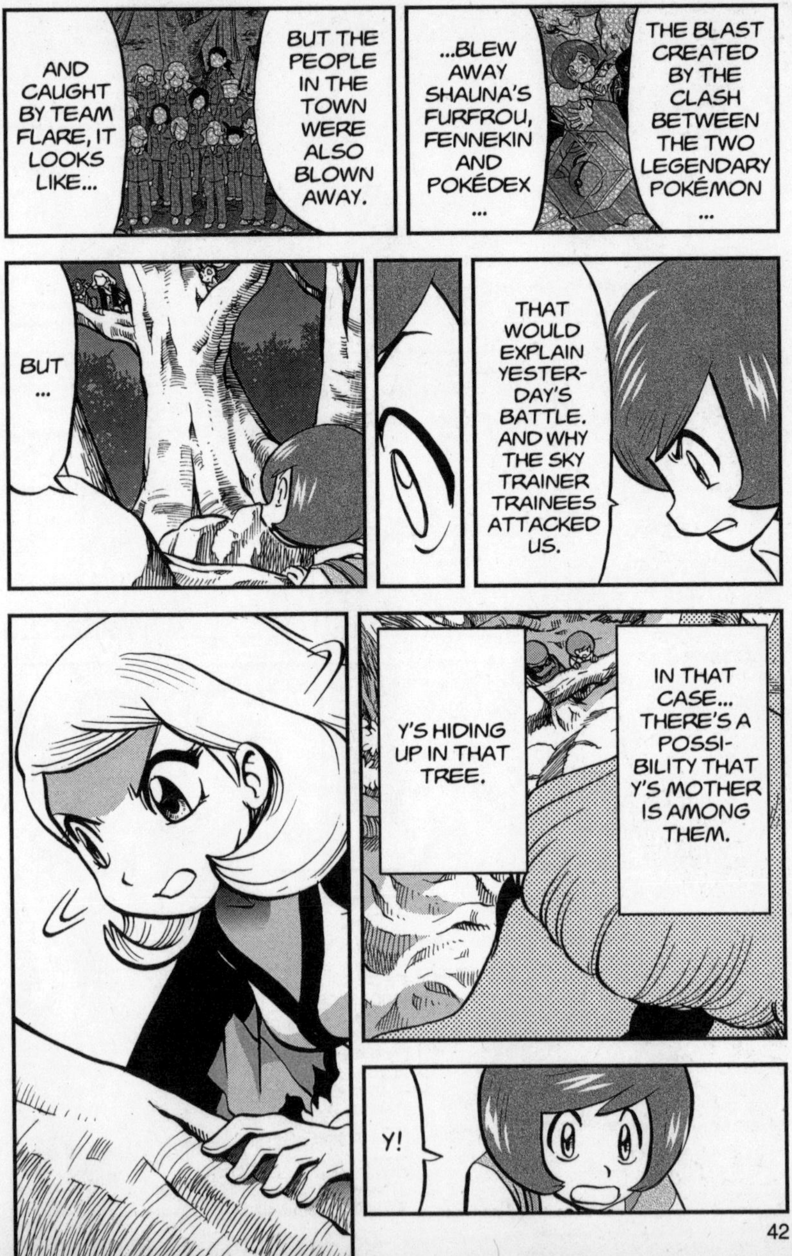
THE BLAST CREATED BY THE CLASH BETWEEN THE TWO LEGENDARY POKÉMON ...
...BLEW AWAY SHAUNA'S FURFROU, FENNEKIN AND POKÉDEX ...
BUT THE PEOPLE IN THE TOWN WERE ALSO BLOWN AWAY.
AND CAUGHT BY TEAM FLARE, IT LOOKS LIKE...
THAT WOULD EXPLAIN YESTERDAY'S BATTLE. AND WHY THE SKY TRAINER TRAINEES ATTACKED US.
BUT ...
IN THAT CASE... THERE'S A POSSIBILITY THAT Y'S MOTHER IS AMONG THEM.
Y'S HIDING UP IN THAT TREE.
Y!

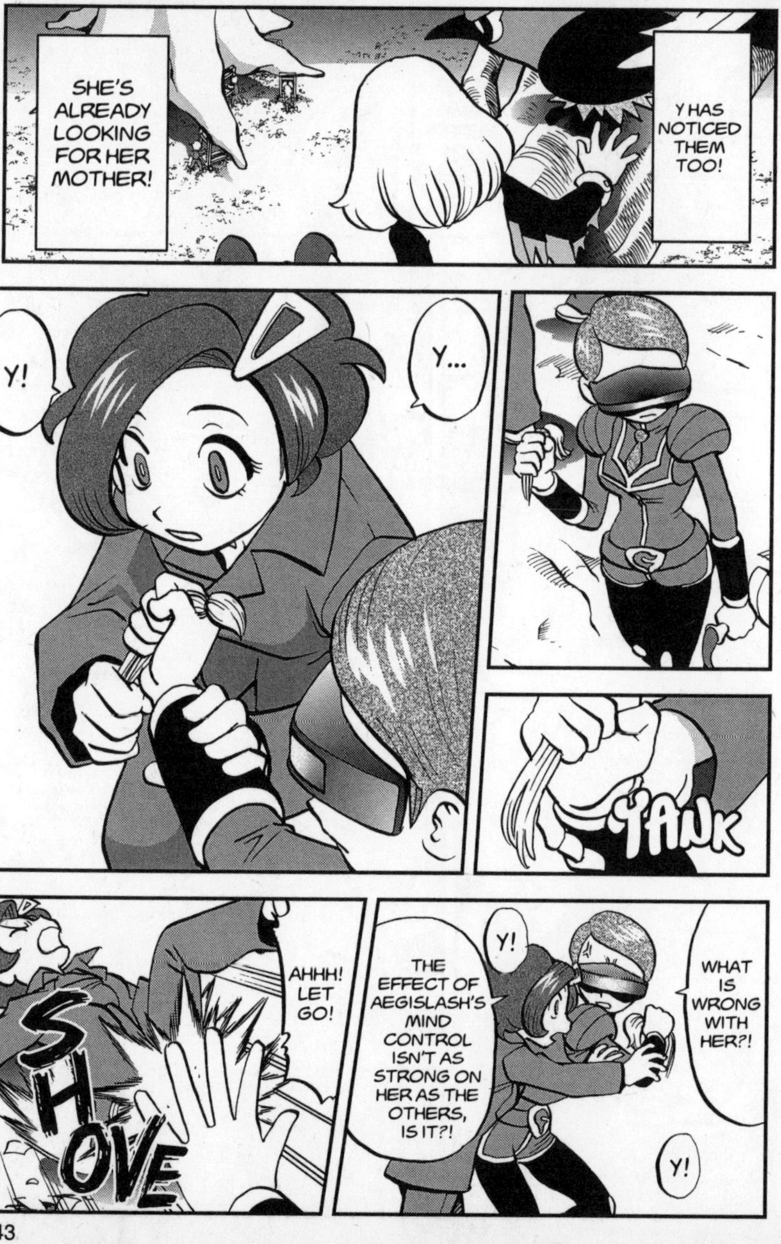
Y HAS NOTICED THEM TOO!
SHE'S ALREADY LOOKING FOR HER MOTHER!
YANK
Y...
Y!
WHAT IS WRONG WITH HER?!
Y!
THE EFFECT OF AEGISLASH'S MIND CONTROL ISN'T AS STRONG ON HER AS THE OTHERS, IS IT?!
Y!
AHHH! LET GO!
SHOVE

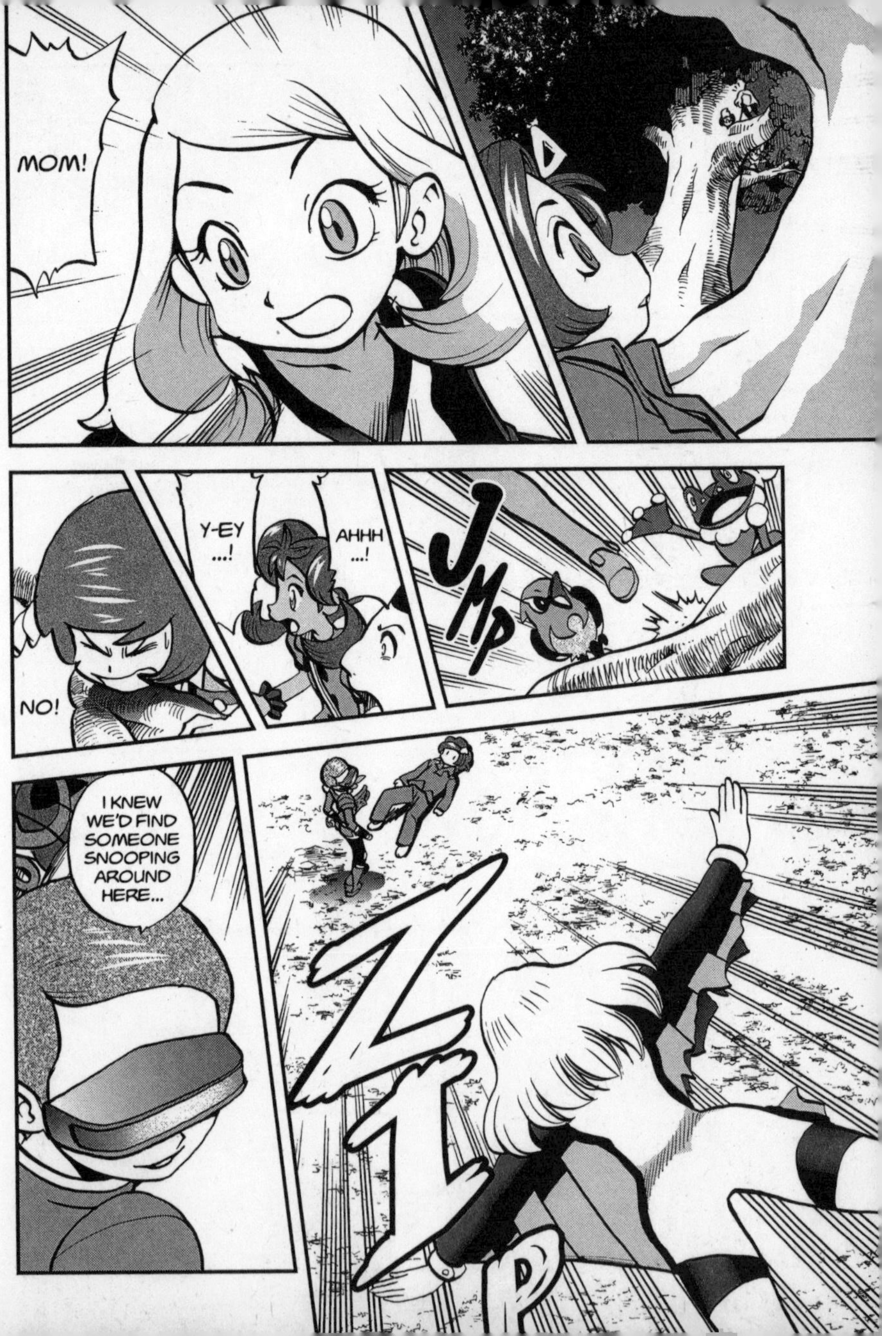
MOM!
JMP
AHHH ...!
Y-EY ...!
NO!
ZIP
I KNEW WE'D FIND SOMEONE SNOOPING AROUND HERE...

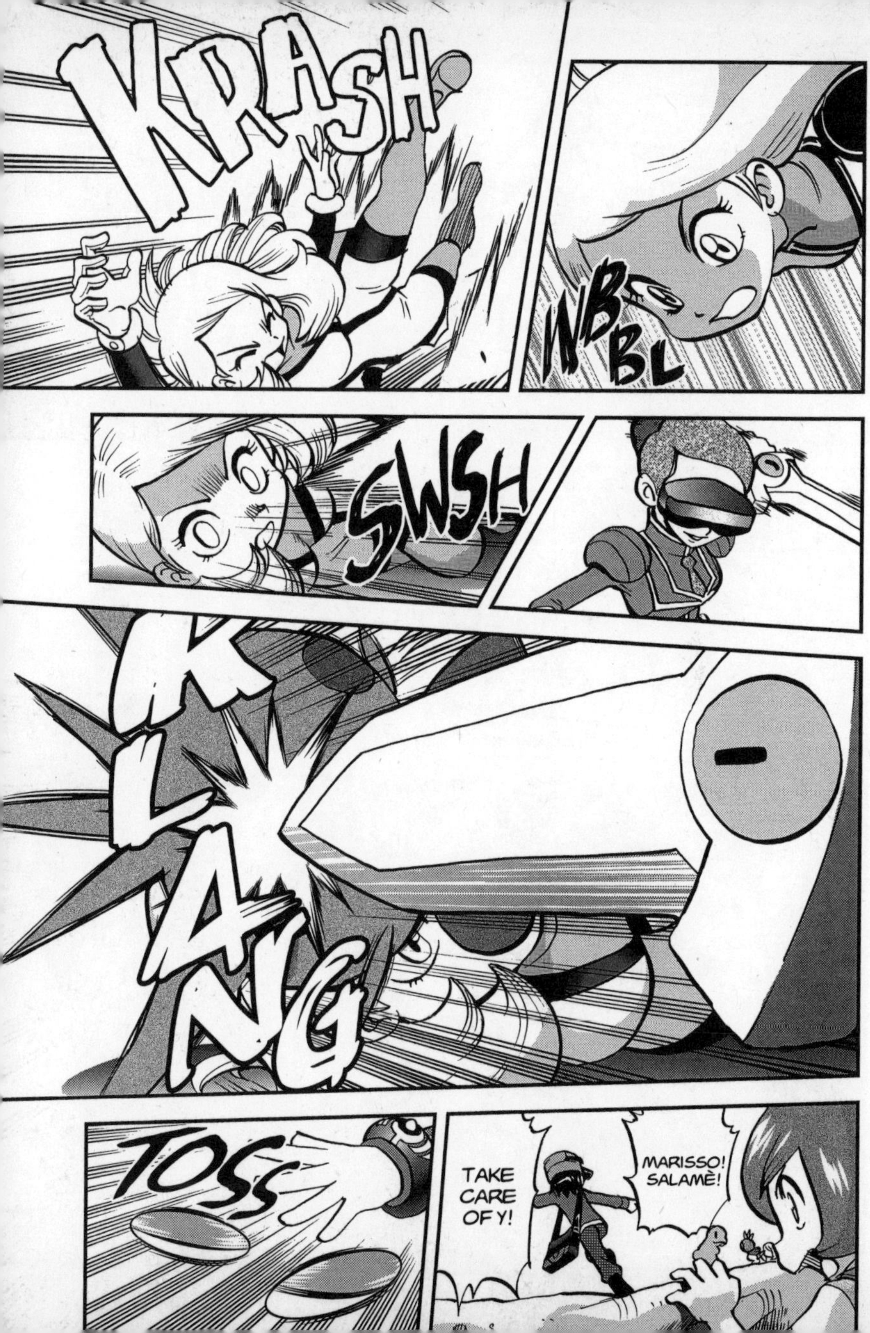
WBBL
KRASH
SWSH
KLANG
MARISSO! SALAMÈ!
TAKE CARE OF Y!
TOSS

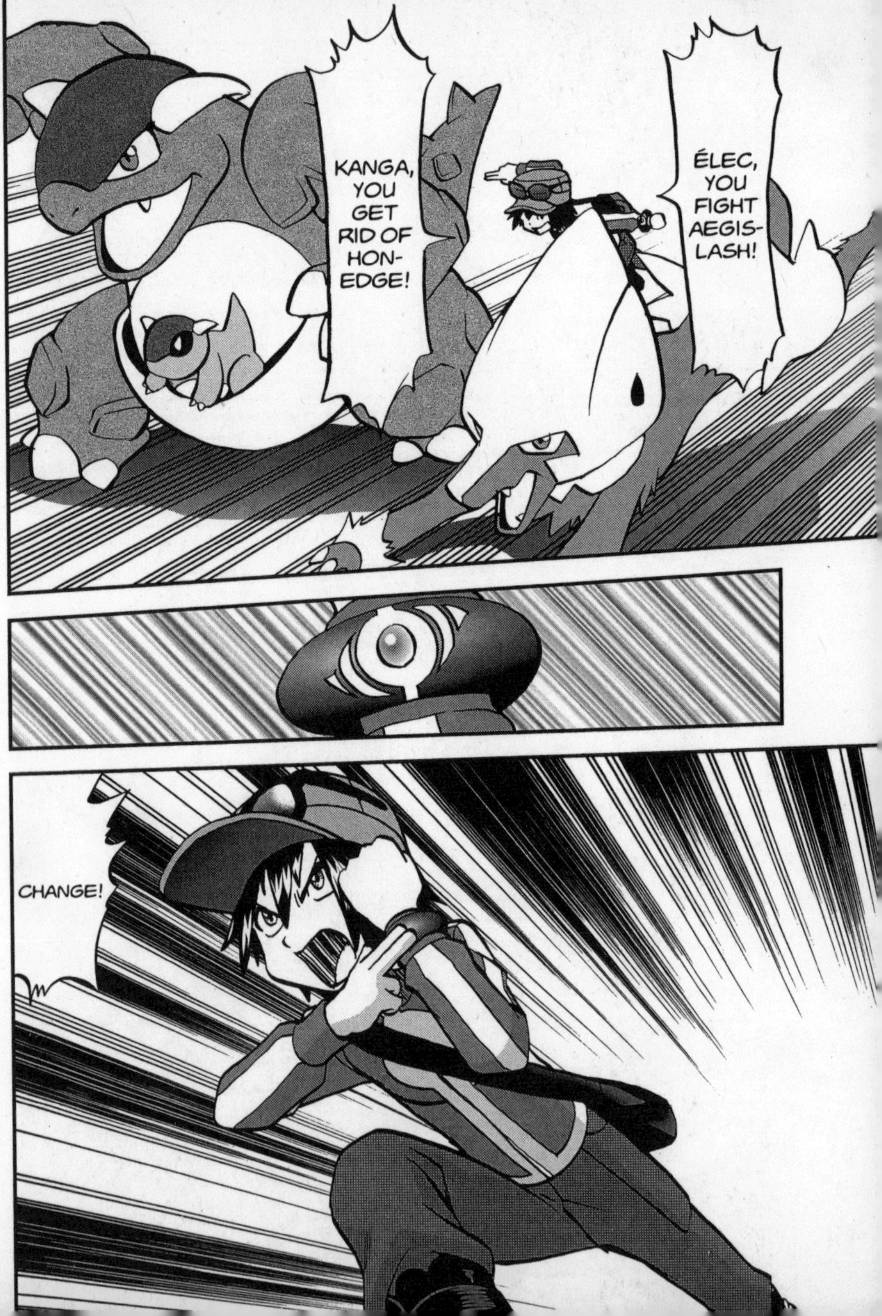
ÉLEC, YOU FIGHT AEGISLASH!
KANGA, YOU GET RID OF HONEDGE!
CHANGE!

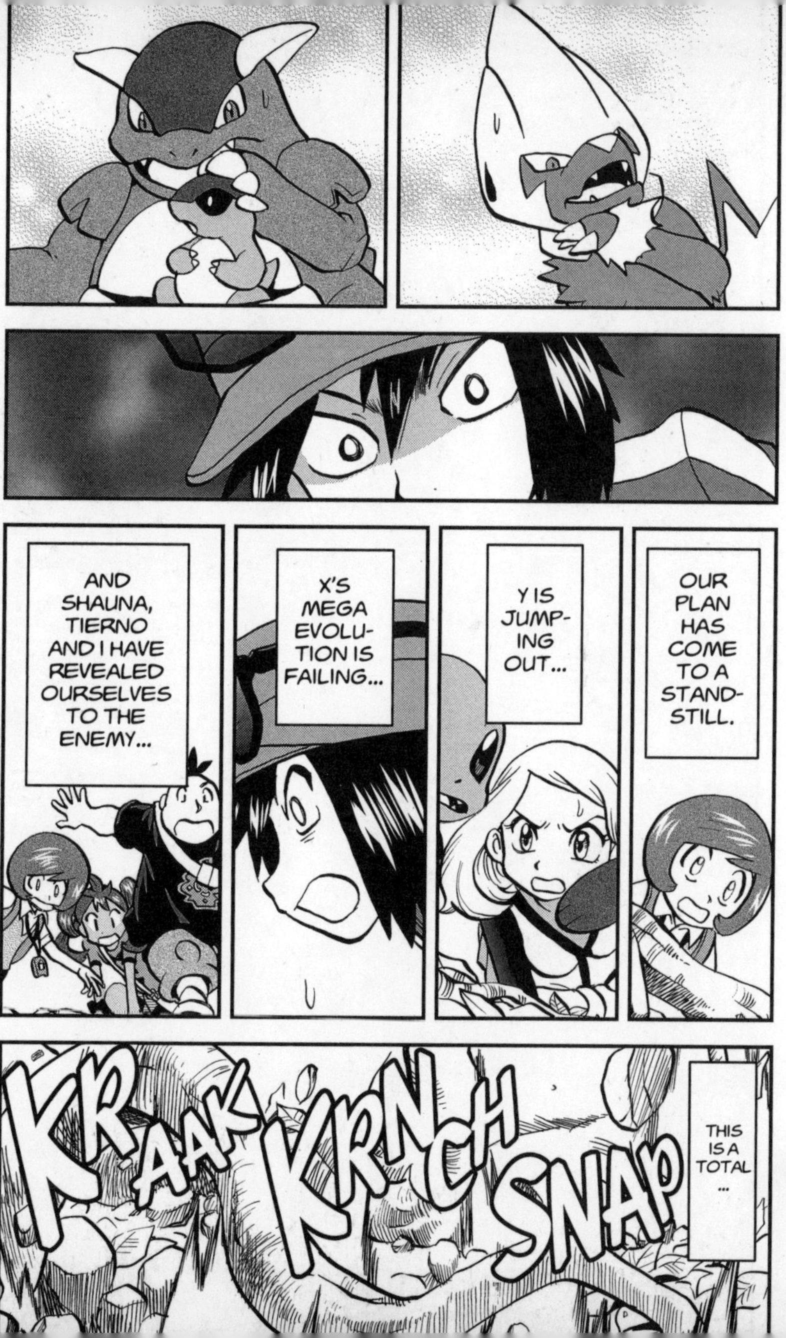
OUR PLAN HAS COME TO A STANDSTILL.
Y IS JUMPING OUT...
X'S MEGA EVOLUTION IS FAILING...
AND SHAUNA, TIERNO AND I HAVE REVEALED OURSELVES TO THE ENEMY...
THIS IS A TOTAL ...
SNAP
KRNCH
KRAAK

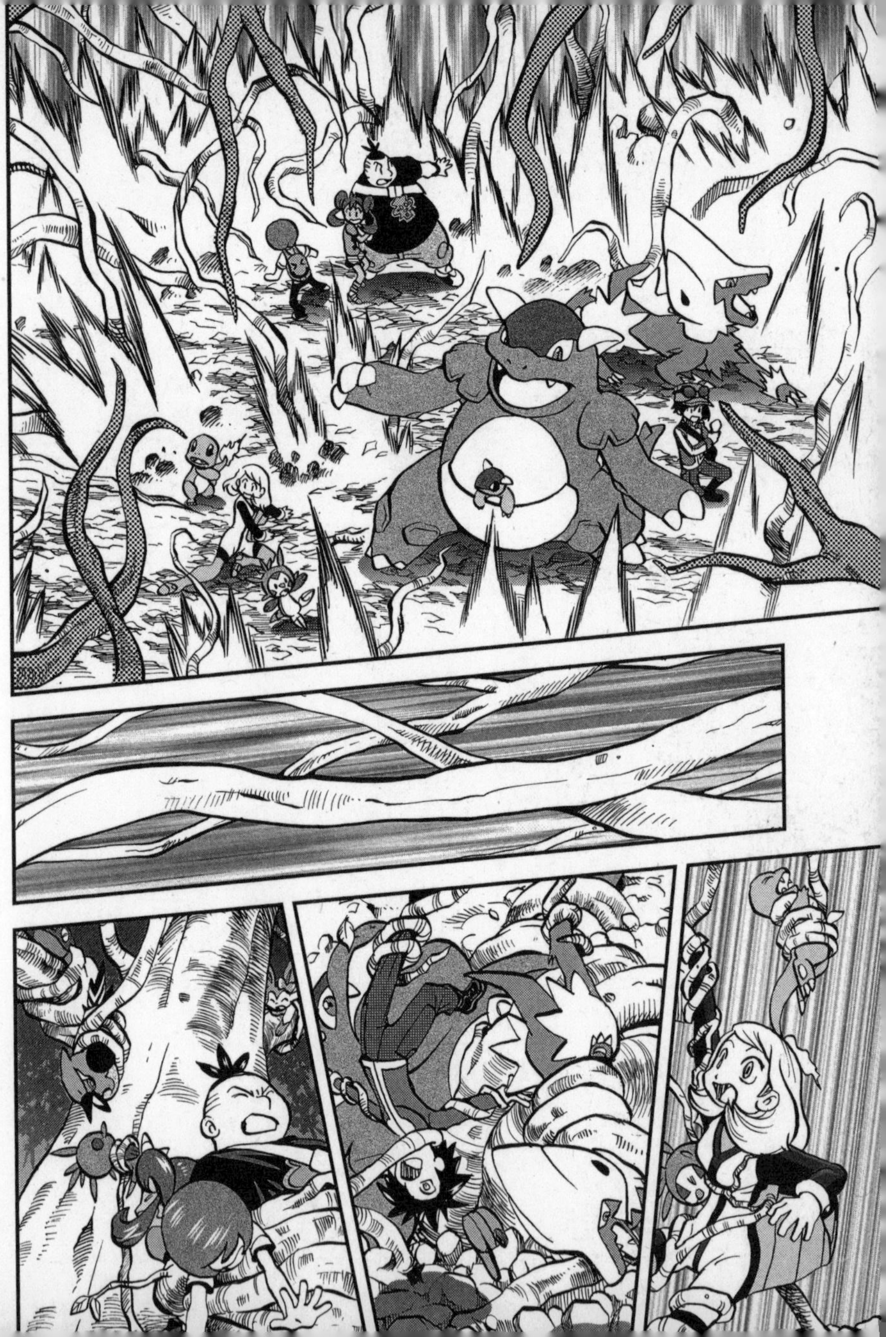

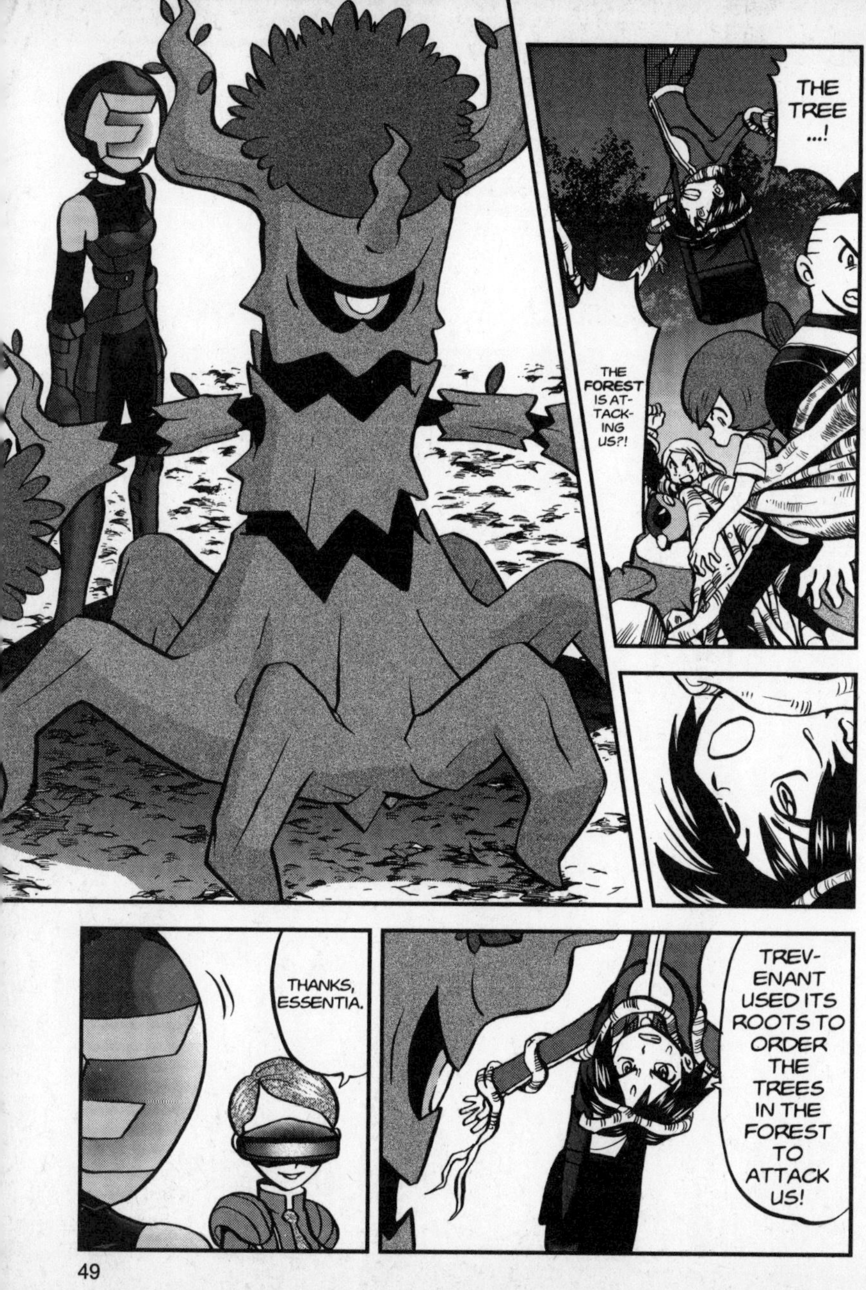
THE TREE ...!
THE FOREST IS AT-TACK-ING US?!
TREV-ENANT USED ITS ROOTS TO ORDER THE TREES IN THE FOREST TO ATTACK US!
THANKS, ESSENTIA.

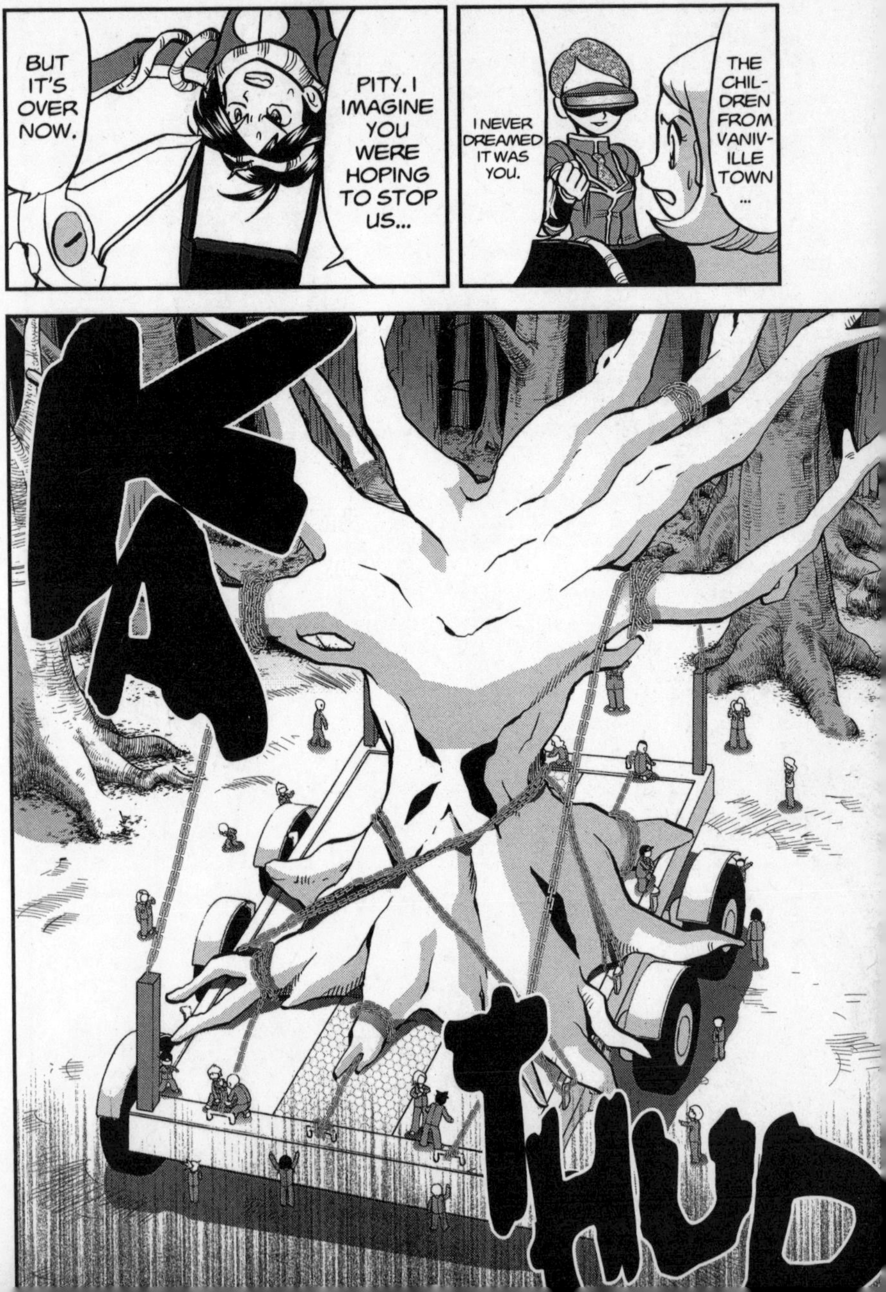
THE CHILDREN FROM VANIVILLE TOWN...
I NEVER DREAMED IT WAS YOU.
PITY. I IMAGINE YOU WERE HOPING TO STOP US...
BUT IT'S OVER NOW.
KA
THUD

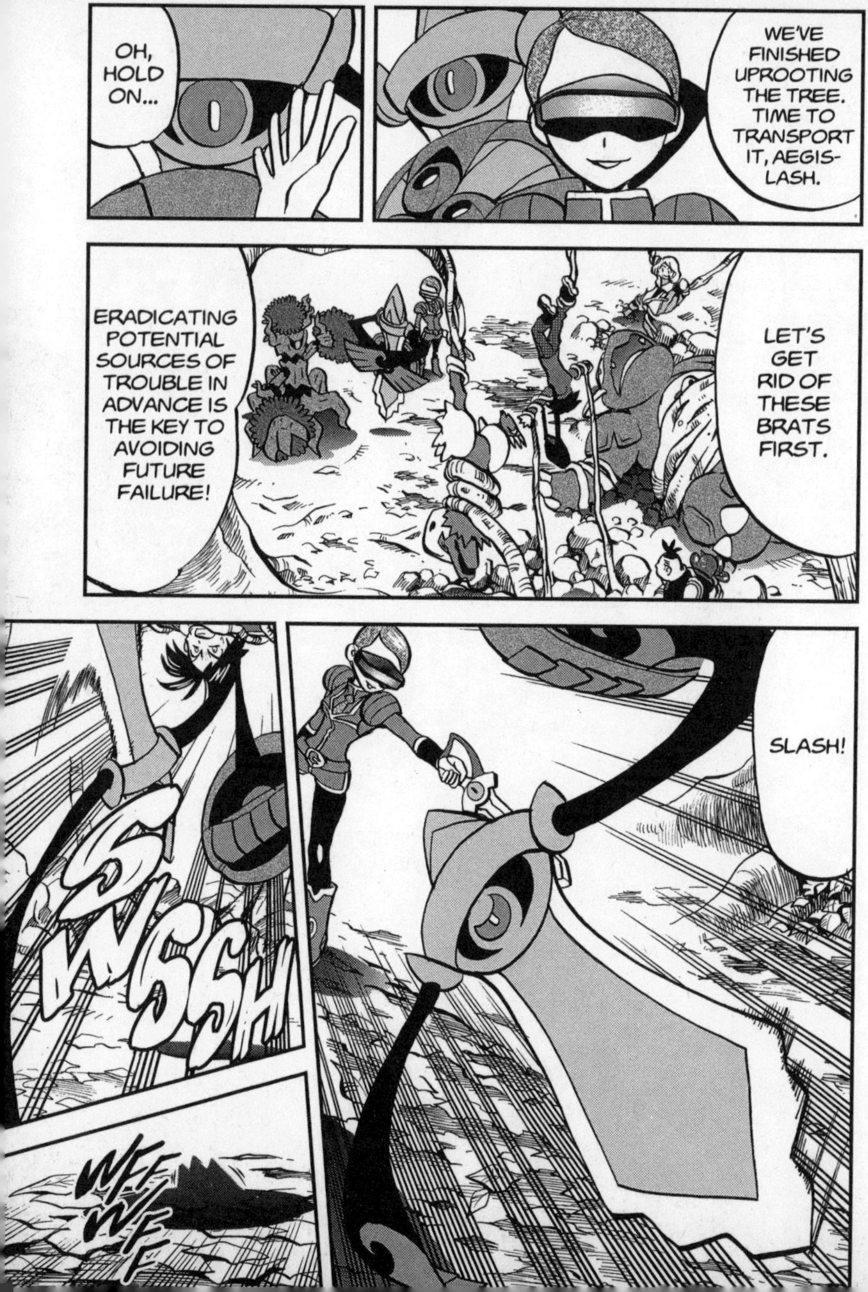

WE'VE FINISHED UPROOTING THE TREE. TIME TO TRANSPORT IT, AEGISLASH.
OH, HOLD ON...
LET'S GET RID OF THESE BRATS FIRST.
ERADICATING POTENTIAL SOURCES OF TROUBLE IN ADVANCE IS THE KEY TO AVOIDING FUTURE FAILURE!
SLASH!
SWSSCH
WF WF

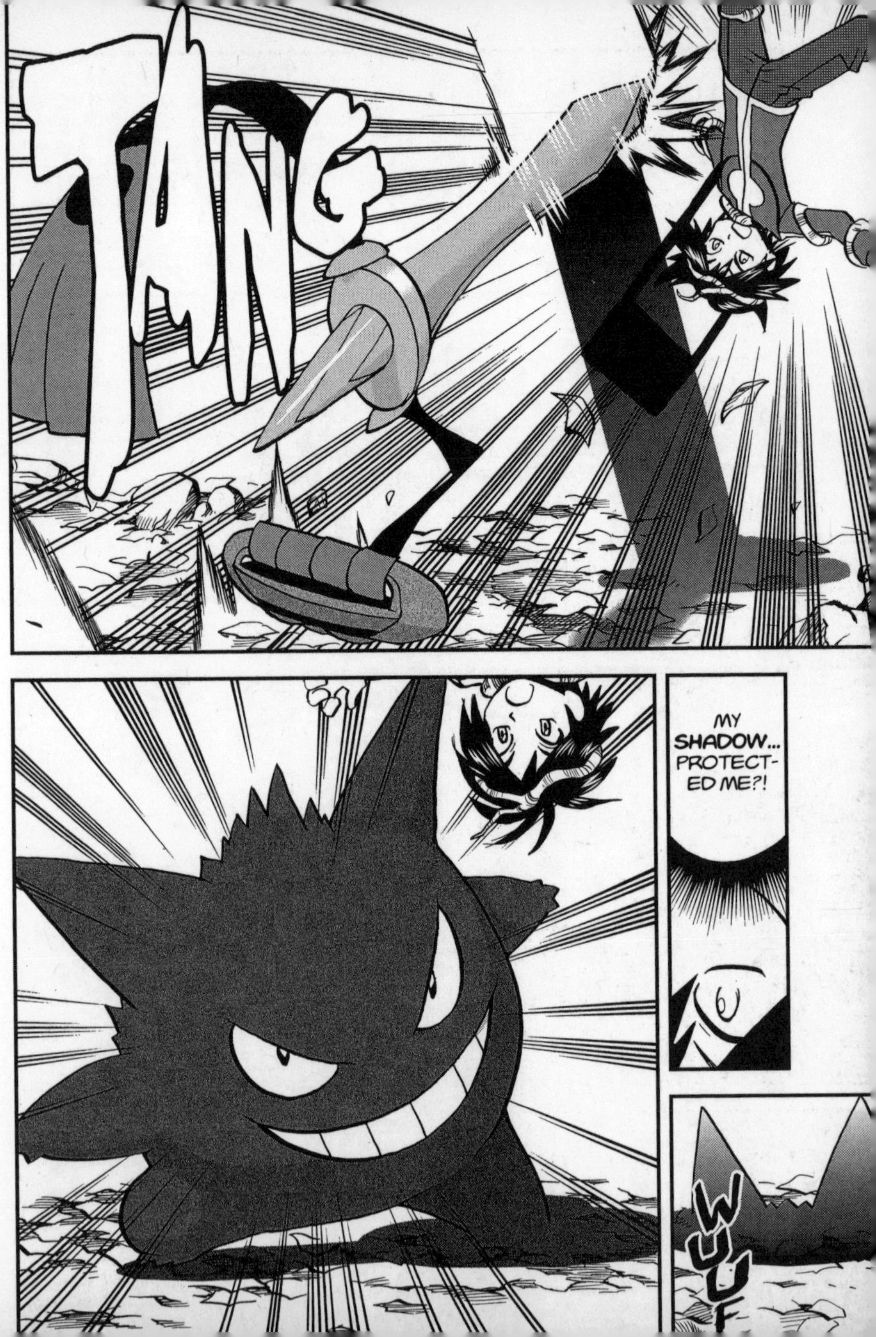
TANG
MY SHADOW... PROTECTED ME?!
WULF

WHO'S THERE ?!

GEN-GAR ?!

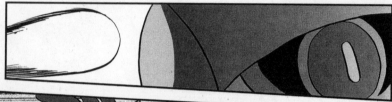

THUMMP

YOU...!

I'M GLAD WE MADE IT.

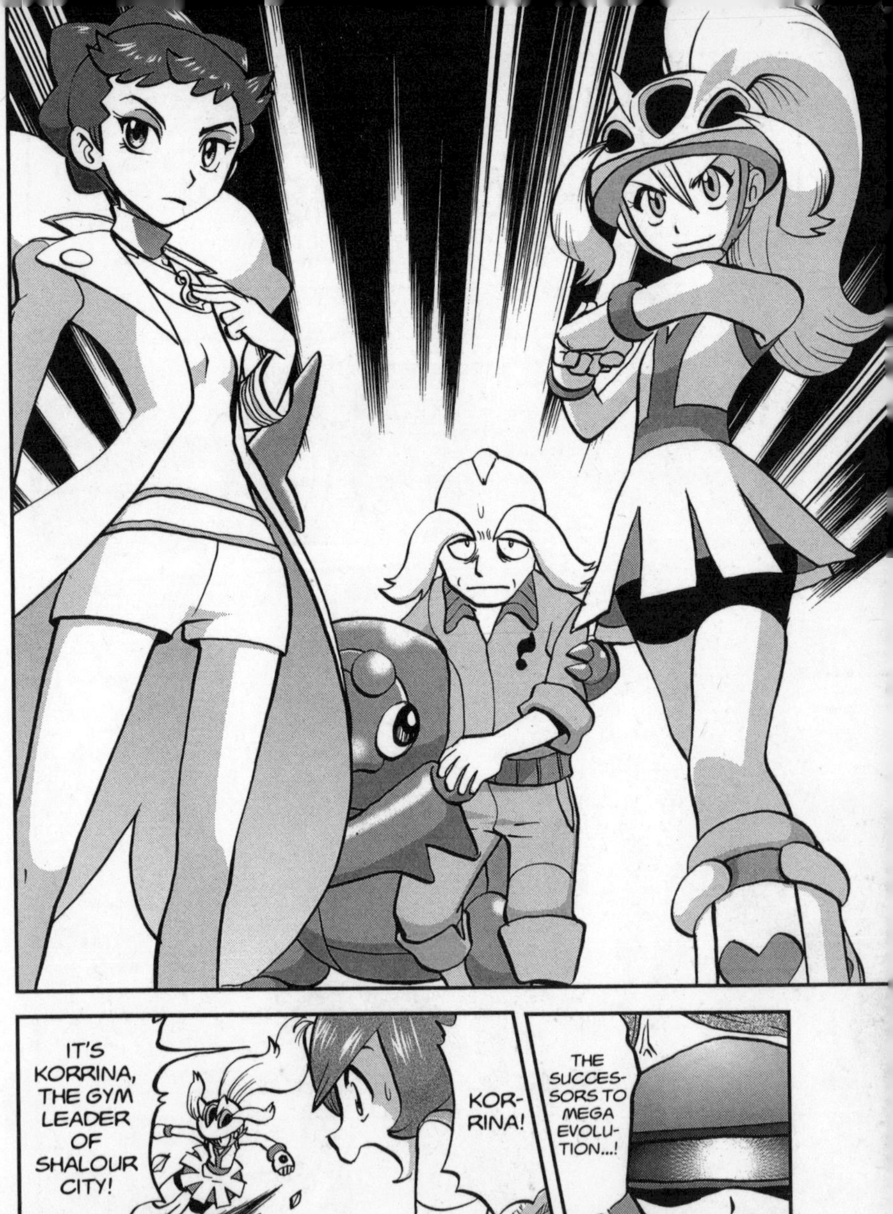
THE SUCCESSORS TO MEGA EVOLUTION...!
KORRINA!
IT'S KORRINA, THE GYM LEADER OF SHALOUR CITY!

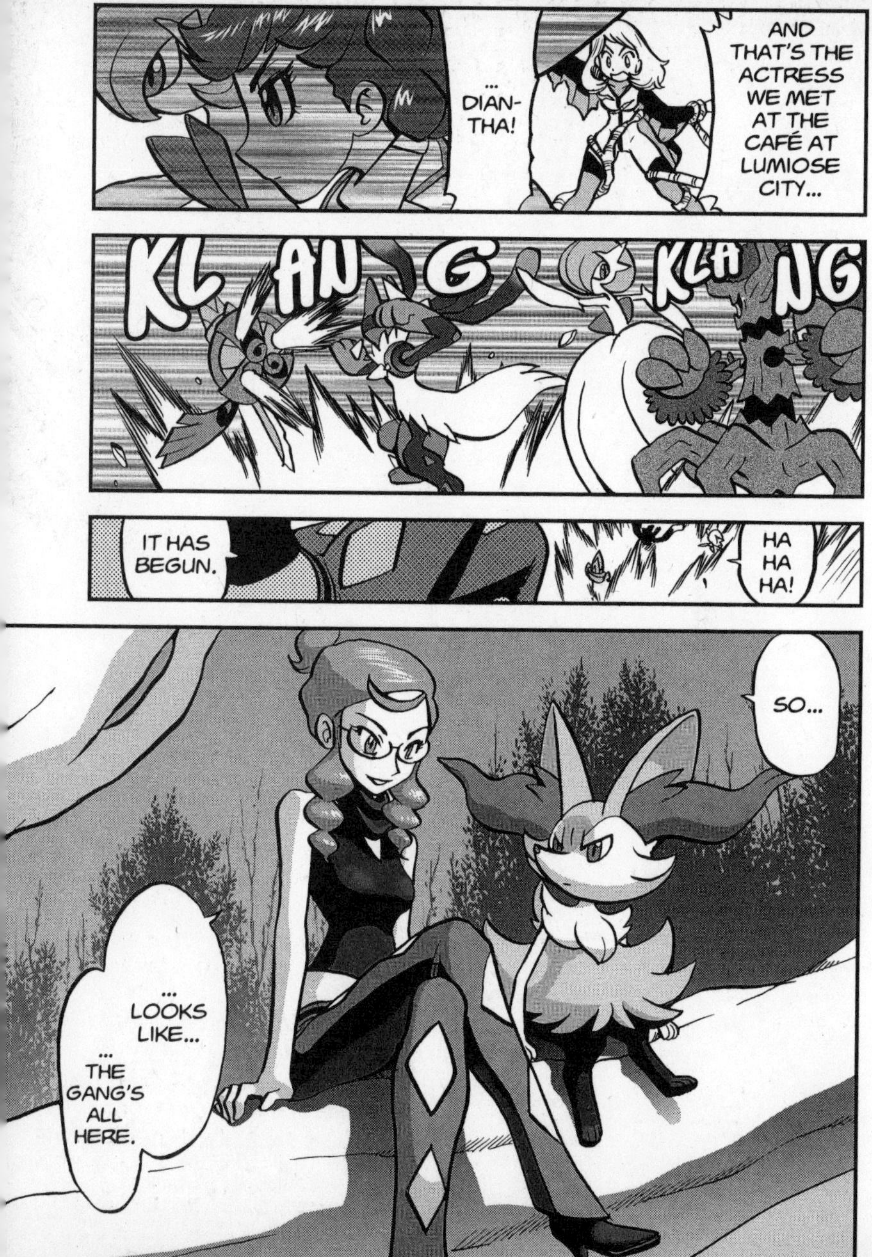
AND THAT'S THE ACTRESS WE MET AT THE CAFÉ AT LUMIOSE CITY...
...DIAN-THA!
KLANG
KLANG
HA HA HA!
IT HAS BEGUN.
SO...
...LOOKS LIKE...
...THE GANG'S ALL HERE.

Current Location

Route 8
Muraille Coast

This is a road of great contrasts,
from the harsh rock of the cliffs
to the soft sands of the beach.

Adventure 20 Changing Gengar

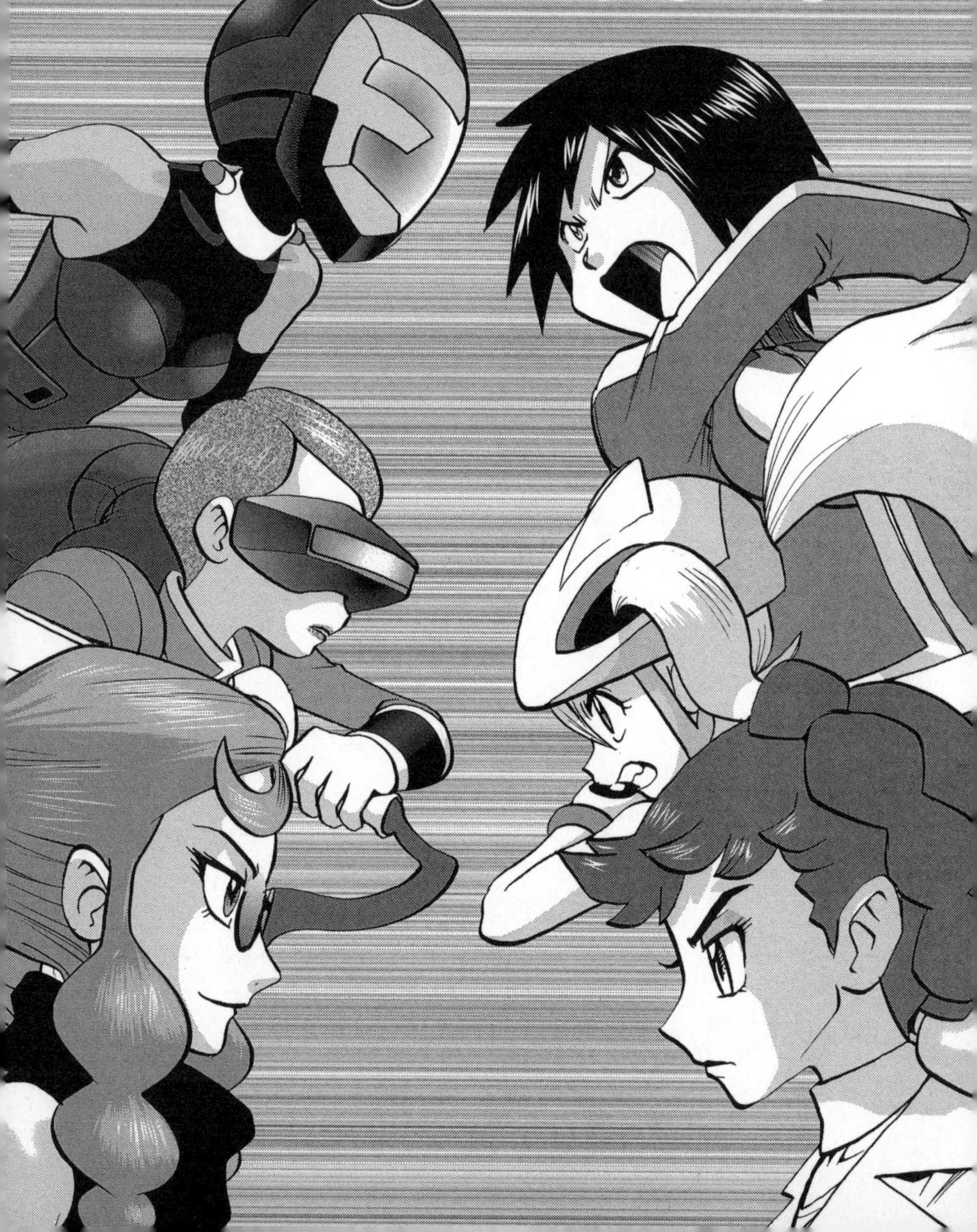

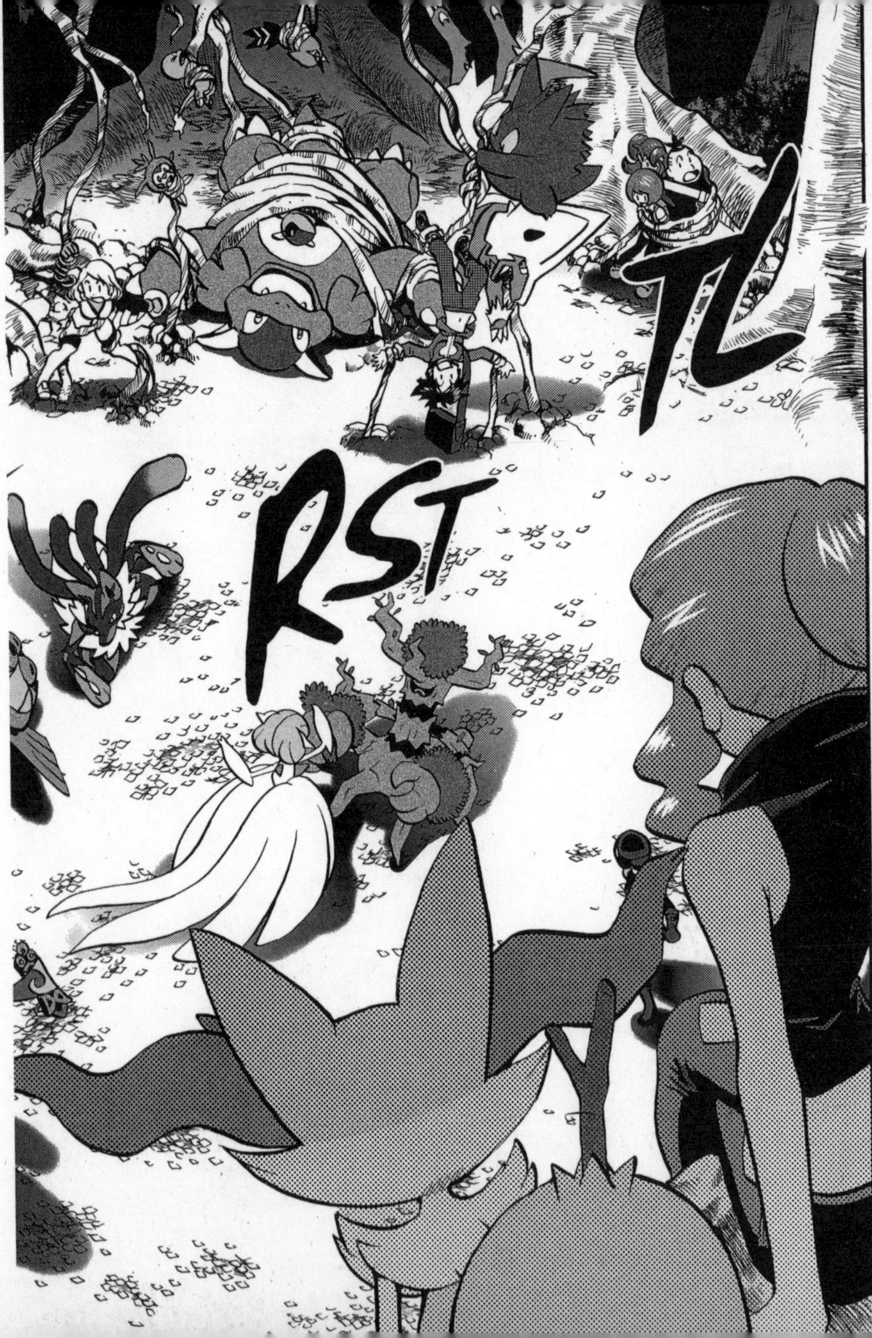
TL
RST

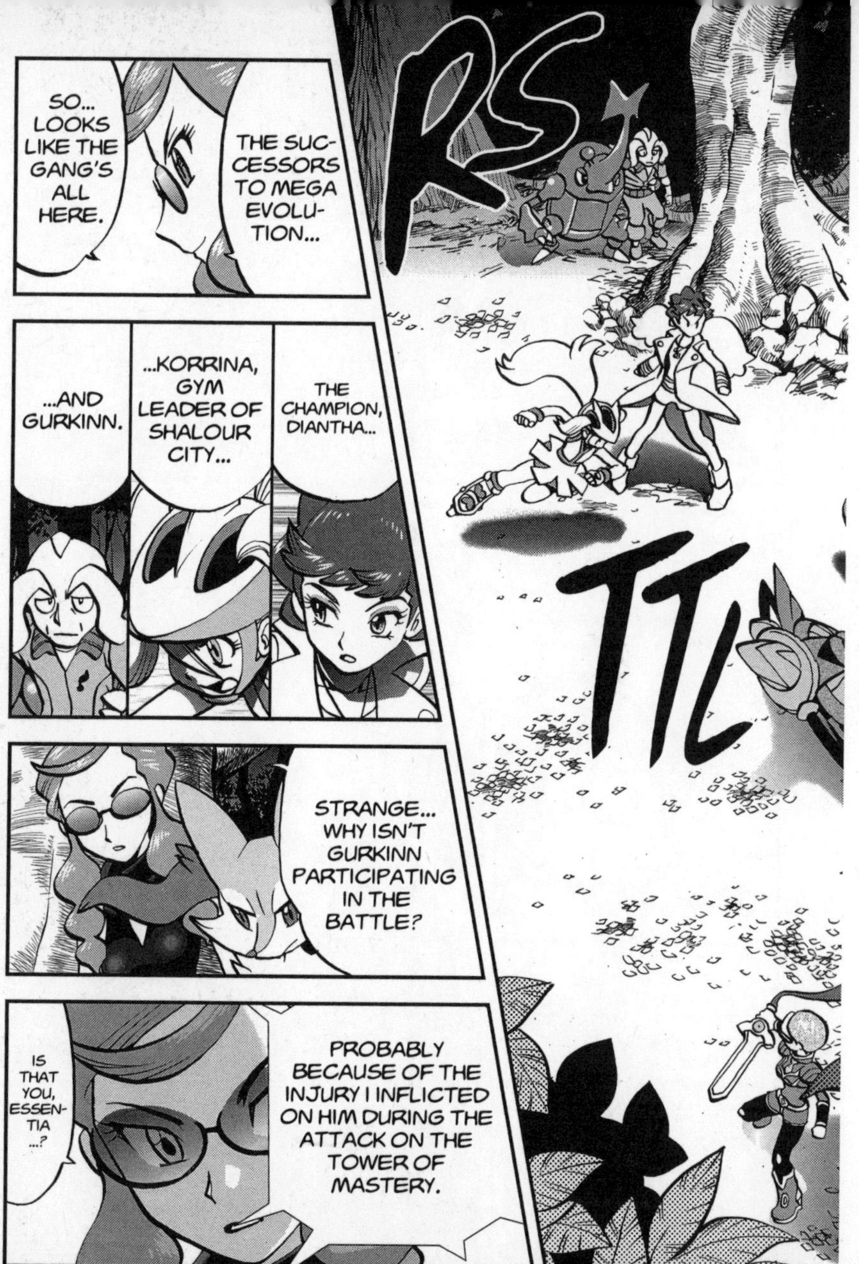
RS
TTL
THE SUC-CESSORS TO MEGA EVOLU-TION...
SO... LOOKS LIKE THE GANG'S ALL HERE.
THE CHAMPION, DIANTHA...
...KORRINA, GYM LEADER OF SHALOUR CITY...
...AND GURKINN.
STRANGE... WHY ISN'T GURKINN PARTICIPATING IN THE BATTLE?
PROBABLY BECAUSE OF THE INJURY I INFLICTED ON HIM DURING THE ATTACK ON THE TOWER OF MASTERY.
IS THAT YOU, ESSEN-TIA ...?

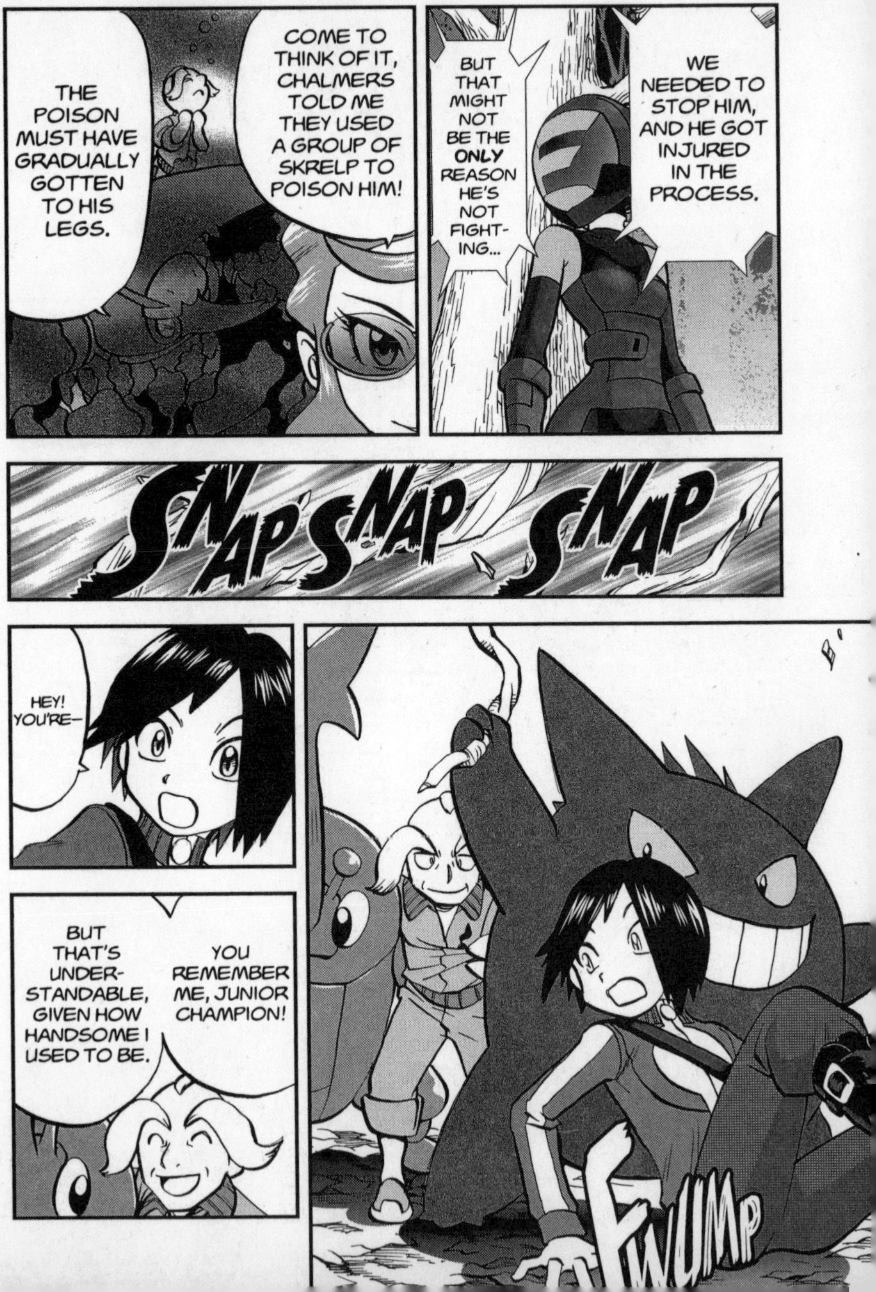
WE NEEDED TO STOP HIM, AND HE GOT INJURED IN THE PROCESS.
BUT THAT MIGHT NOT BE THE ONLY REASON HE'S NOT FIGHT-ING...
COME TO THINK OF IT, CHALMERS TOLD ME THEY USED A GROUP OF SKRELP TO POISON HIM!
THE POISON MUST HAVE GRADUALLY GOTTEN TO HIS LEGS.
SNAP SNAP SNAP
FWUMP
HEY! YOU'RE—
YOU REMEMBER ME, JUNIOR CHAMPION!
BUT THAT'S UNDER-STANDABLE, GIVEN HOW HANDSOME I USED TO BE.

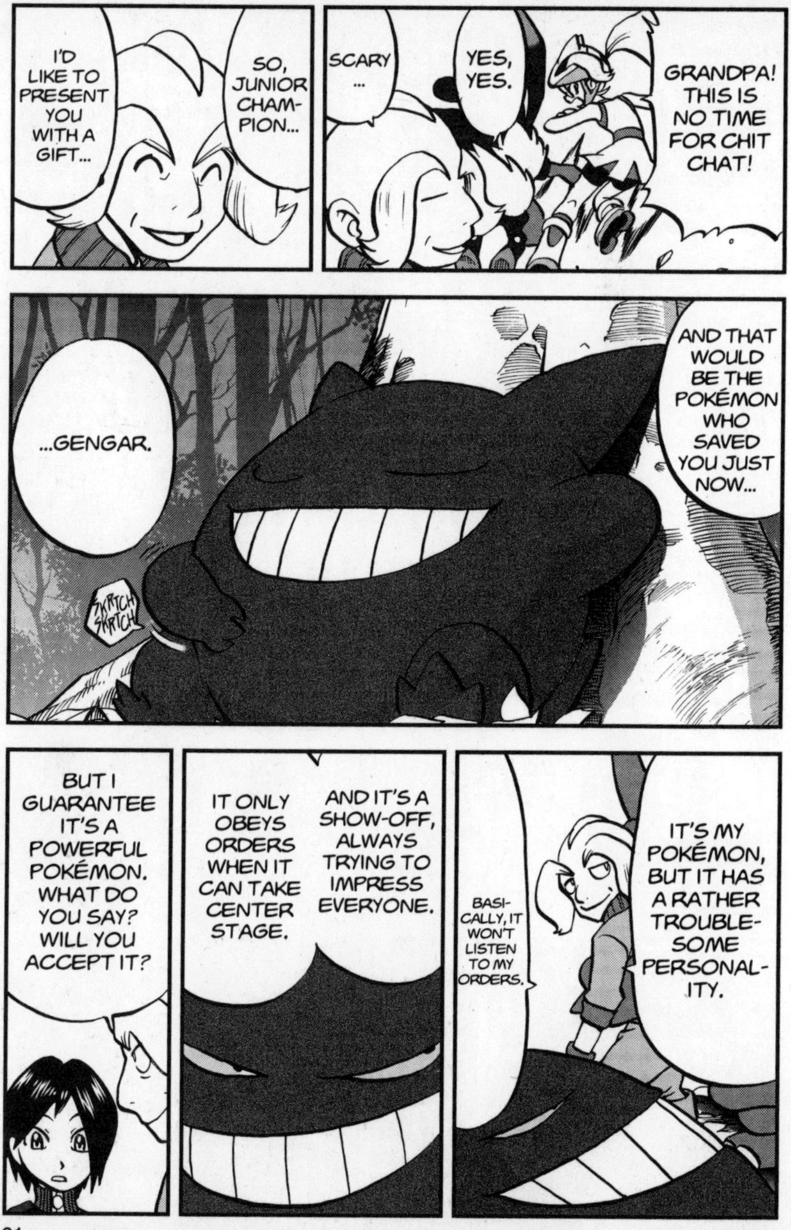
GRANDPA! THIS IS NO TIME FOR CHIT CHAT!
YES, YES.
SCARY ...
SO, JUNIOR CHAMPION...
I'D LIKE TO PRESENT YOU WITH A GIFT...
AND THAT WOULD BE THE POKÉMON WHO SAVED YOU JUST NOW...
...GENGAR.
SKRTCH SKRTCH
IT'S MY POKÉMON, BUT IT HAS A RATHER TROUBLE-SOME PERSONAL-ITY.
BASI-CALLY, IT WON'T LISTEN TO MY ORDERS.
AND IT'S A SHOW-OFF, ALWAYS TRYING TO IMPRESS EVERYONE.
IT ONLY OBEYS ORDERS WHEN IT CAN TAKE CENTER STAGE.
BUT I GUARANTEE IT'S A POWERFUL POKÉMON. WHAT DO YOU SAY? WILL YOU ACCEPT IT?

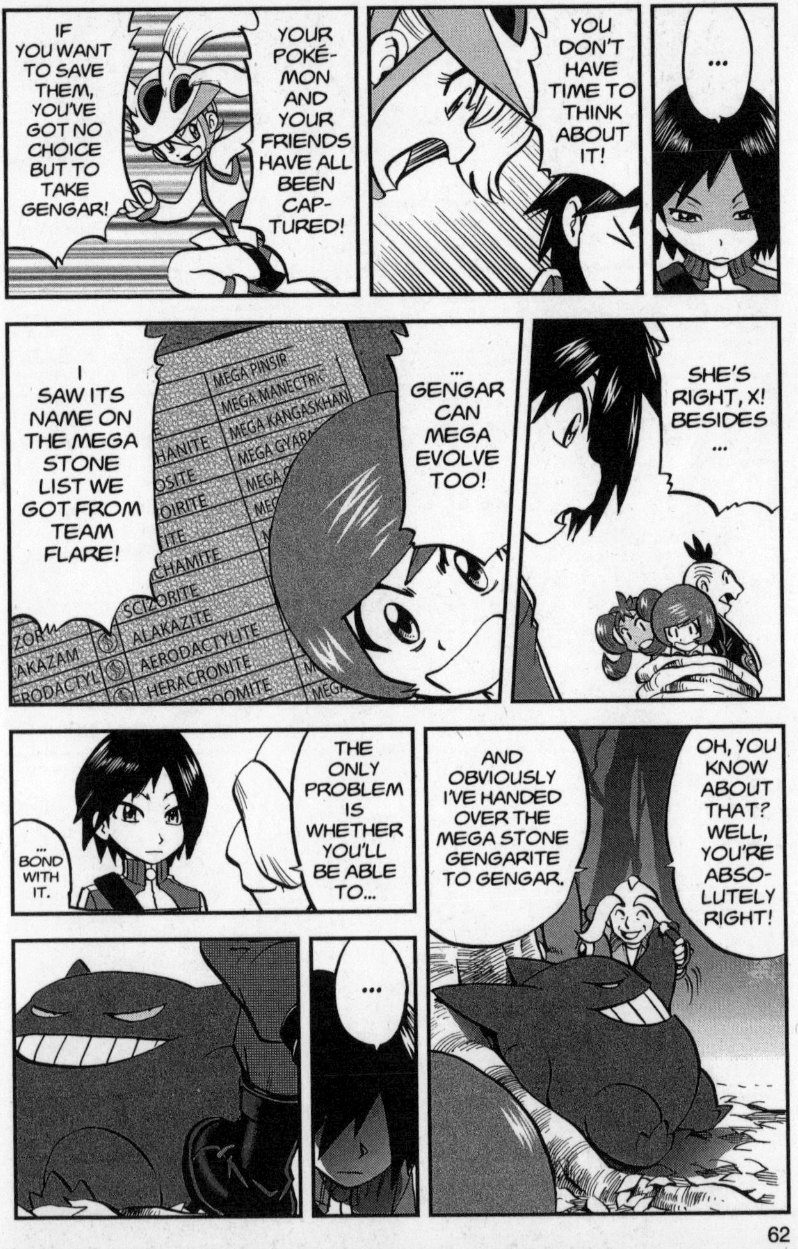
...
YOU DON'T HAVE TIME TO THINK ABOUT IT!
YOUR POKÉ-MON AND YOUR FRIENDS HAVE ALL BEEN CAP-TURED!
IF YOU WANT TO SAVE THEM, YOU'VE GOT NO CHOICE BUT TO TAKE GENGAR!
SHE'S RIGHT, X! BESIDES...
... GENGAR CAN MEGA EVOLVE TOO!
MEGA PINSIR
MEGA KANGASKHAN
I SAW ITS NAME ON THE MEGA STONE LIST WE GOT FROM TEAM FLARE!
SCIZORITE
ALAKAZITE
AERODACTYLITE
HERACRONITE
OH, YOU KNOW ABOUT THAT? WELL, YOU'RE ABSO-LUTELY RIGHT!
AND OBVIOUSLY I'VE HANDED OVER THE MEGA STONE GENGARITE TO GENGAR.
THE ONLY PROBLEM IS WHETHER YOU'LL BE ABLE TO...
... BOND WITH IT.
...

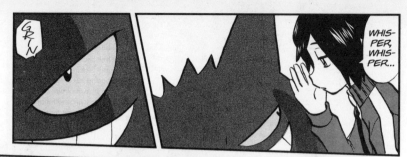

GRIN

WHIS-PER, WHIS-PER...

DASH

SHAD-OW PUNCH!

OOH!

63

KRACKTACK

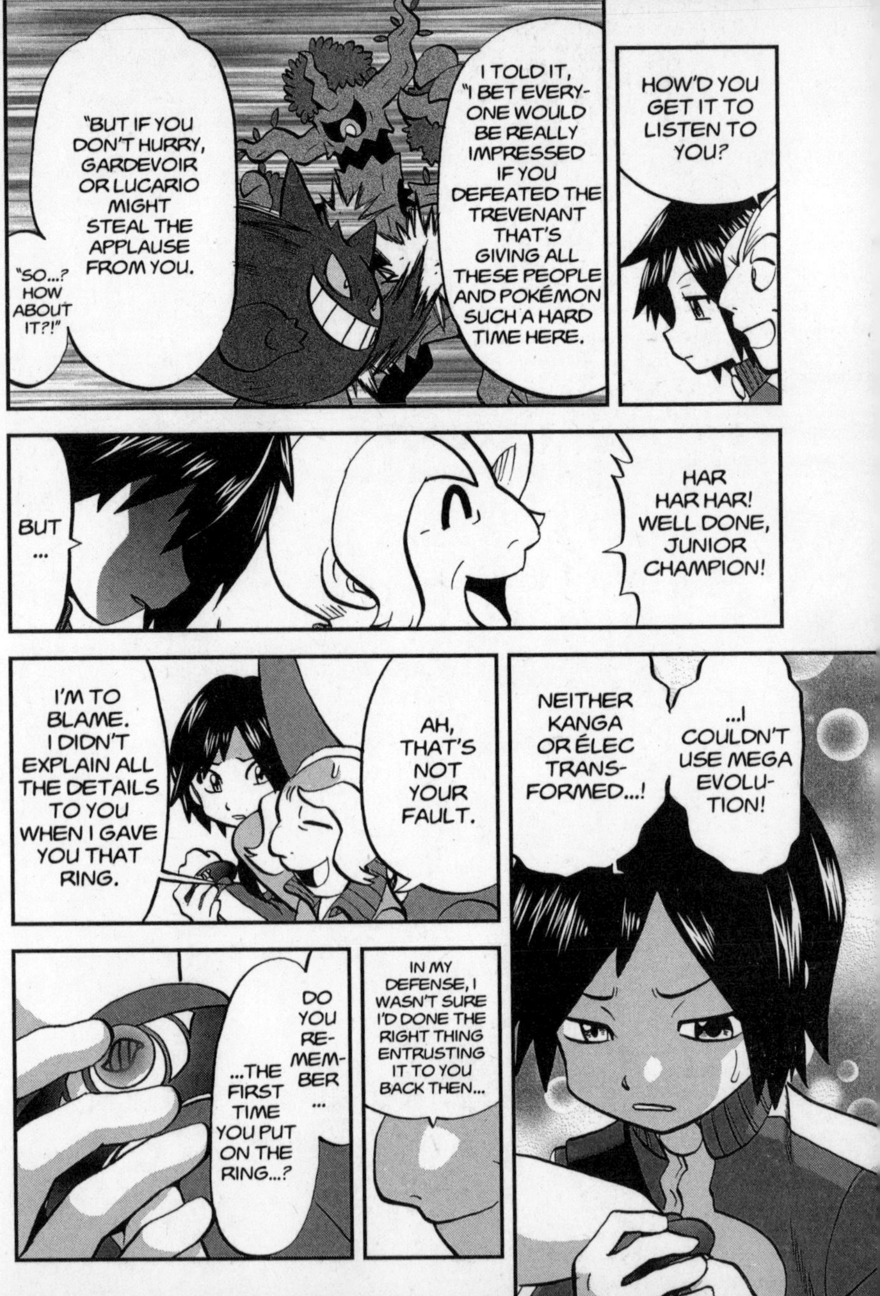
HOW'D YOU GET IT TO LISTEN TO YOU?
I TOLD IT, "I BET EVERY-ONE WOULD BE REALLY IMPRESSED IF YOU DEFEATED THE TREVENANT THAT'S GIVING ALL THESE PEOPLE AND POKÉMON SUCH A HARD TIME HERE.
"BUT IF YOU DON'T HURRY, GARDEVOIR OR LUCARIO MIGHT STEAL THE APPLAUSE FROM YOU.
"SO...? HOW ABOUT IT?!"
HAR HAR HAR! WELL DONE, JUNIOR CHAMPION!
BUT ...
...I COULDN'T USE MEGA EVOLU-TION!
NEITHER KANGA OR ÉLEC TRANS-FORMED...!
AH, THAT'S NOT YOUR FAULT.
I'M TO BLAME. I DIDN'T EXPLAIN ALL THE DETAILS TO YOU WHEN I GAVE YOU THAT RING.
IN MY DEFENSE, I WASN'T SURE I'D DONE THE RIGHT THING ENTRUSTING IT TO YOU BACK THEN...
DO YOU RE-MEM-BER ...
...THE FIRST TIME YOU PUT ON THE RING...?

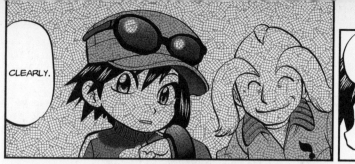

YES ...
CLEARLY.
HOW CAN I PUT IT...? IT FELT LIKE...
...MY STRENGTH AND MY EMOTIONS... WERE ALL GETTING CONCENTRATED INTO THE RING—OR THE KEY STONE EMBEDDED IN THE CENTER OF THE RING, TO BE EXACT.
IT WAS LIKE I HAD ANOTHER BRAIN OR HEART...
...ON MY LEFT ARM.
YOUR SENSES WERE CORRECT.
HOWEVER, NOT EVERYBODY ...
...HAS THAT EXPERIENCE.

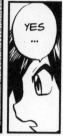

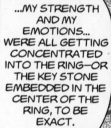

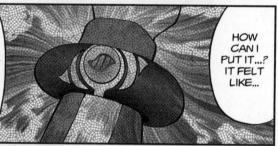

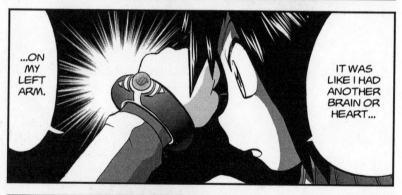

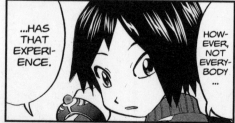

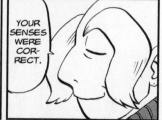

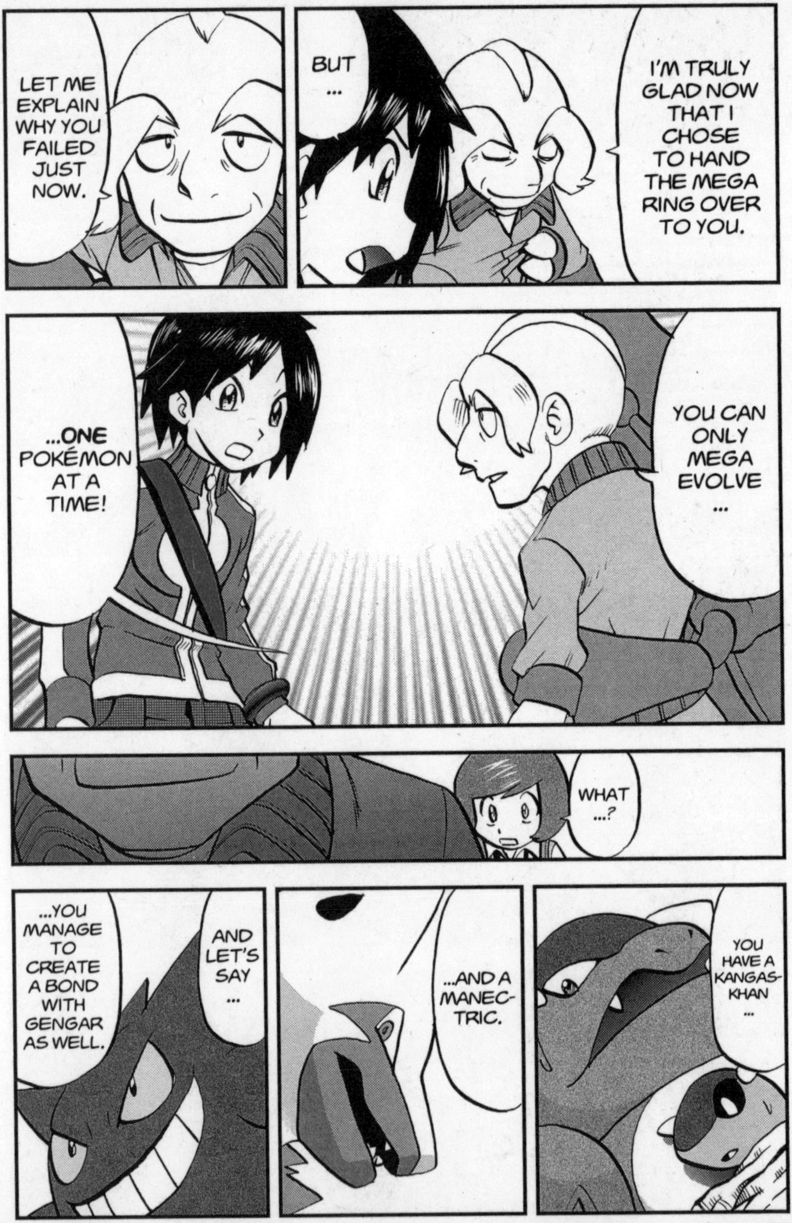
I'M TRULY GLAD NOW THAT I CHOSE TO HAND THE MEGA RING OVER TO YOU.
BUT ...
LET ME EXPLAIN WHY YOU FAILED JUST NOW.
YOU CAN ONLY MEGA EVOLVE ...
...ONE POKÉMON AT A TIME!
WHAT ...?
YOU HAVE A KANGAS-KHAN ...
...AND A MANEC-TRIC.
AND LET'S SAY ...
...YOU MANAGE TO CREATE A BOND WITH GENGAR AS WELL.

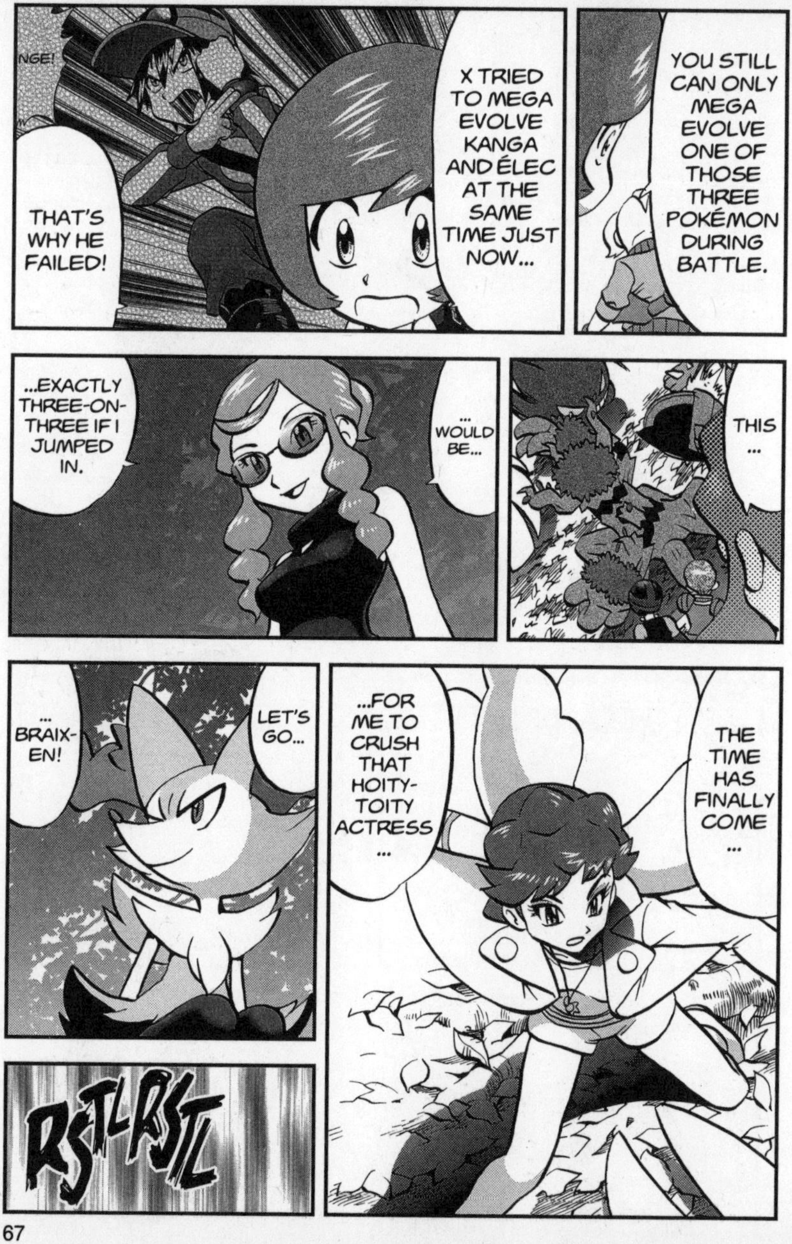
YOU STILL CAN ONLY MEGA EVOLVE ONE OF THOSE THREE POKÉMON DURING BATTLE.
X TRIED TO MEGA EVOLVE KANGA AND ÉLEC AT THE SAME TIME JUST NOW...
THAT'S WHY HE FAILED!
THIS ...
... WOULD BE...
...EXACTLY THREE-ON-THREE IF I JUMPED IN.
THE TIME HAS FINALLY COME ...
...FOR ME TO CRUSH THAT HOITY-TOITY ACTRESS ...
LET'S GO...
... BRAIX-EN!
RSTL RSTL

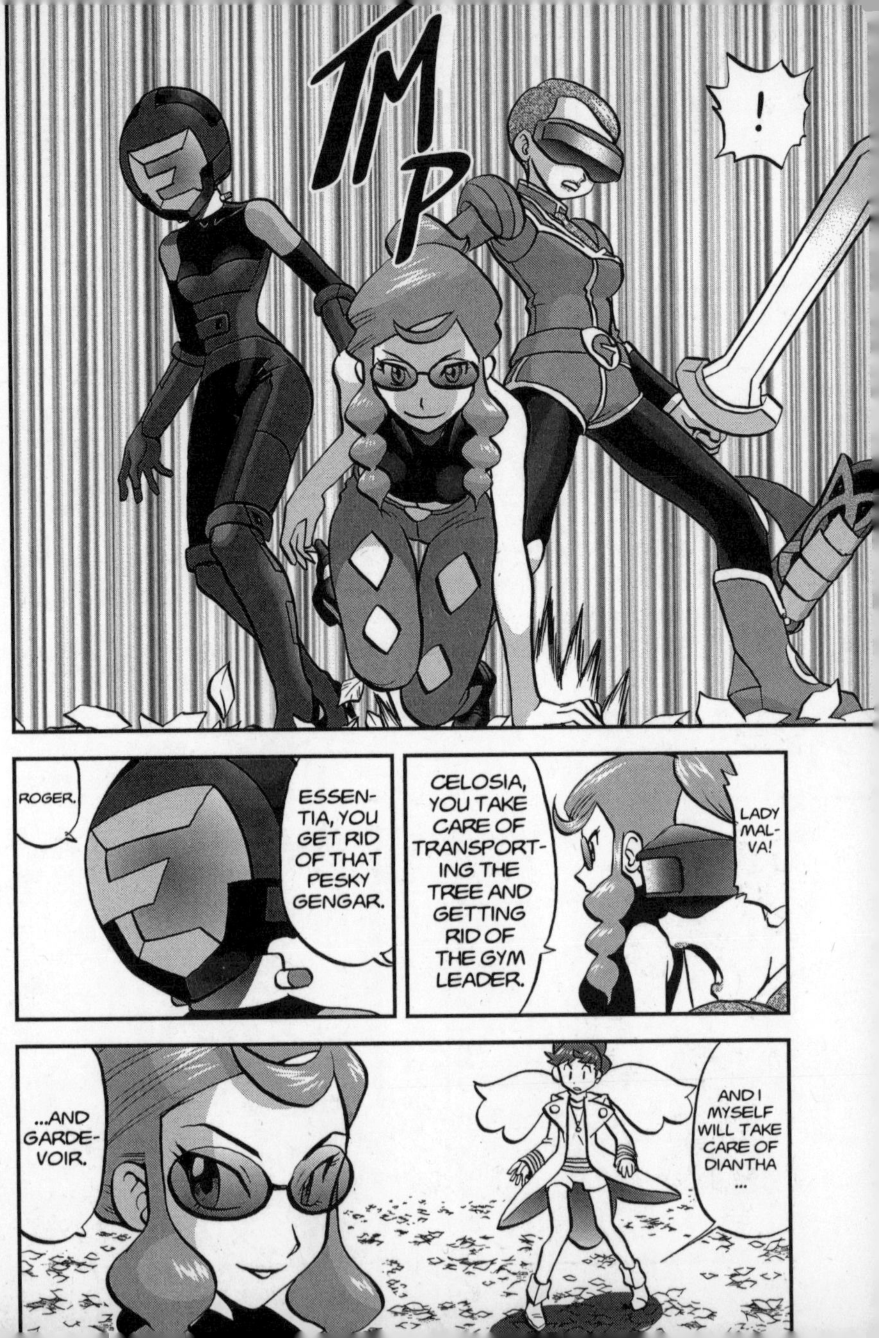
!
TMP
LADY MALVA!
CELOSIA, YOU TAKE CARE OF TRANSPORTING THE TREE AND GETTING RID OF THE GYM LEADER.
ESSENTIA, YOU GET RID OF THAT PESKY GENGAR.
ROGER.
AND I MYSELF WILL TAKE CARE OF DIANTHA ...
...AND GARDEVOIR.

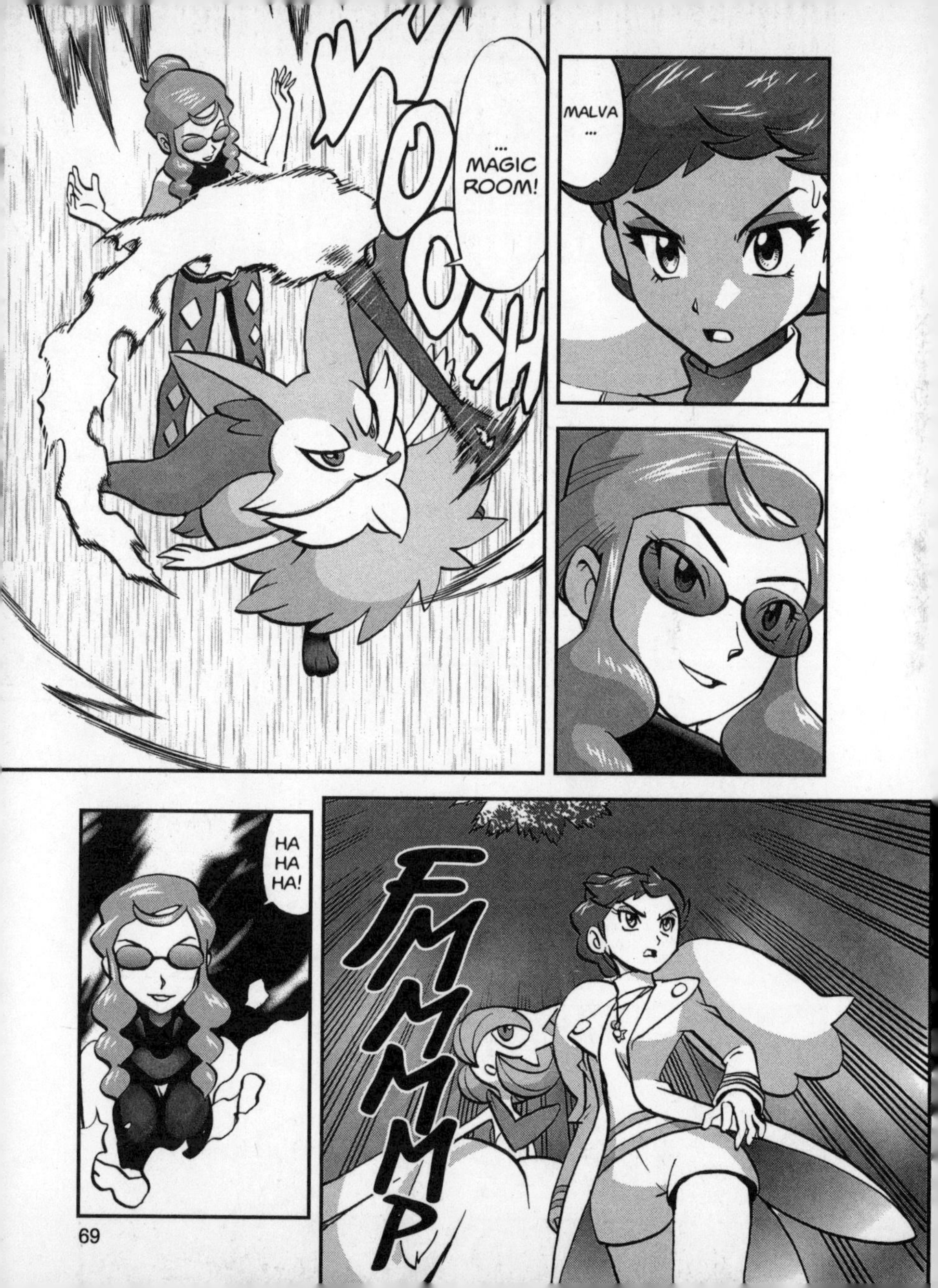
MALVA ...
... MAGIC ROOM!
WHOOSH
FMMMMP
HA HA HA!

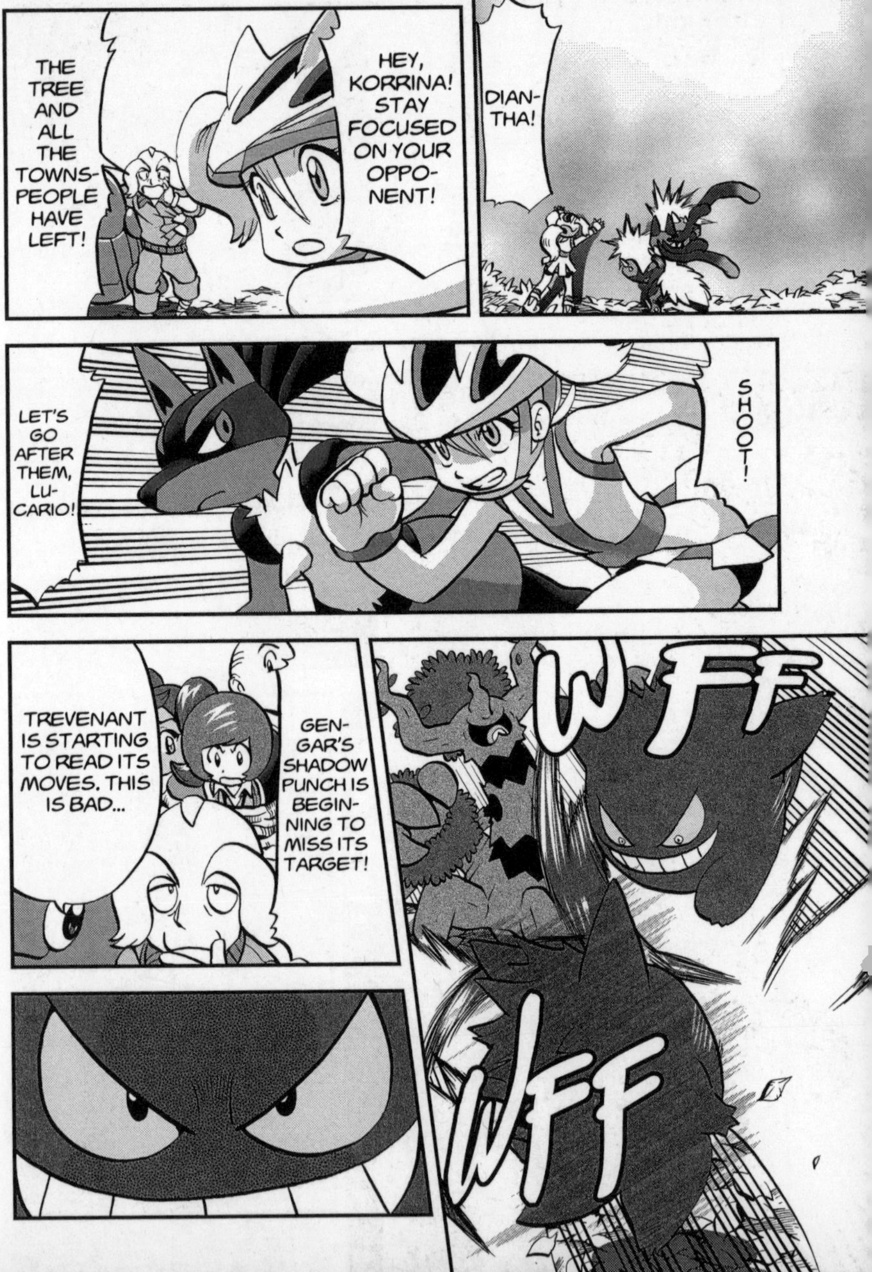
DIANTHA!
HEY, KORRINA! STAY FOCUSED ON YOUR OPPONENT!
THE TREE AND ALL THE TOWNSPEOPLE HAVE LEFT!
SHOOT!
LET'S GO AFTER THEM, LUCARIO!
WFF
WFF
GENGAR'S SHADOW PUNCH IS BEGINNING TO MISS ITS TARGET!
TREVENANT IS STARTING TO READ ITS MOVES. THIS IS BAD...

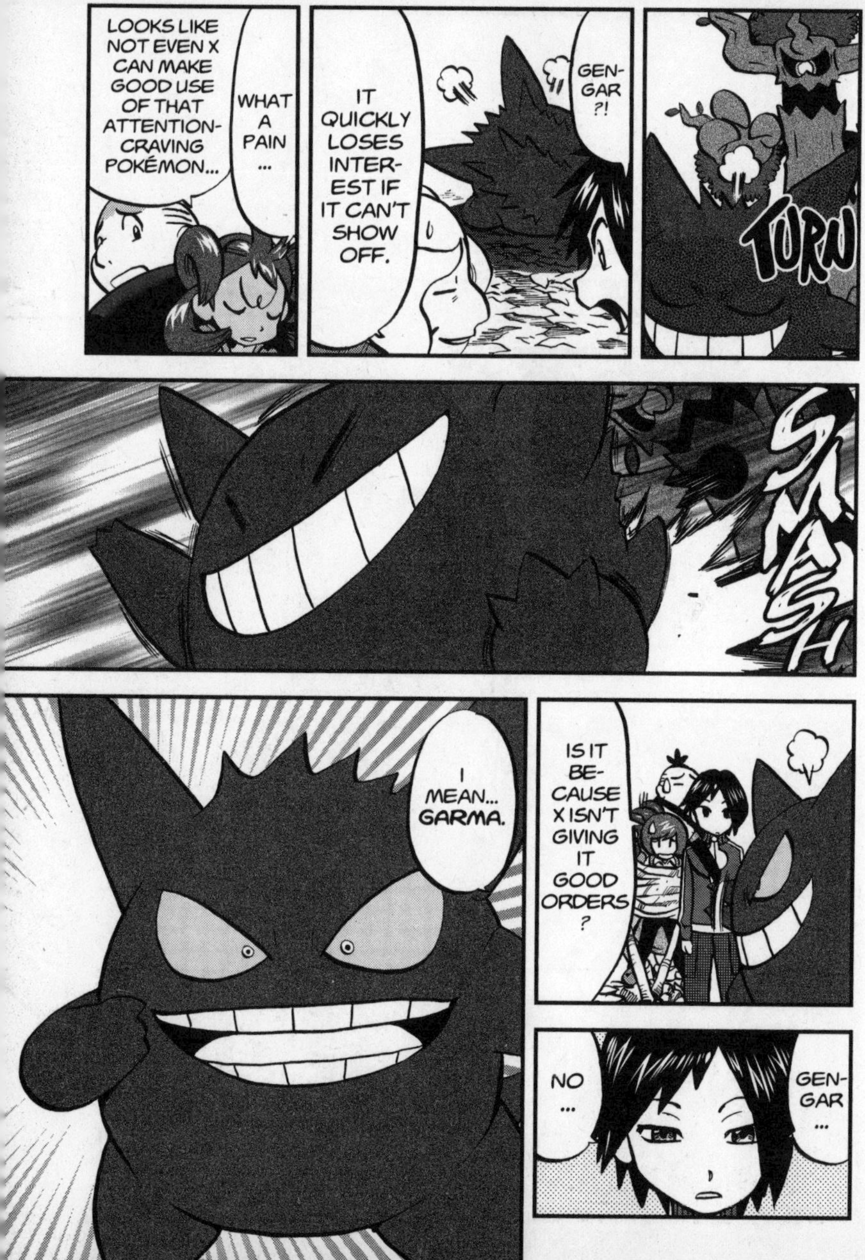
TURN
GEN-GAR?!
IT QUICKLY LOSES INTEREST IF IT CAN'T SHOW OFF.
WHAT A PAIN...
LOOKS LIKE NOT EVEN X CAN MAKE GOOD USE OF THAT ATTENTION-CRAVING POKÉMON...
SMASH
IS IT BECAUSE X ISN'T GIVING IT GOOD ORDERS?
GEN-GAR...
NO...
I MEAN... **GARMA.**

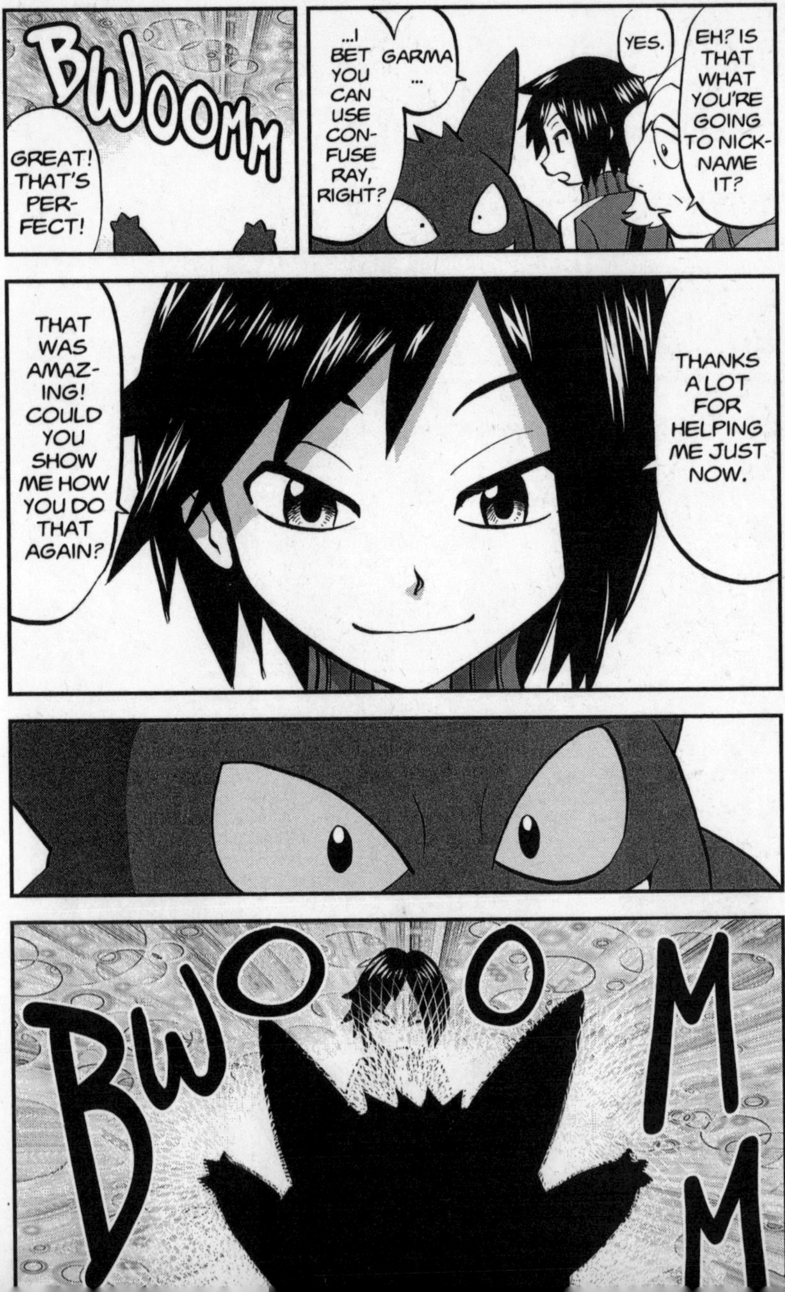
EH? IS THAT WHAT YOU'RE GOING TO NICKNAME IT?
YES.
GARMA ...
...I BET YOU CAN USE CONFUSE RAY, RIGHT?
BWOOMM
GREAT! THAT'S PERFECT!
THANKS A LOT FOR HELPING ME JUST NOW.
THAT WAS AMAZING! COULD YOU SHOW ME HOW YOU DO THAT AGAIN?
BWOOMMM

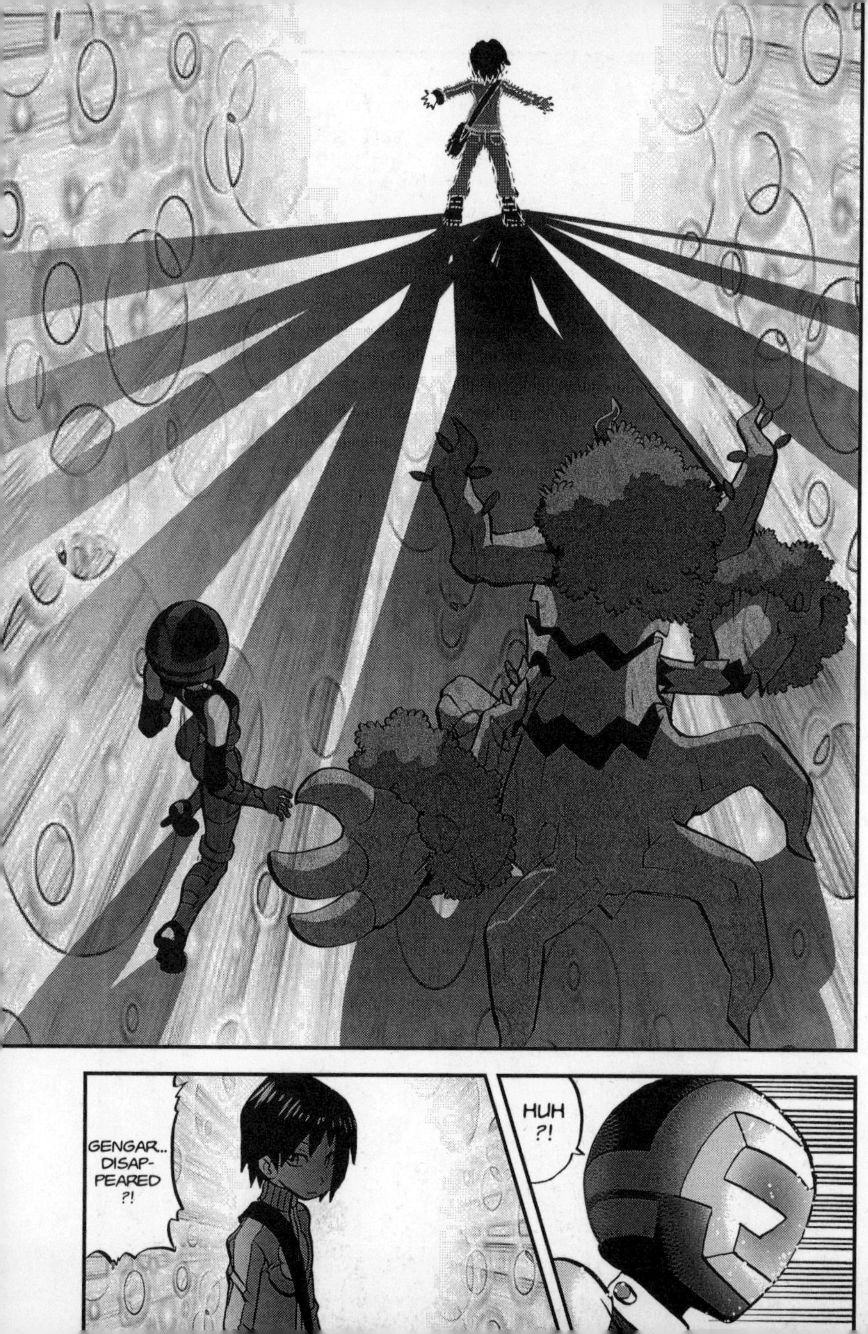
HUH ?!
GENGAR.. DISAP- PEARED ?!

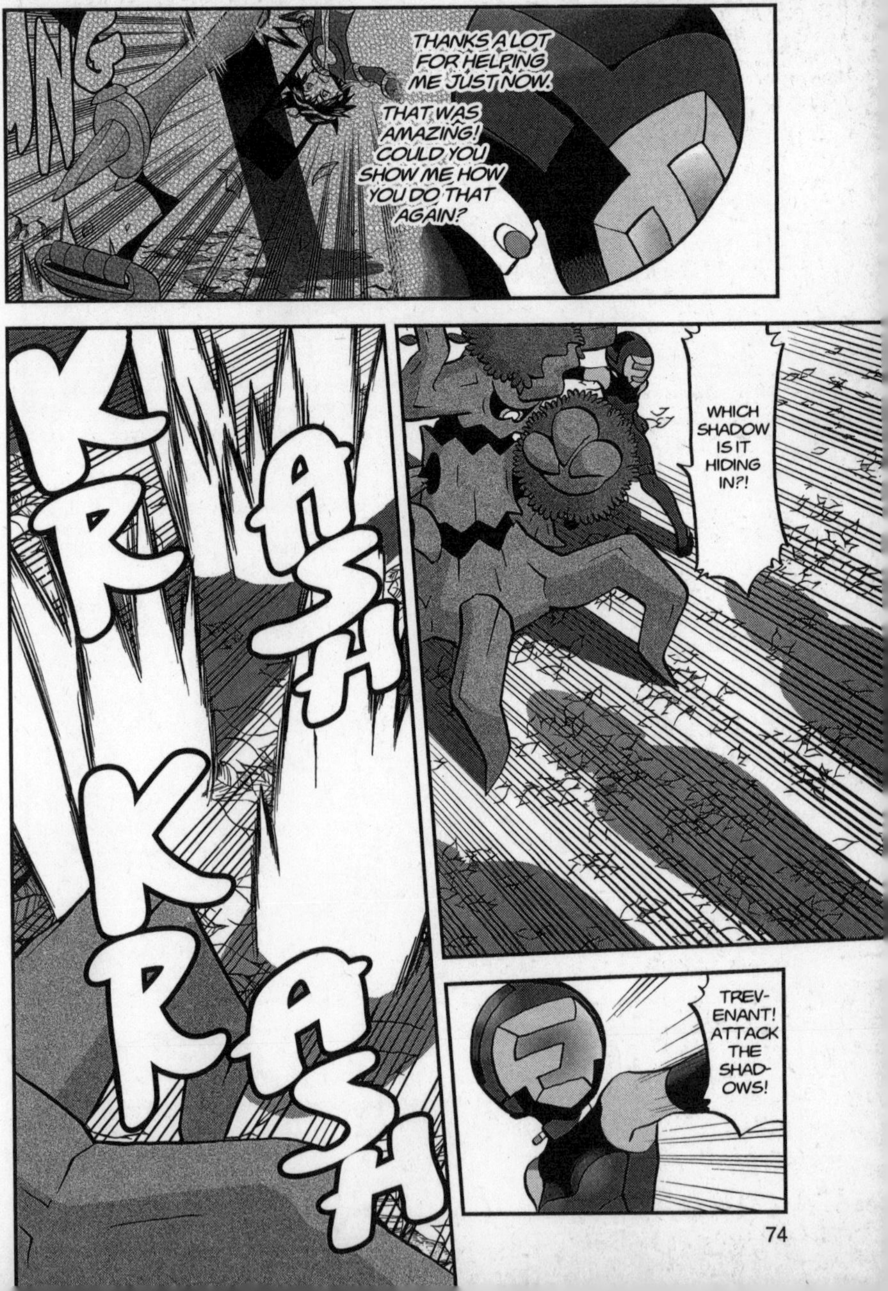
THANKS A LOT FOR HELPING ME JUST NOW.
THAT WAS AMAZING! COULD YOU SHOW ME HOW YOU DO THAT AGAIN?
WHICH SHADOW IS IT HIDING IN?!
TREV-ENANT! ATTACK THE SHAD-OWS!
KRASH
KRASH

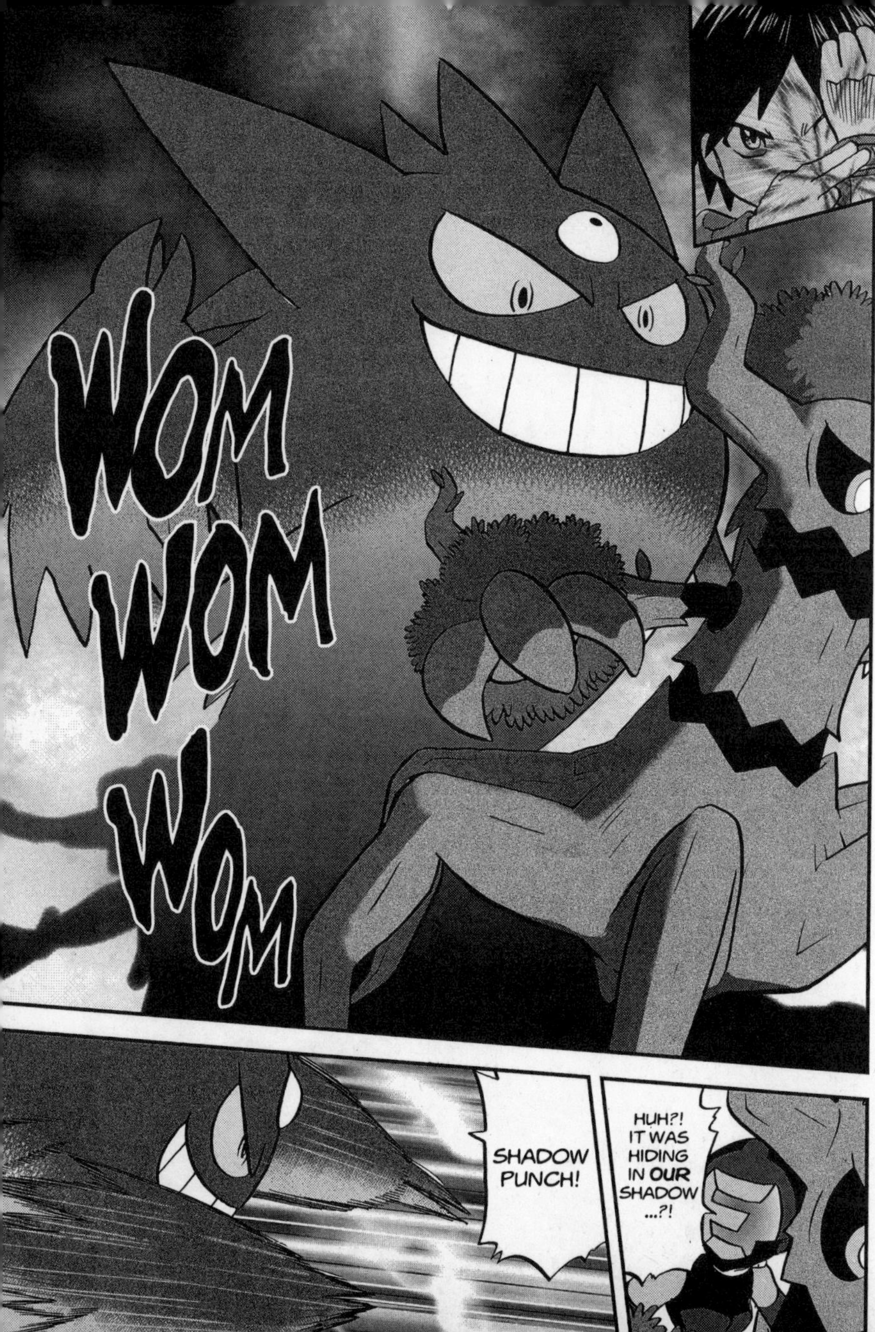
WOM WOM WOM WOM
HUH?! IT WAS HIDING IN **OUR** SHADOW ...?!
SHADOW PUNCH!

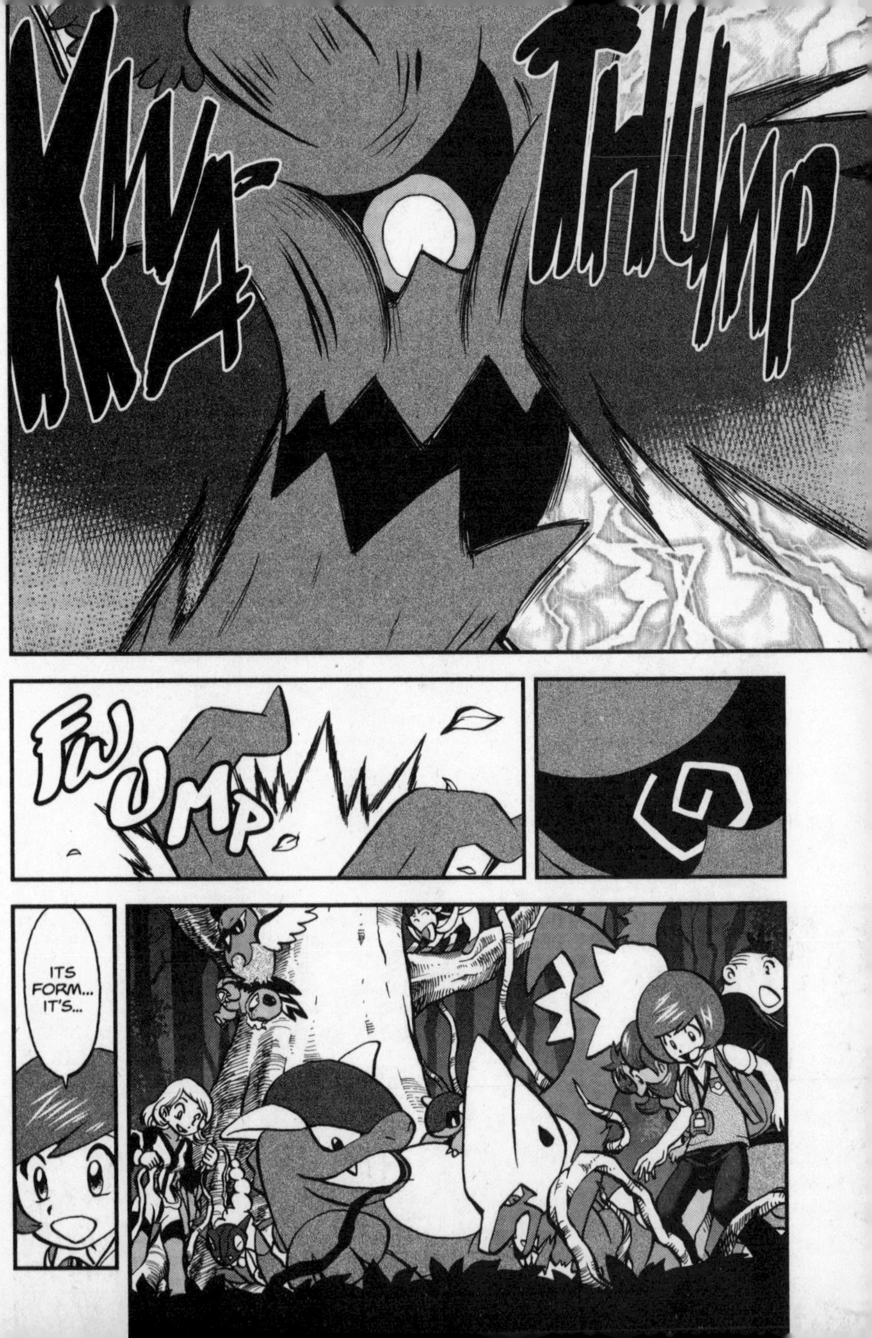
KWA-THUMP
FWUMP
ITS FORM... IT'S...

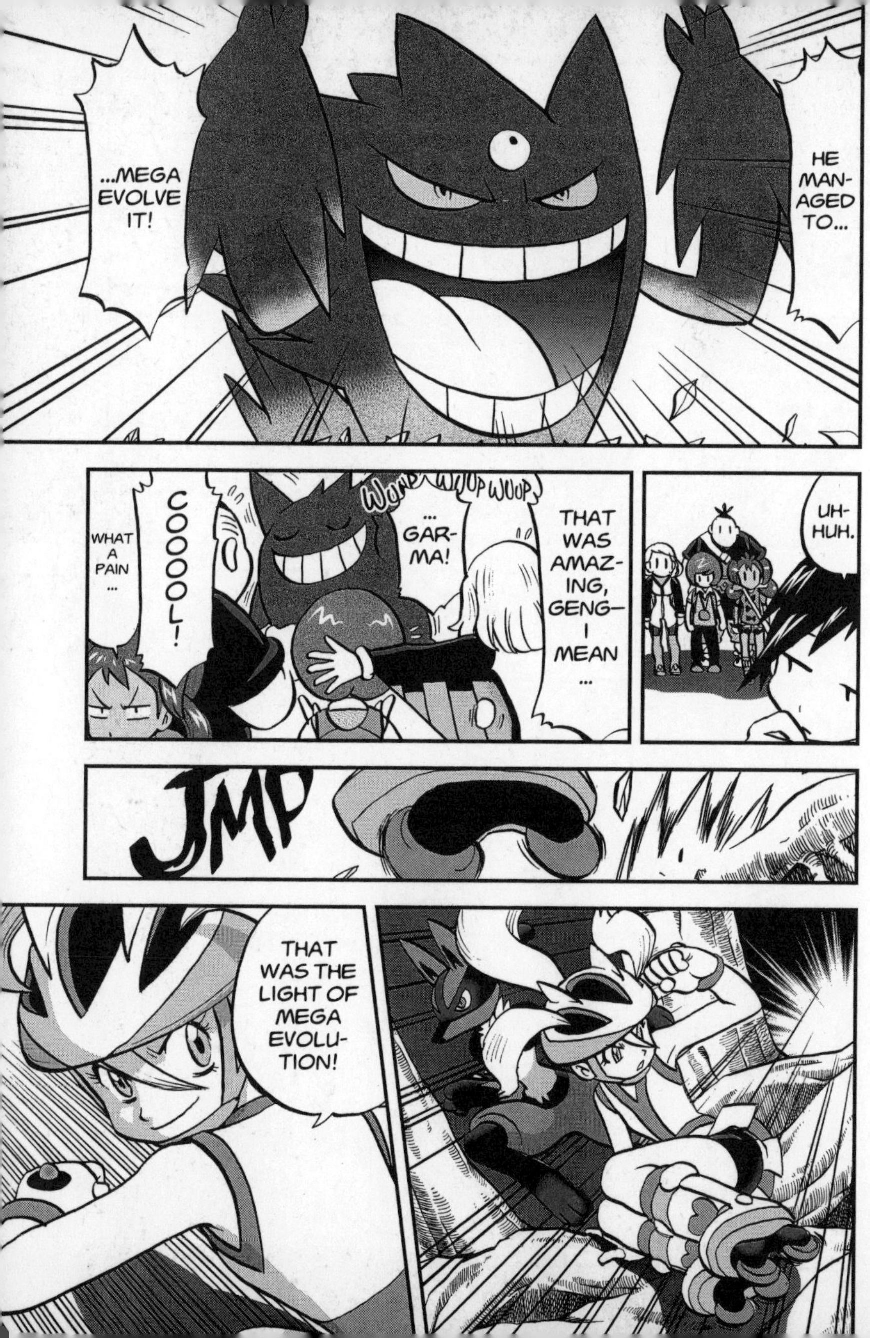
HE MANAGED TO...
...MEGA EVOLVE IT!
UH-HUH.
THAT WAS AMAZING, GENG— I MEAN ...
WOMP WUUP WUUP
... GARMA!
COOOOOL!
WHAT A PAIN ...
JMP
THAT WAS THE LIGHT OF MEGA EVOLUTION!

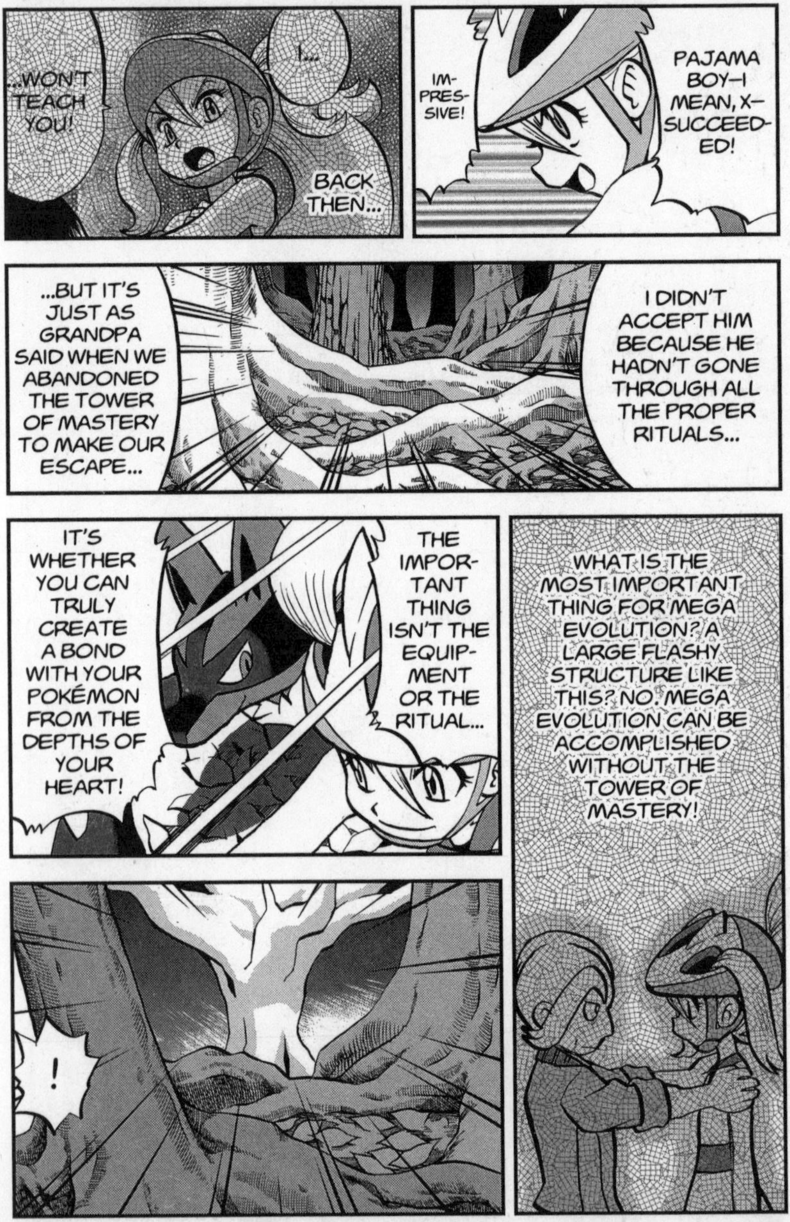
PAJAMA BOY—I MEAN, X—SUCCEEDED!
IM-PRES-SIVE!
I...
...WON'T TEACH YOU!
BACK THEN...
I DIDN'T ACCEPT HIM BECAUSE HE HADN'T GONE THROUGH ALL THE PROPER RITUALS...
...BUT IT'S JUST AS GRANDPA SAID WHEN WE ABANDONED THE TOWER OF MASTERY TO MAKE OUR ESCAPE...
WHAT IS THE MOST IMPORTANT THING FOR MEGA EVOLUTION? A LARGE FLASHY STRUCTURE LIKE THIS? NO. MEGA EVOLUTION CAN BE ACCOMPLISHED WITHOUT THE TOWER OF MASTERY!
THE IMPORTANT THING ISN'T THE EQUIPMENT OR THE RITUAL...
IT'S WHETHER YOU CAN TRULY CREATE A BOND WITH YOUR POKÉMON FROM THE DEPTHS OF YOUR HEART!
!

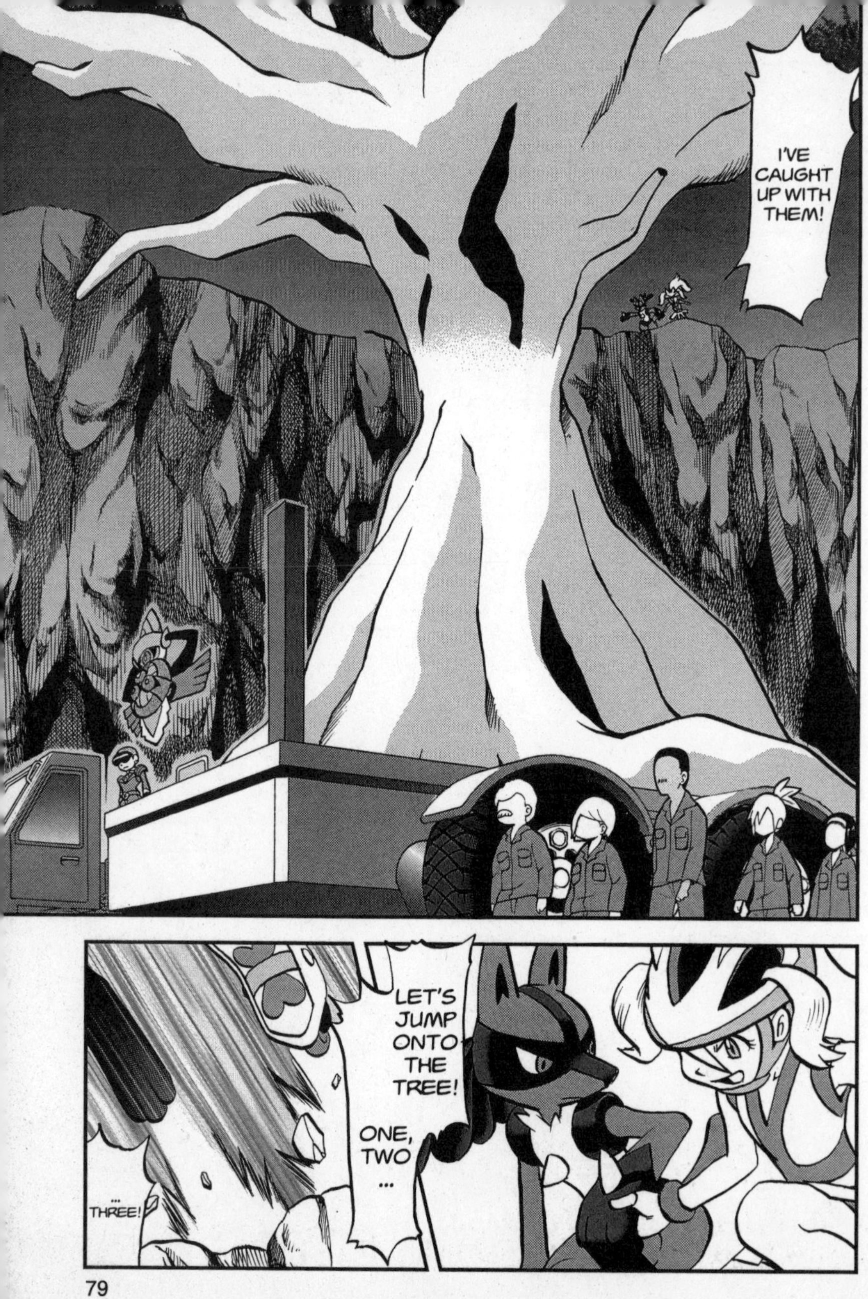
I'VE CAUGHT UP WITH THEM!
LET'S JUMP ONTO THE TREE!
ONE, TWO ...
... THREE!

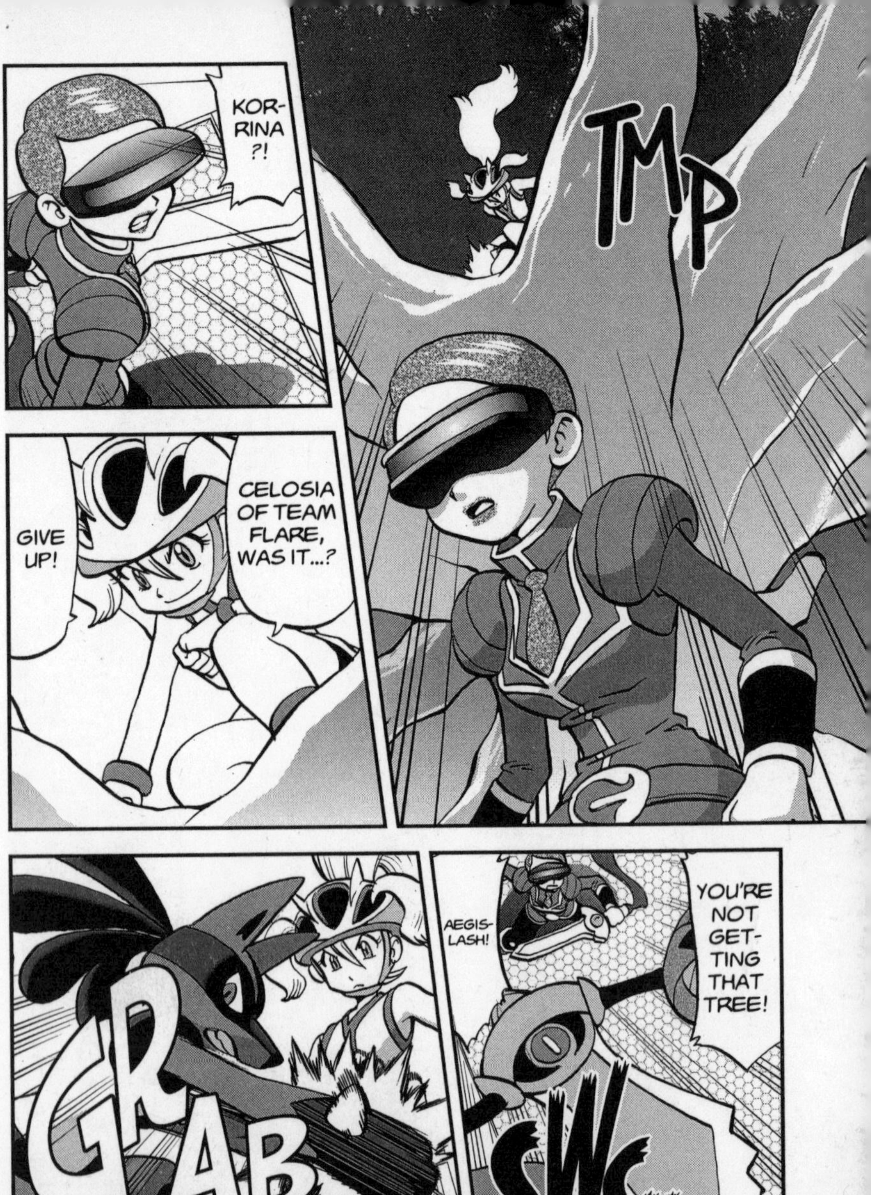
TMP
KOR-RINA ?!
CELOSIA OF TEAM FLARE, WAS IT...?
GIVE UP!
YOU'RE NOT GET-TING THAT TREE!
AEGIS-LASH!
SWSH
GRAB

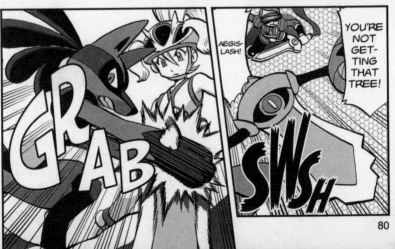

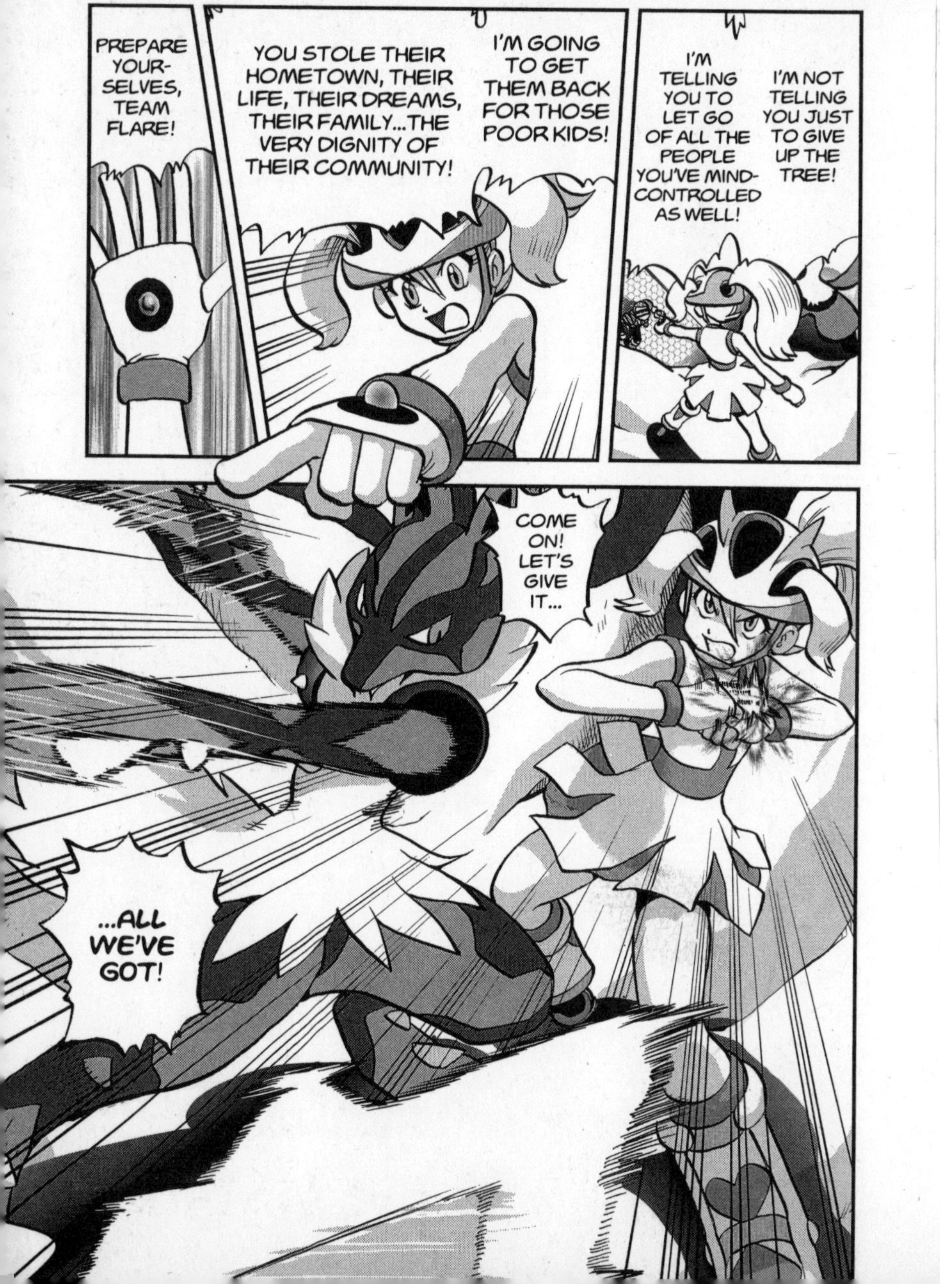
I'M NOT TELLING YOU JUST TO GIVE UP THE TREE!
I'M TELLING YOU TO LET GO OF ALL THE PEOPLE YOU'VE MIND-CONTROLLED AS WELL!
I'M GOING TO GET THEM BACK FOR THOSE POOR KIDS!
YOU STOLE THEIR HOMETOWN, THEIR LIFE, THEIR DREAMS, THEIR FAMILY...THE VERY DIGNITY OF THEIR COMMUNITY!
PREPARE YOUR-SELVES, TEAM FLARE!
COME ON! LET'S GIVE IT...
...ALL WE'VE GOT!

Current Location

Route 8
Muraille Coast

This is a road of great contrasts, from the harsh rock of the cliffs to the soft sands of the beach.

Adventure 21 Surrounding Braixen

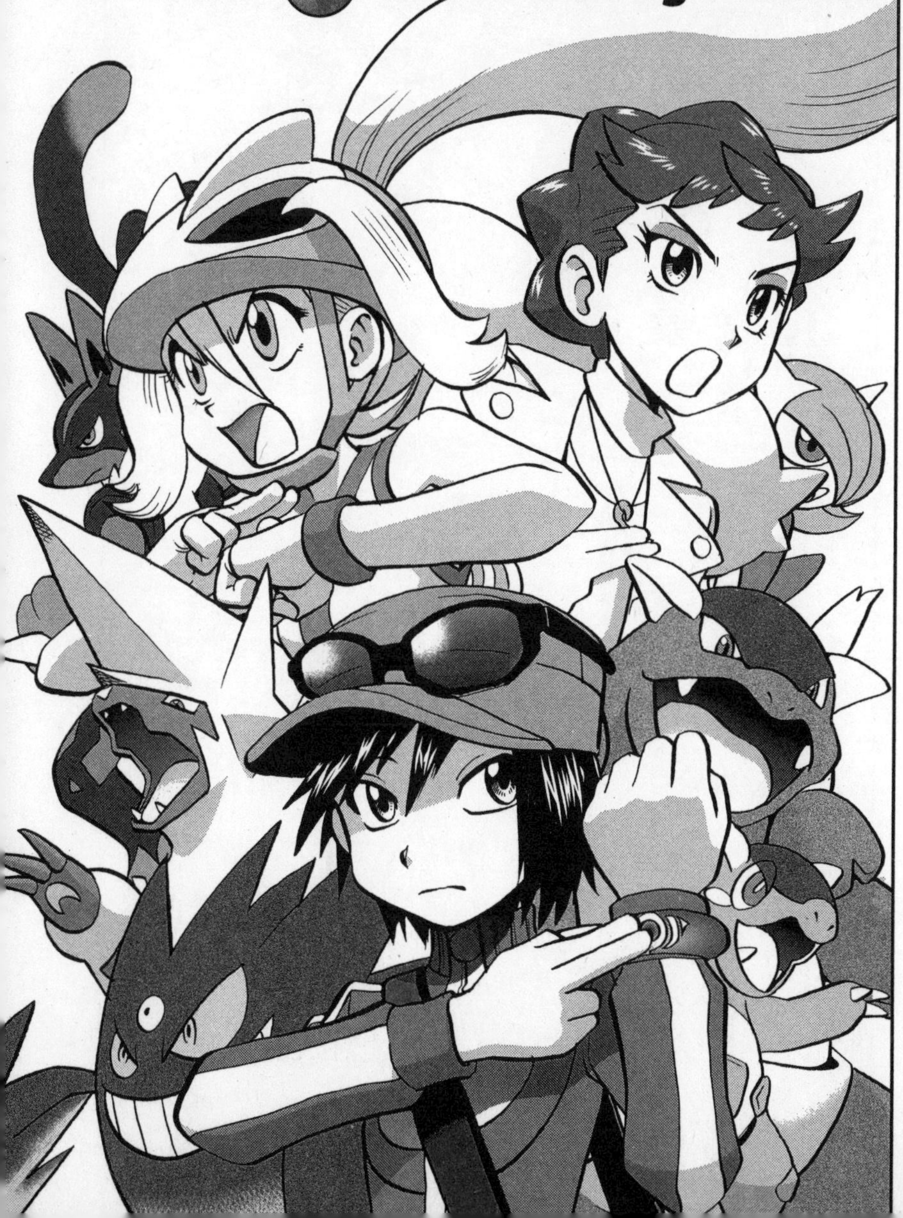

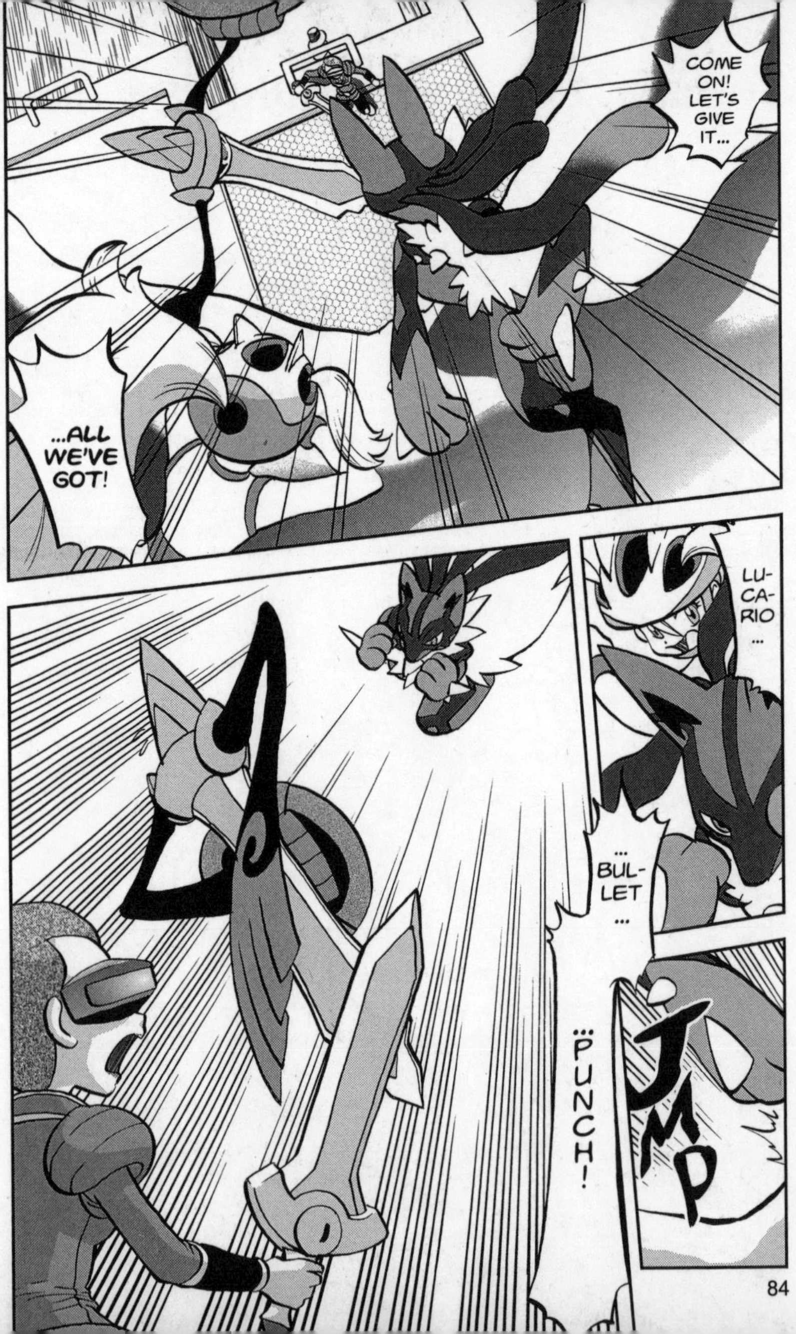
COME ON! LET'S GIVE IT...
...ALL WE'VE GOT!
LU-CA-RIO...
...BUL-LET...
...PUNCH!
JMP

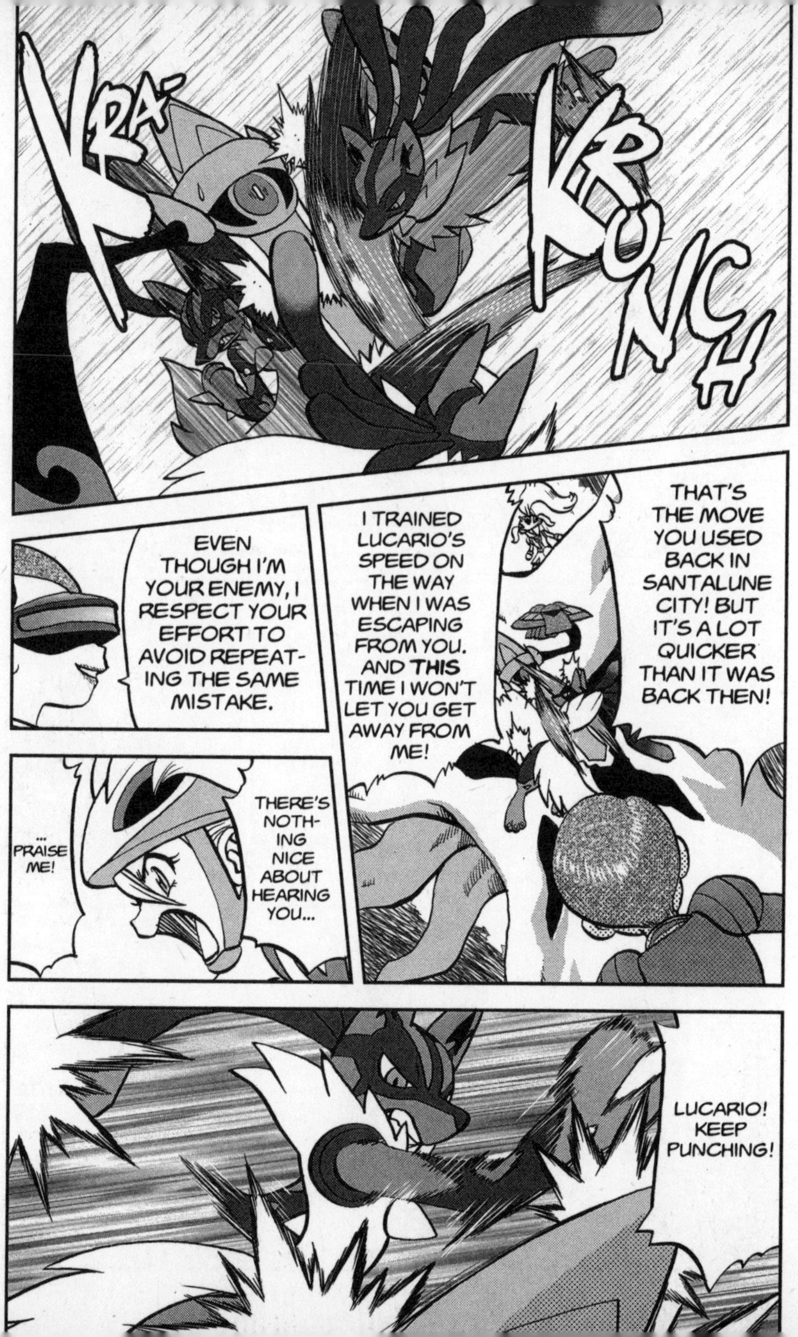
KRUNCH
VRA-
THAT'S THE MOVE YOU USED BACK IN SANTALUNE CITY! BUT IT'S A LOT QUICKER THAN IT WAS BACK THEN!
I TRAINED LUCARIO'S SPEED ON THE WAY WHEN I WAS ESCAPING FROM YOU. AND **THIS** TIME I WON'T LET YOU GET AWAY FROM ME!
EVEN THOUGH I'M YOUR ENEMY, I RESPECT YOUR EFFORT TO AVOID REPEATING THE SAME MISTAKE.
THERE'S NOTHING NICE ABOUT HEARING YOU...
... PRAISE ME!
LUCARIO! KEEP PUNCHING!

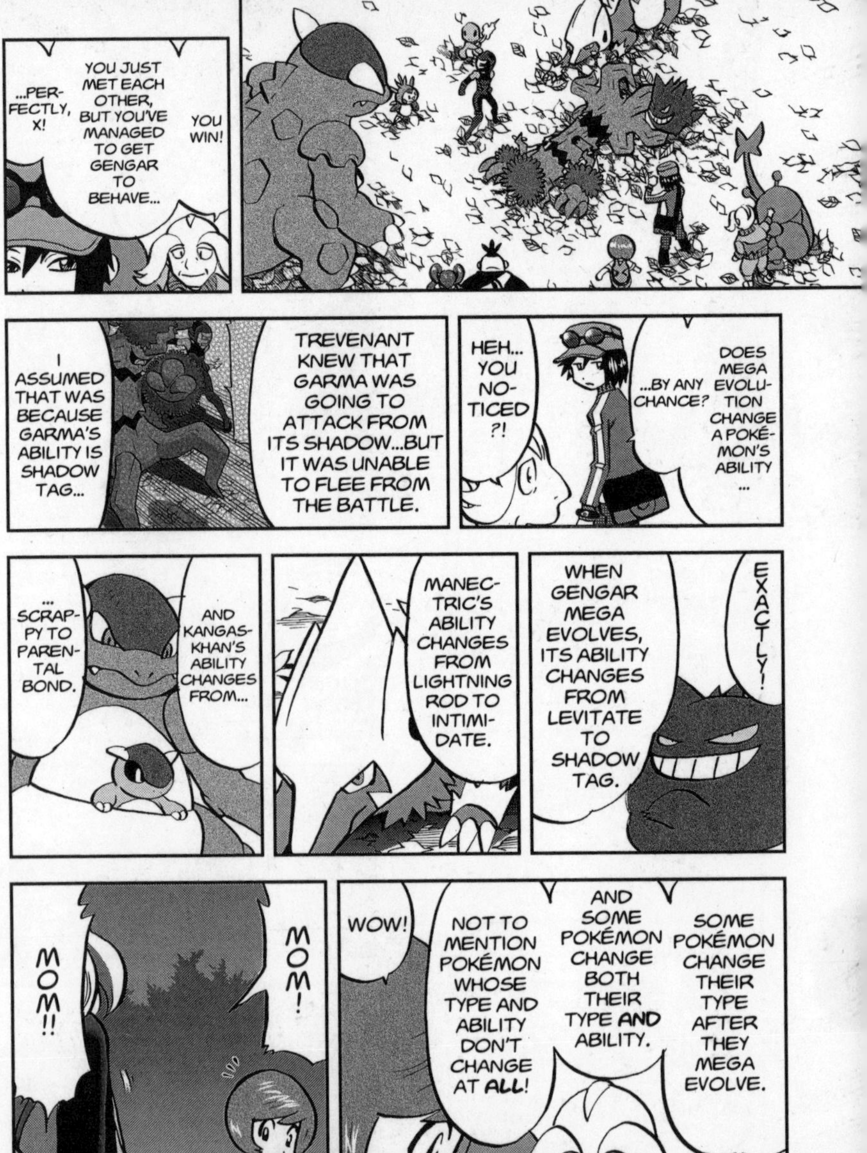
YOU WIN!
YOU JUST MET EACH OTHER, BUT YOU'VE MANAGED TO GET GENGAR TO BEHAVE...
...PERFECTLY, X!
DOES MEGA EVOLUTION CHANGE A POKÉMON'S ABILITY...
...BY ANY CHANCE?
HEH... YOU NOTICED?!
TREVENANT KNEW THAT GARMA WAS GOING TO ATTACK FROM ITS SHADOW...BUT IT WAS UNABLE TO FLEE FROM THE BATTLE.
I ASSUMED THAT WAS BECAUSE GARMA'S ABILITY IS SHADOW TAG...
EXACTLY!
WHEN GENGAR MEGA EVOLVES, ITS ABILITY CHANGES FROM LEVITATE TO SHADOW TAG.
MANECTRIC'S ABILITY CHANGES FROM LIGHTNING ROD TO INTIMIDATE.
AND KANGASKHAN'S ABILITY CHANGES FROM...
...SCRAPPY TO PARENTAL BOND.
SOME POKÉMON CHANGE THEIR TYPE AFTER THEY MEGA EVOLVE.
AND SOME POKÉMON CHANGE BOTH THEIR TYPE **AND** ABILITY.
NOT TO MENTION POKÉMON WHOSE TYPE AND ABILITY DON'T CHANGE AT **ALL**!
WOW!
MOM!
MOM!!

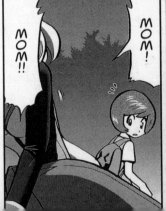

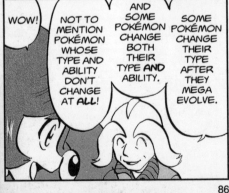

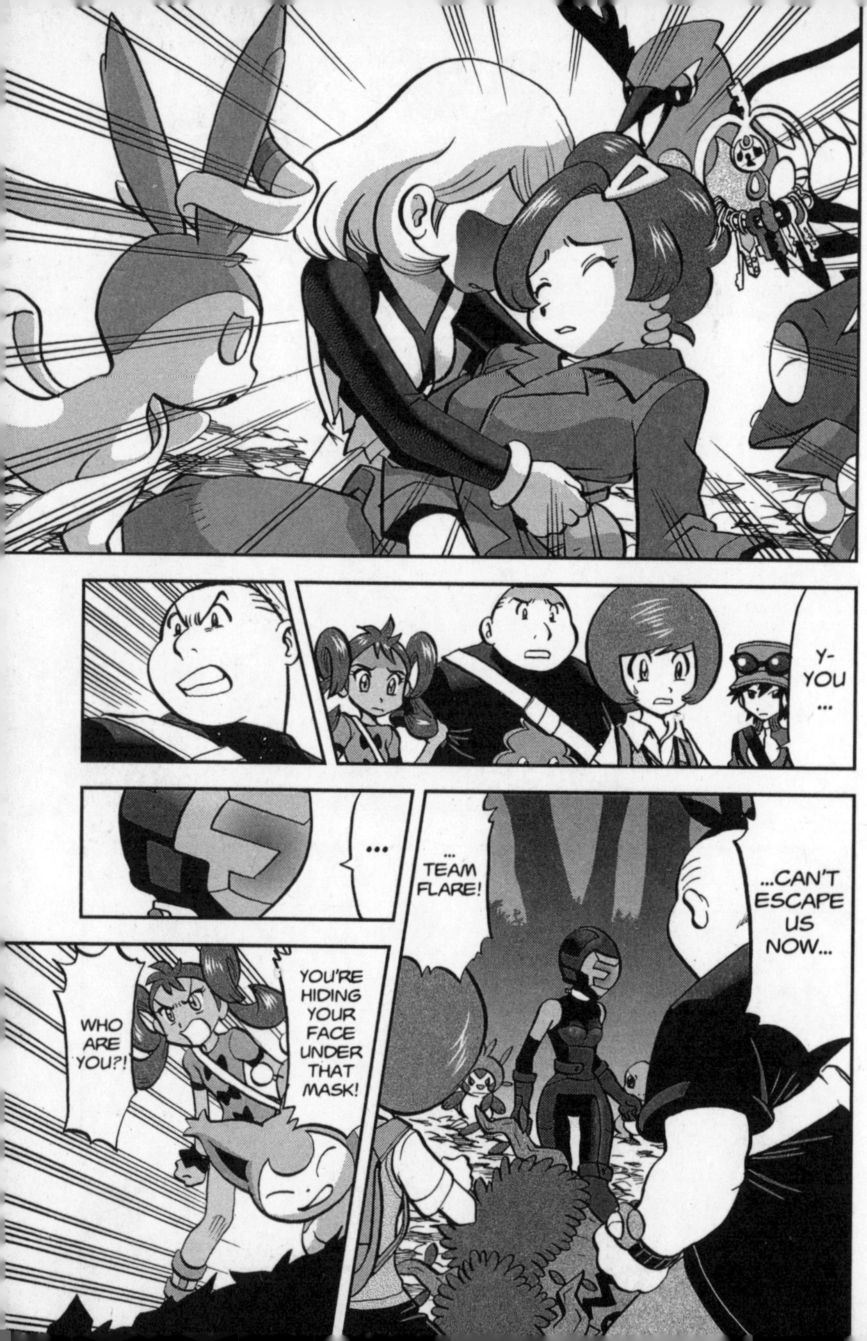
Y-YOU ...
...CAN'T ESCAPE US NOW...
... TEAM FLARE!
...
YOU'RE HIDING YOUR FACE UNDER THAT MASK!
WHO ARE YOU?!

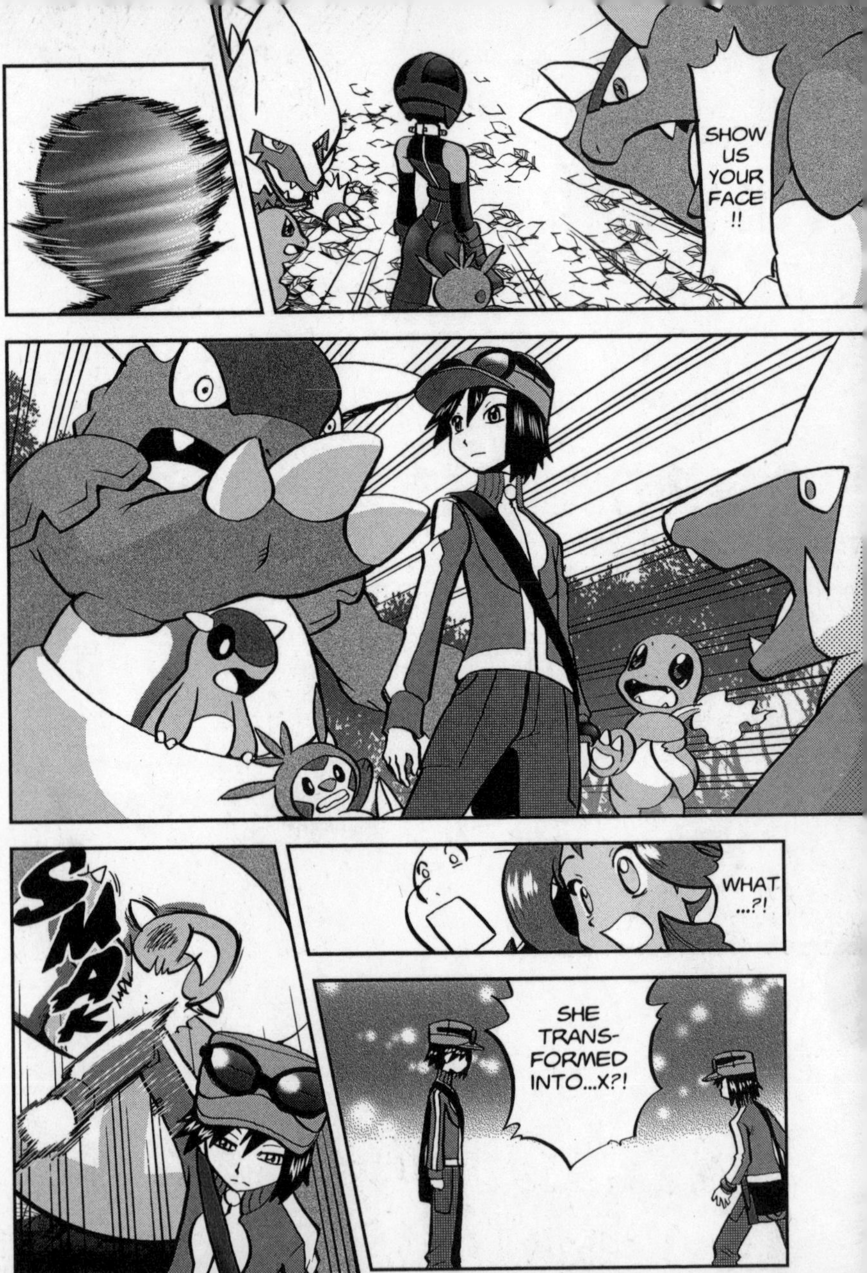
SHOW US YOUR FACE!!
WHAT ...?!
SHE TRANS-FORMED INTO...X?!
SNAP

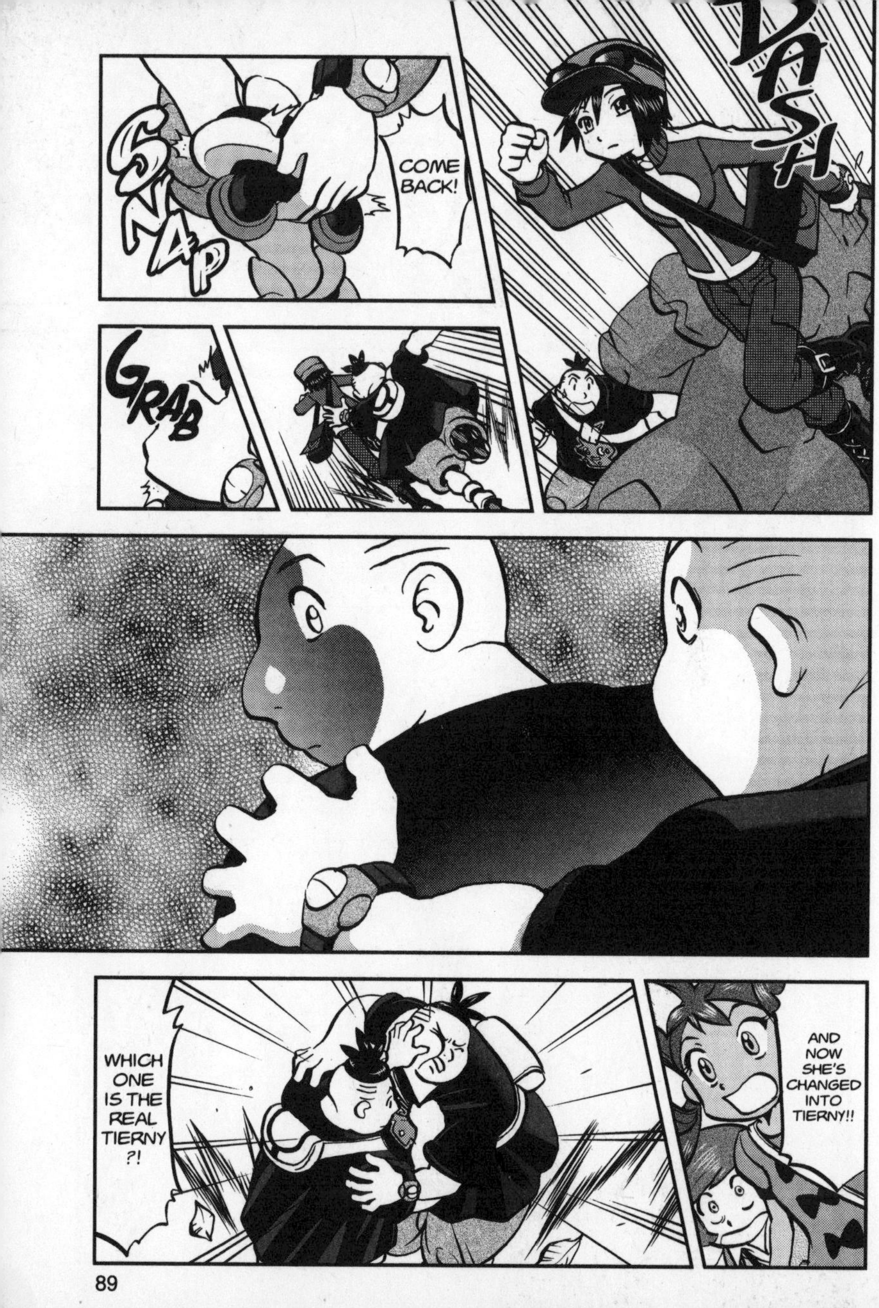
DASH
COME BACK!
SNAP
GRAB
AND NOW SHE'S CHANGED INTO TIERNY!!
WHICH ONE IS THE REAL TIERNY?!

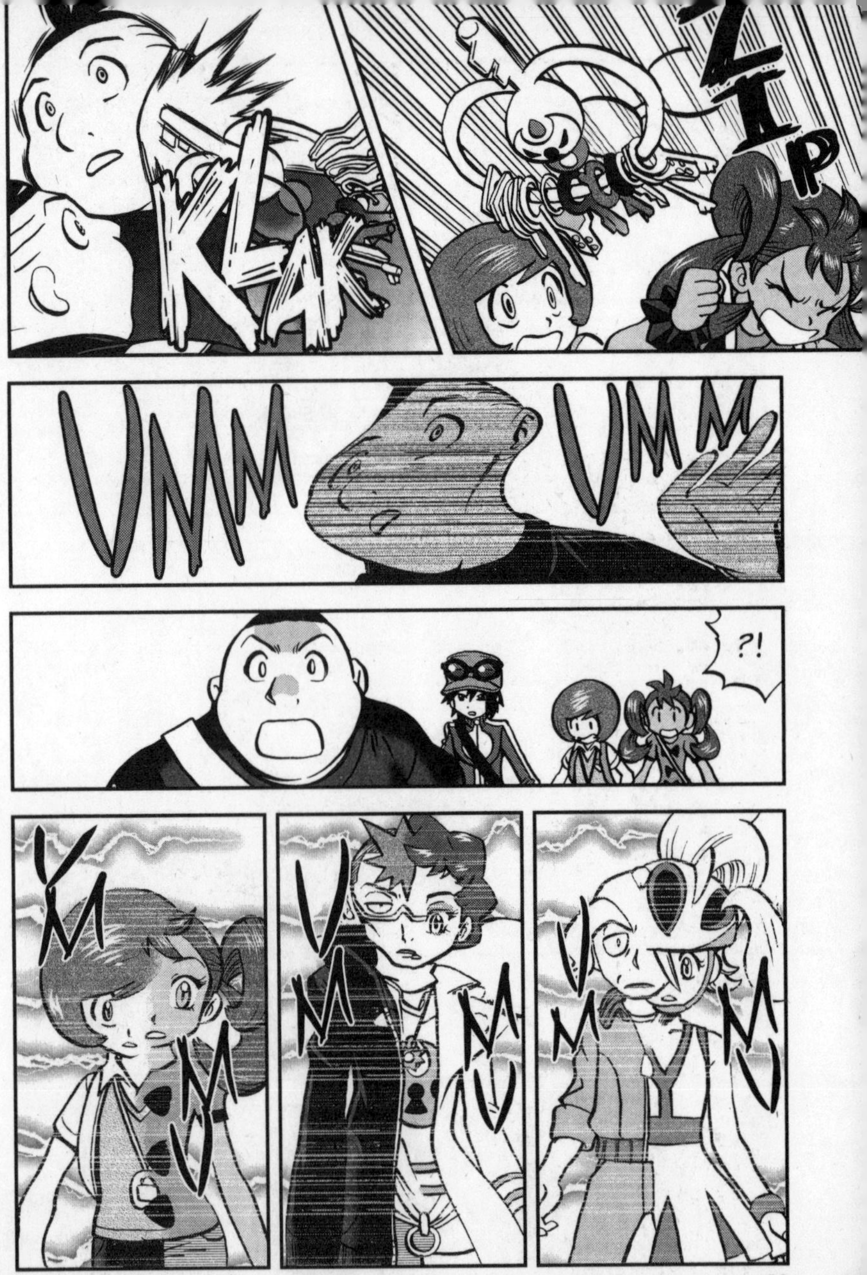
ZIP
KLAK
VMMM
VMMM
?!
VMMM
VMMM
VMMM
VMMM

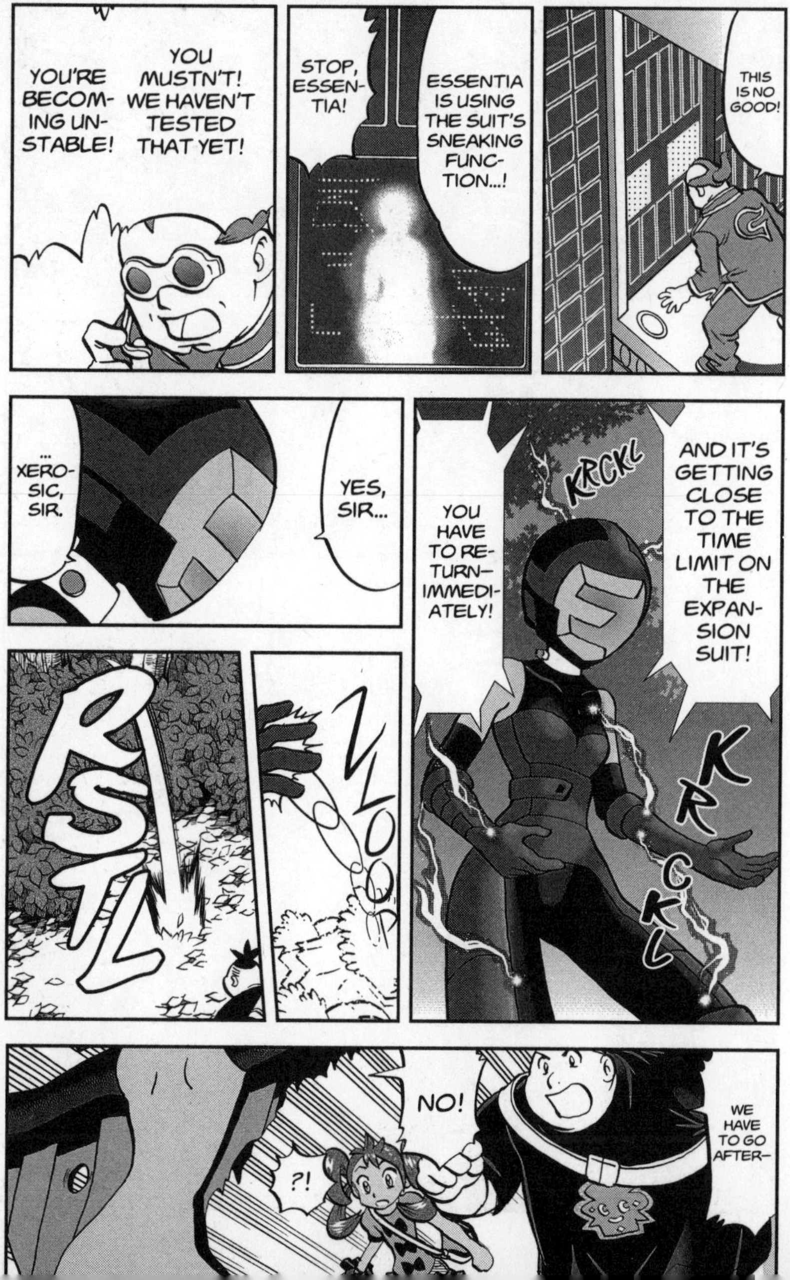

THIS IS NO GOOD!
ESSENTIA IS USING THE SUIT'S SNEAKING FUNCTION...!
STOP, ESSENTIA!
YOU MUSTN'T! WE HAVEN'T TESTED THAT YET!
YOU'RE BECOMING UNSTABLE!
AND IT'S GETTING CLOSE TO THE TIME LIMIT ON THE EXPANSION SUIT!
KRCKL
YOU HAVE TO RETURN—IMMEDIATELY!
KRRCKL
YES, SIR...
... XEROSIC, SIR.
RSTL
WE HAVE TO GO AFTER—
NO!
?!

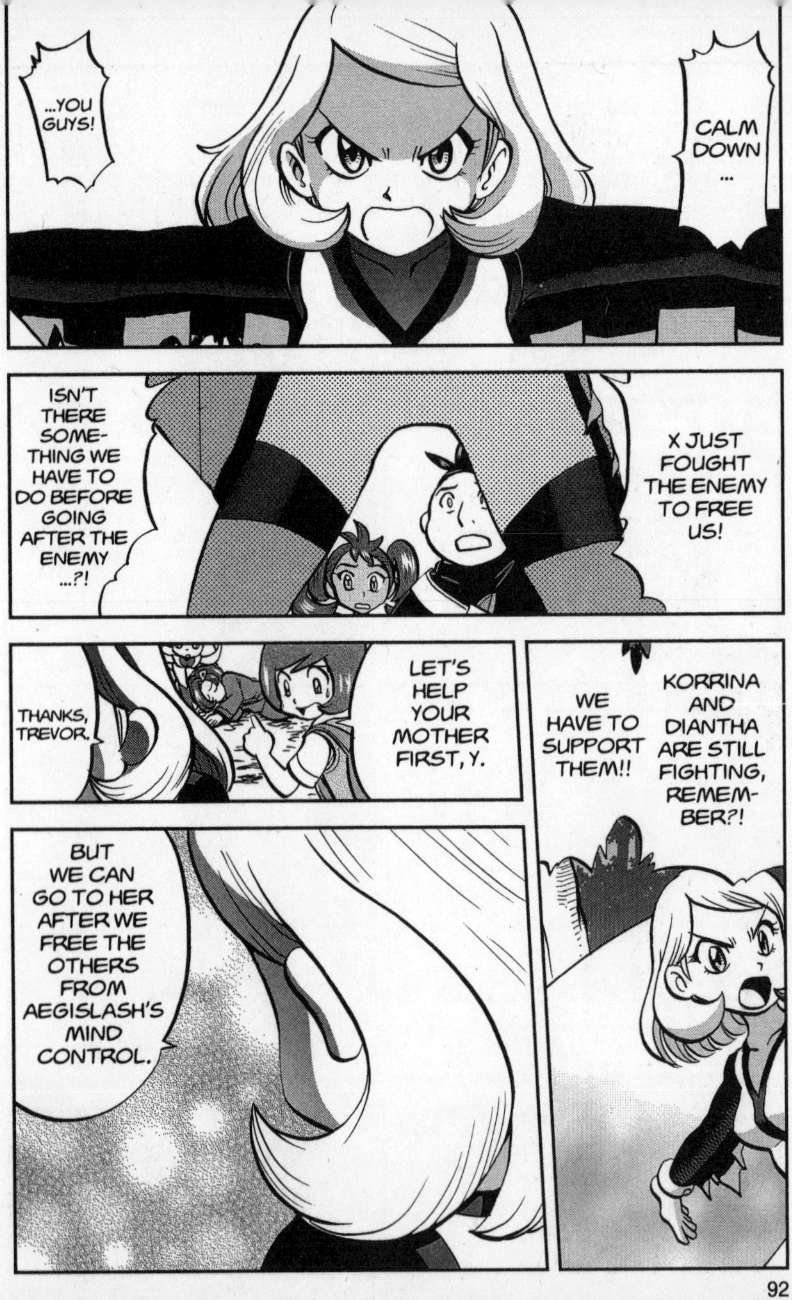
CALM DOWN ...
...YOU GUYS!
X JUST FOUGHT THE ENEMY TO FREE US!
ISN'T THERE SOME-THING WE HAVE TO DO BEFORE GOING AFTER THE ENEMY ...?!
KORRINA AND DIANTHA ARE STILL FIGHTING, REMEM-BER?!
WE HAVE TO SUPPORT THEM!!
LET'S HELP YOUR MOTHER FIRST, Y.
THANKS, TREVOR.
BUT WE CAN GO TO HER AFTER WE FREE THE OTHERS FROM AEGISLASH'S MIND CONTROL.

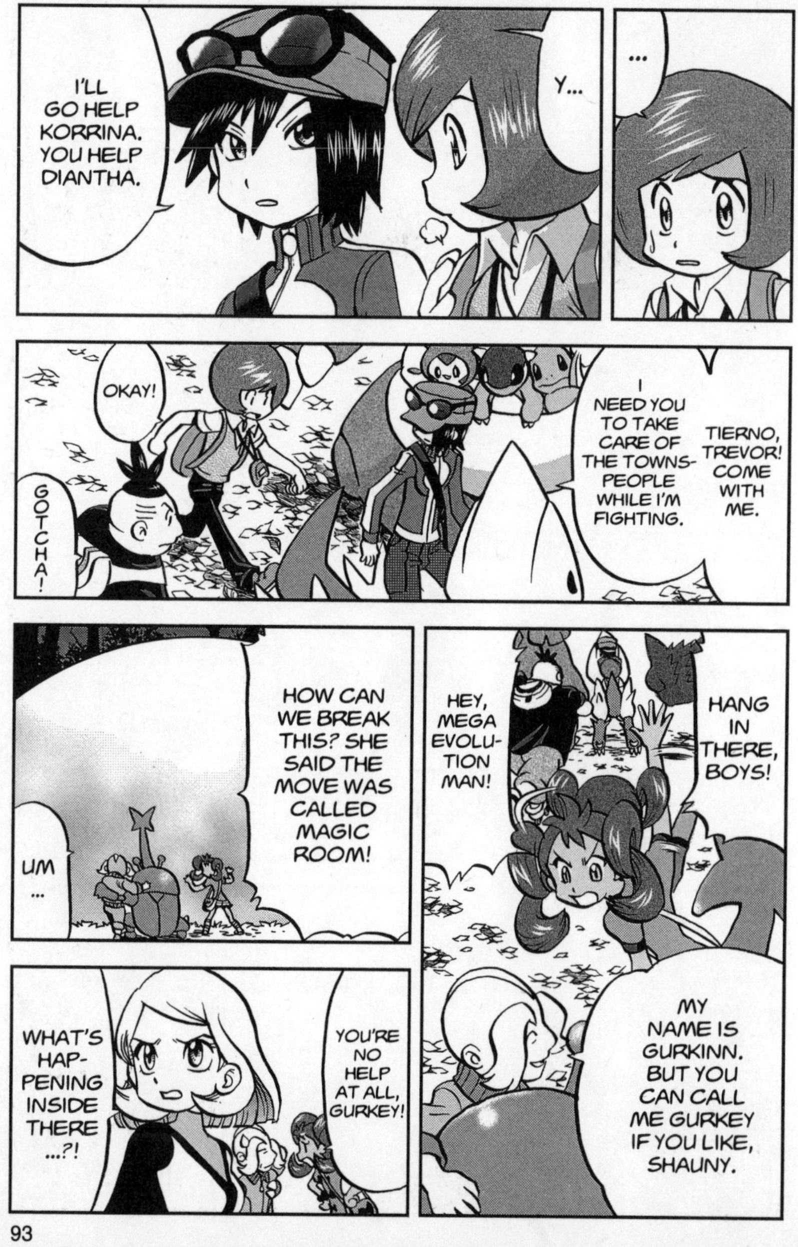
...
Y...
I'LL GO HELP KORRINA. YOU HELP DIANTHA.
TIERNO, TREVOR! COME WITH ME.
I NEED YOU TO TAKE CARE OF THE TOWNS-PEOPLE WHILE I'M FIGHTING.
OKAY!
GOTCHA!
HANG IN THERE, BOYS!
HEY, MEGA EVOLU-TION MAN!
HOW CAN WE BREAK THIS? SHE SAID THE MOVE WAS CALLED MAGIC ROOM!
UM ...
MY NAME IS GURKINN. BUT YOU CAN CALL ME GURKEY IF YOU LIKE, SHAUNY.
YOU'RE NO HELP AT ALL, GURKEY!
WHAT'S HAP-PENING INSIDE THERE ...?!

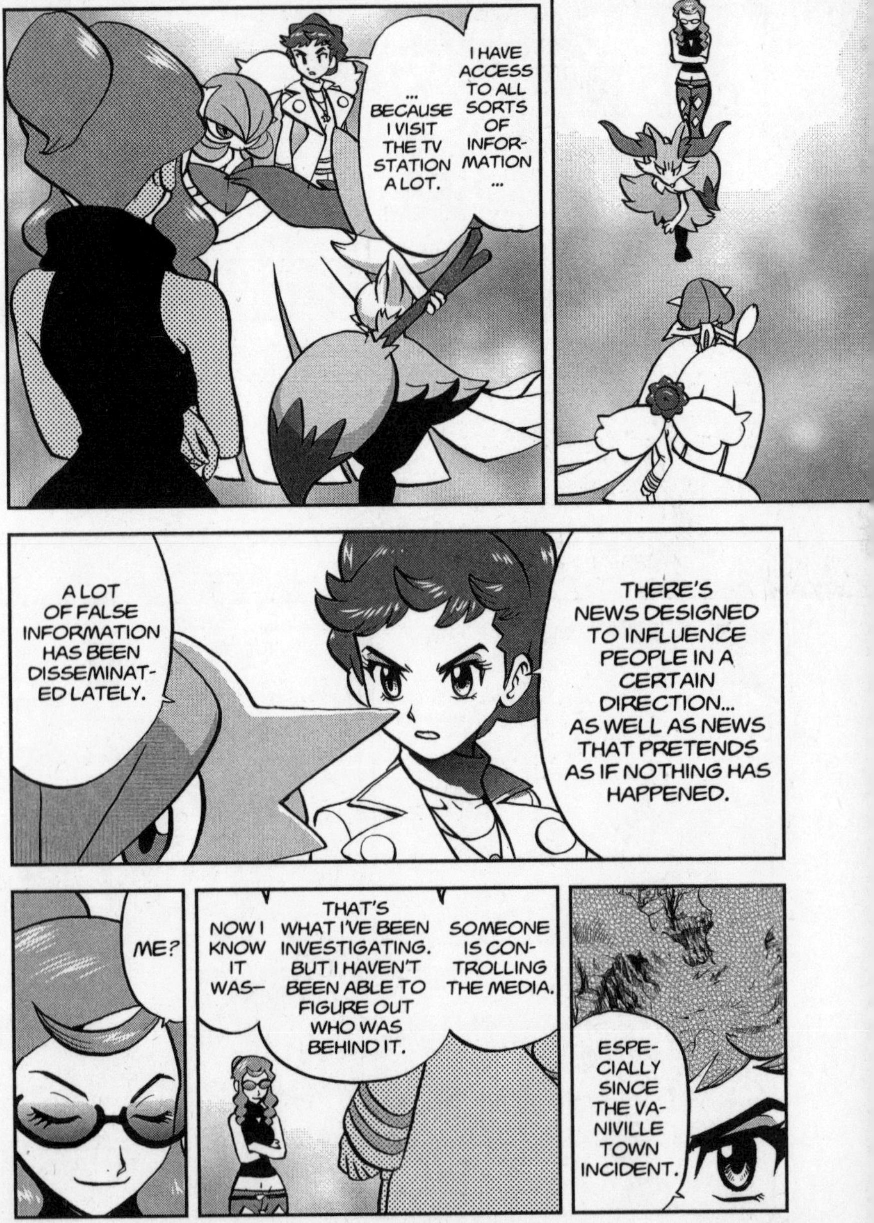

I HAVE ACCESS TO ALL SORTS OF INFORMATION...
... BECAUSE I VISIT THE TV STATION A LOT.
THERE'S NEWS DESIGNED TO INFLUENCE PEOPLE IN A CERTAIN DIRECTION... AS WELL AS NEWS THAT PRETENDS AS IF NOTHING HAS HAPPENED.
A LOT OF FALSE INFORMATION HAS BEEN DISSEMINAT-ED LATELY.
ESPE-CIALLY SINCE THE VA-NIVILLE TOWN INCIDENT.
SOMEONE IS CON-TROLLING THE MEDIA.
THAT'S WHAT I'VE BEEN INVESTIGATING. BUT I HAVEN'T BEEN ABLE TO FIGURE OUT WHO WAS BEHIND IT.
NOW I KNOW IT WAS—
ME?

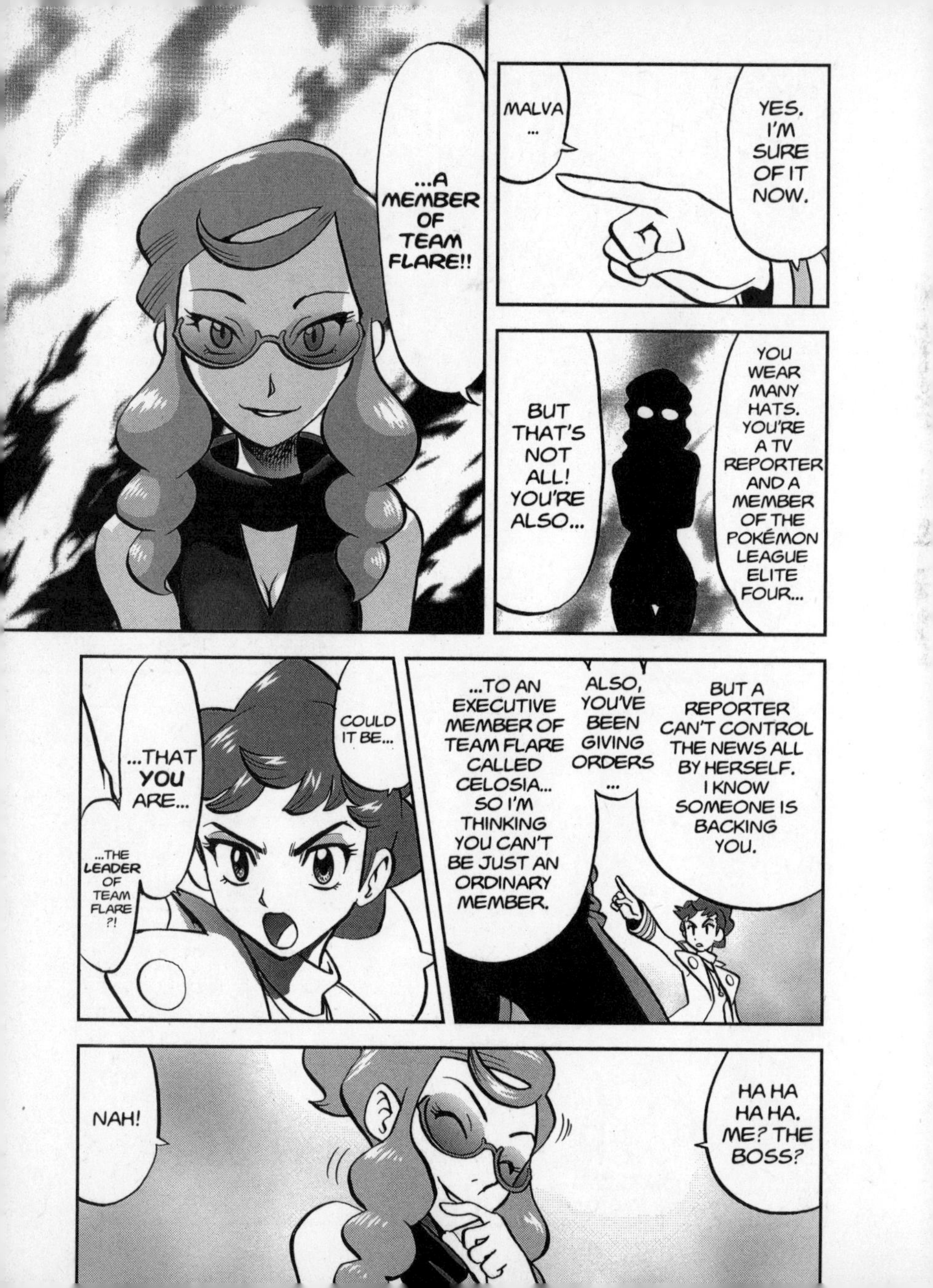
YES. I'M SURE OF IT NOW.
MALVA...
YOU WEAR MANY HATS. YOU'RE A TV REPORTER AND A MEMBER OF THE POKÉMON LEAGUE ELITE FOUR...
BUT THAT'S NOT ALL! YOU'RE ALSO...
...A MEMBER OF TEAM FLARE!!
BUT A REPORTER CAN'T CONTROL THE NEWS ALL BY HERSELF. I KNOW SOMEONE IS BACKING YOU.
ALSO, YOU'VE BEEN GIVING ORDERS...
...TO AN EXECUTIVE MEMBER OF TEAM FLARE CALLED CELOSIA... SO I'M THINKING YOU CAN'T BE JUST AN ORDINARY MEMBER.
COULD IT BE...
...THAT YOU ARE...
...THE LEADER OF TEAM FLARE?!
HA HA HA HA. ME? THE BOSS?
NAH!

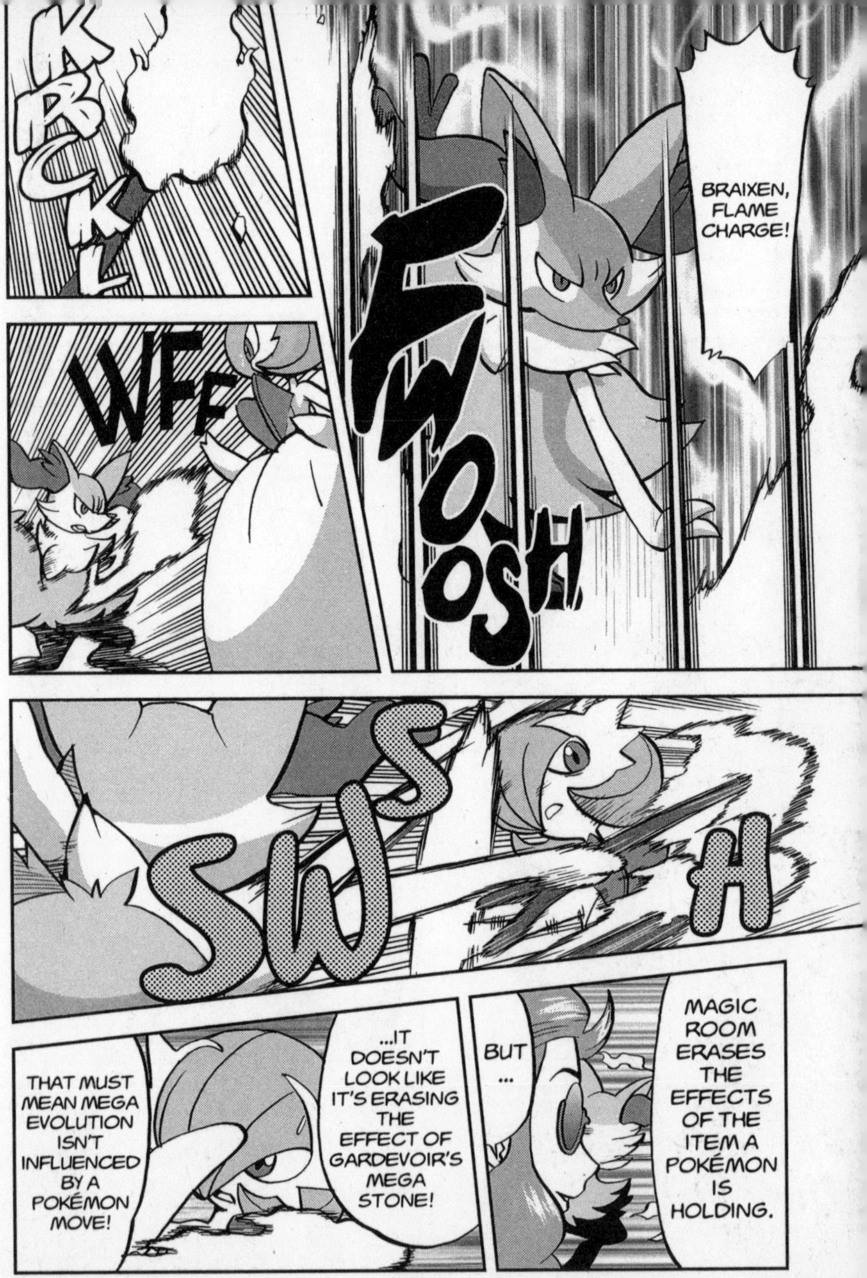
BRAIXEN, FLAME CHARGE!
FWOOSH
KRCKL
WFF
SWSH
MAGIC ROOM ERASES THE EFFECTS OF THE ITEM A POKÉMON IS HOLDING.
BUT ...
...IT DOESN'T LOOK LIKE IT'S ERASING THE EFFECT OF GARDEVOIR'S MEGA STONE!
THAT MUST MEAN MEGA EVOLUTION ISN'T INFLUENCED BY A POKÉMON MOVE!

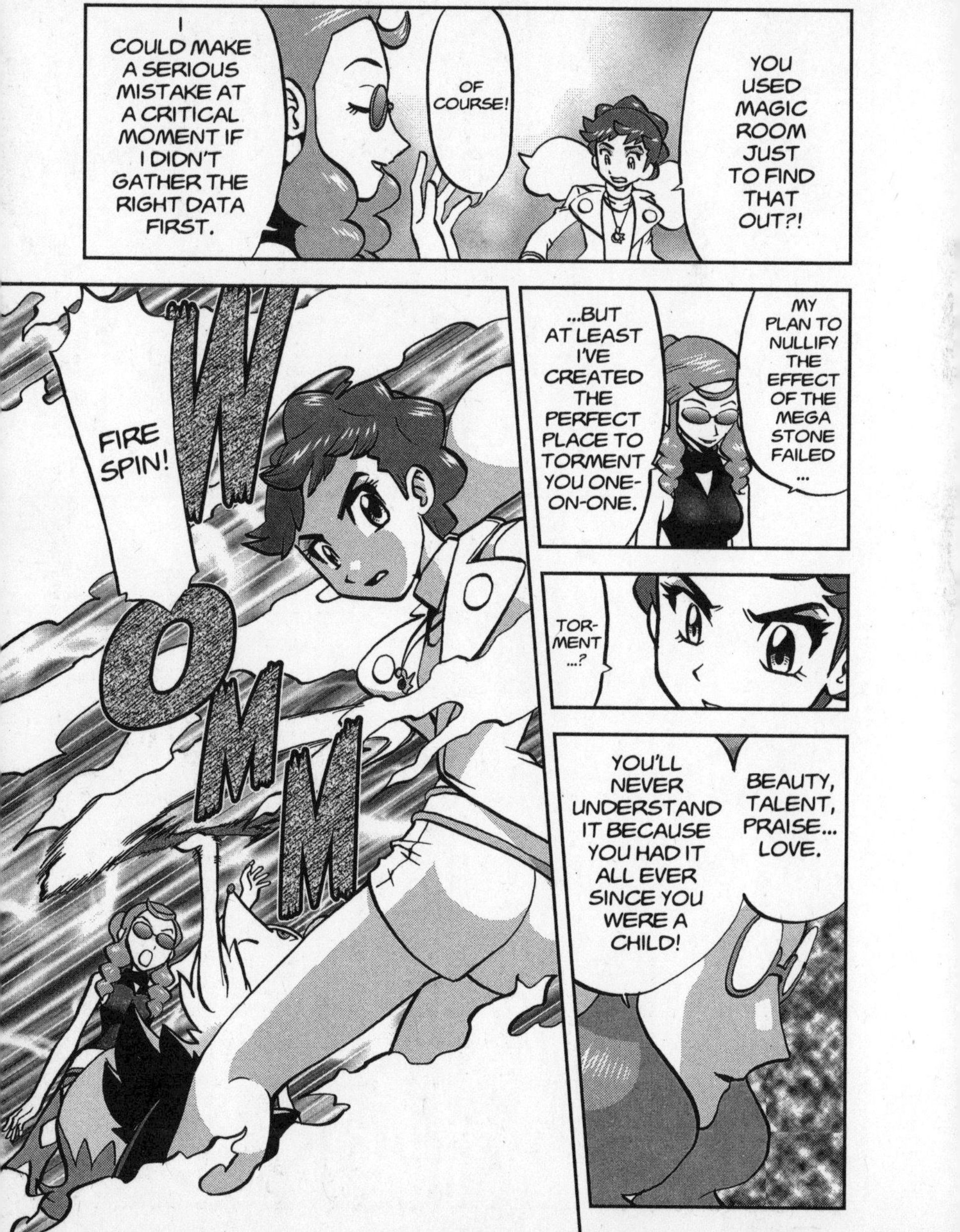
YOU USED MAGIC ROOM JUST TO FIND THAT OUT?!
OF COURSE!
I COULD MAKE A SERIOUS MISTAKE AT A CRITICAL MOMENT IF I DIDN'T GATHER THE RIGHT DATA FIRST.
MY PLAN TO NULLIFY THE EFFECT OF THE MEGA STONE FAILED...
...BUT AT LEAST I'VE CREATED THE PERFECT PLACE TO TORMENT YOU ONE-ON-ONE.
TOR-MENT...?
BEAUTY, TALENT, PRAISE... LOVE.
YOU'LL NEVER UNDERSTAND IT BECAUSE YOU HAD IT ALL EVER SINCE YOU WERE A CHILD!
FIRE SPIN!
WOMM

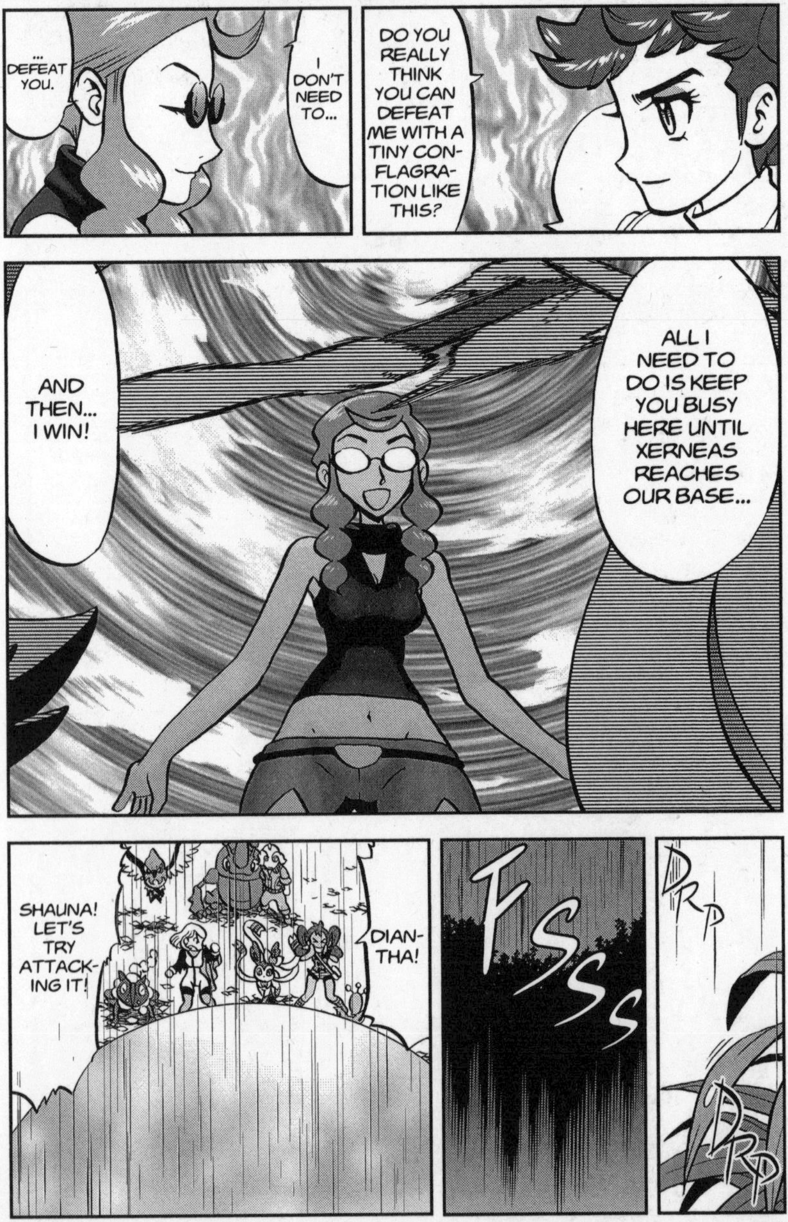
DO YOU REALLY THINK YOU CAN DEFEAT ME WITH A TINY CONFLAGRATION LIKE THIS?
I DON'T NEED TO...
...DEFEAT YOU.
ALL I NEED TO DO IS KEEP YOU BUSY HERE UNTIL XERNEAS REACHES OUR BASE...
AND THEN... I WIN!
DRP
DRP
FSSS
DIANTHA!
SHAUNA! LET'S TRY ATTACKING IT!

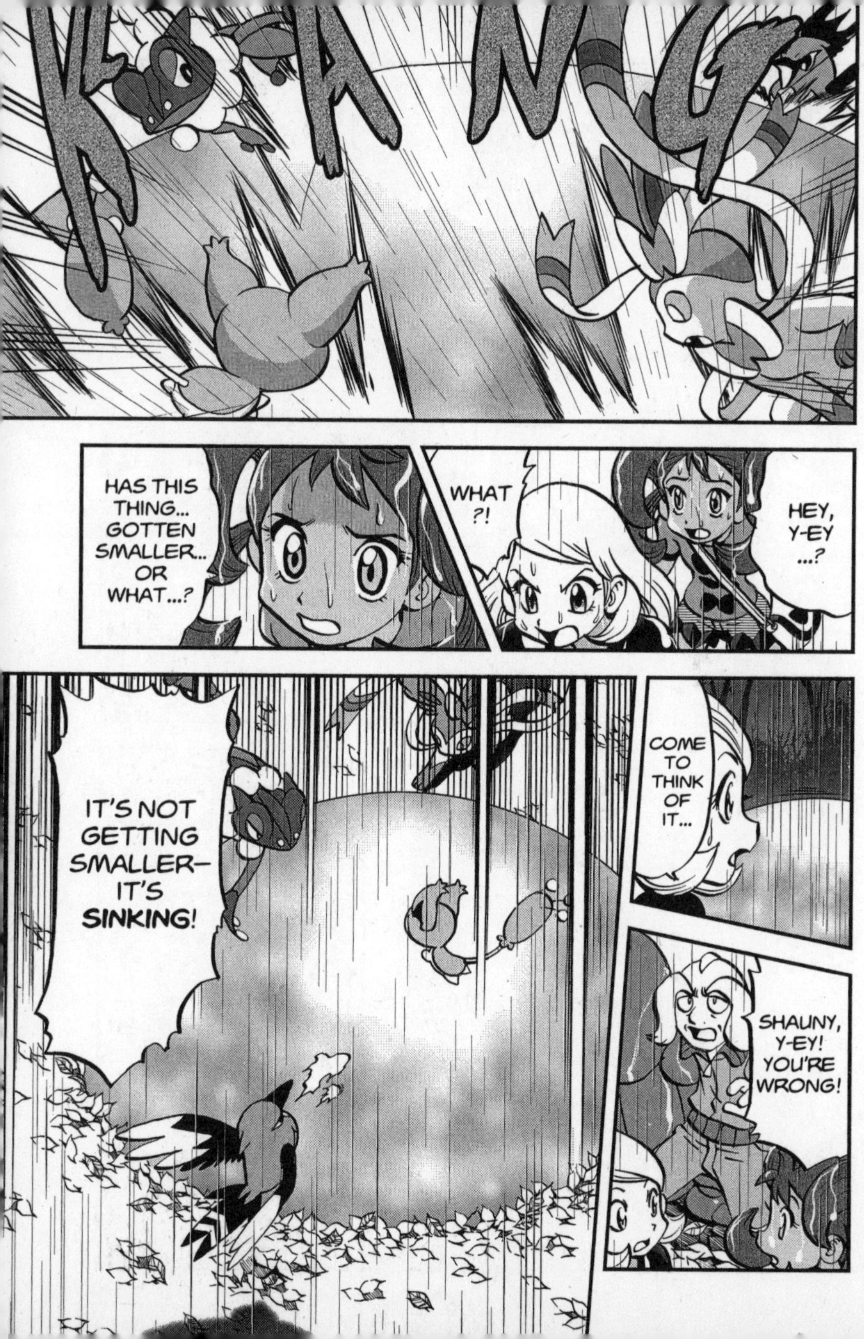
KANG
HEY, Y-EY ...?
WHAT ?!
HAS THIS THING... GOTTEN SMALLER... OR WHAT...?
COME TO THINK OF IT...
SHAUNY, Y-EY! YOU'RE WRONG!
IT'S NOT GETTING SMALLER— IT'S **SINKING**!

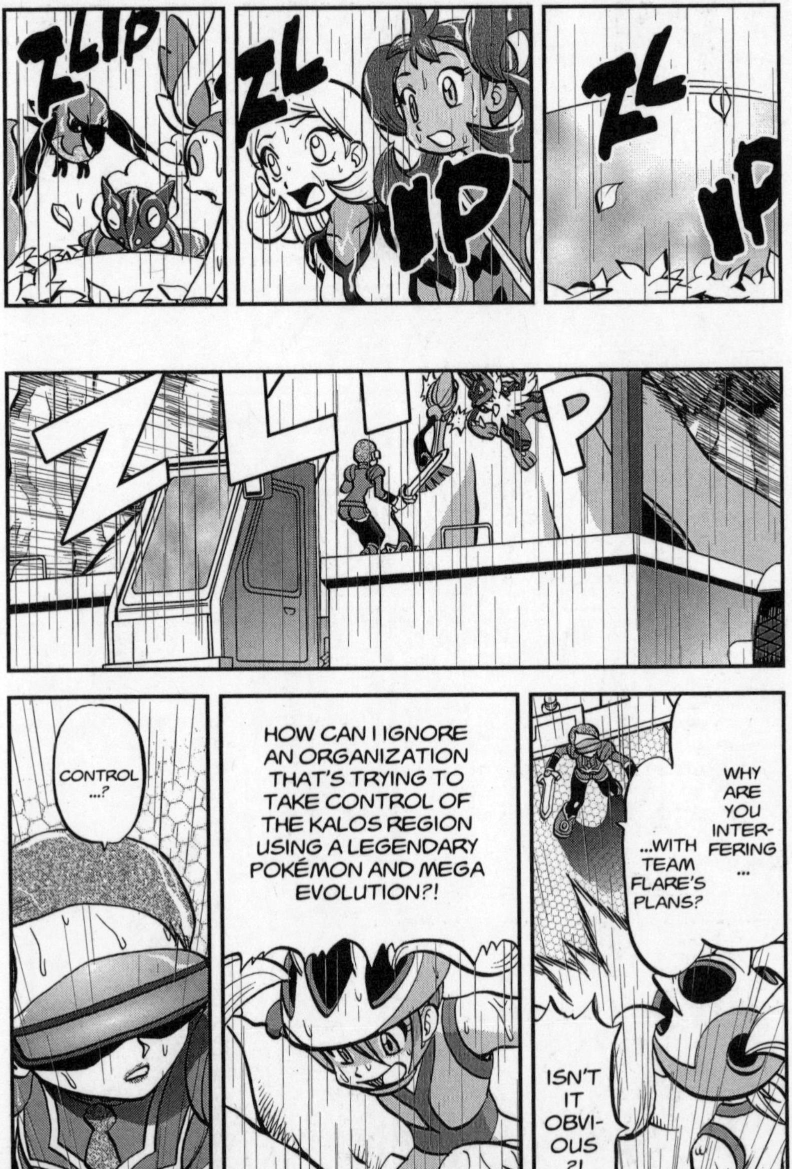
ZL IP
ZL IP
ZLIP
ZLIP
WHY ARE YOU INTER-FERING...
...WITH TEAM FLARE'S PLANS?
ISN'T IT OBVI-OUS?!
HOW CAN I IGNORE AN ORGANIZATION THAT'S TRYING TO TAKE CONTROL OF THE KALOS REGION USING A LEGENDARY POKÉMON AND MEGA EVOLUTION?!
CONTROL ...?

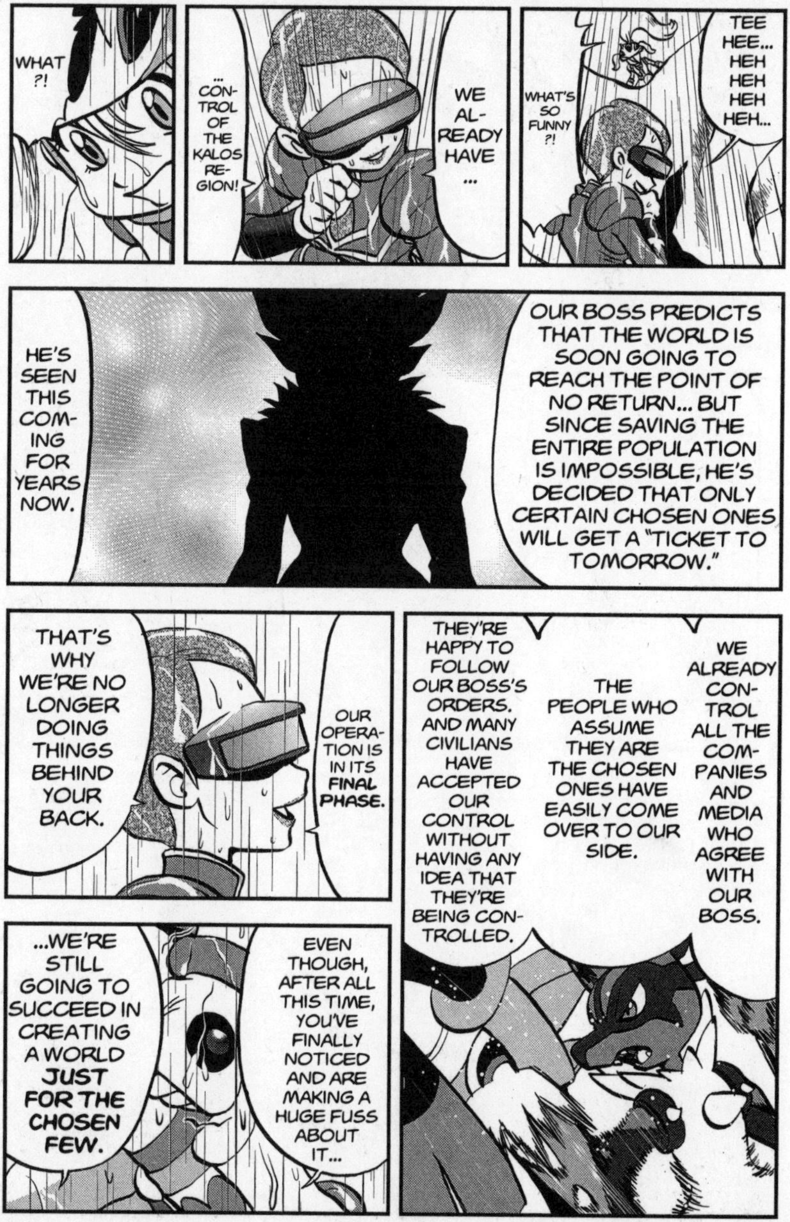
TEE HEE... HEH HEH HEH HEH...
WHAT'S SO FUNNY?!
WE ALREADY HAVE...
...CONTROL OF THE KALOS REGION!
WHAT?!
OUR BOSS PREDICTS THAT THE WORLD IS SOON GOING TO REACH THE POINT OF NO RETURN... BUT SINCE SAVING THE ENTIRE POPULATION IS IMPOSSIBLE, HE'S DECIDED THAT ONLY CERTAIN CHOSEN ONES WILL GET A "TICKET TO TOMORROW."
HE'S SEEN THIS COMING FOR YEARS NOW.
WE ALREADY CONTROL ALL THE COMPANIES AND MEDIA WHO AGREE WITH OUR BOSS.
THE PEOPLE WHO ASSUME THEY ARE THE CHOSEN ONES HAVE EASILY COME OVER TO OUR SIDE.
THEY'RE HAPPY TO FOLLOW OUR BOSS'S ORDERS. AND MANY CIVILIANS HAVE ACCEPTED OUR CONTROL WITHOUT HAVING ANY IDEA THAT THEY'RE BEING CONTROLLED.
OUR OPERATION IS IN ITS **FINAL PHASE.**
THAT'S WHY WE'RE NO LONGER DOING THINGS BEHIND YOUR BACK.
EVEN THOUGH, AFTER ALL THIS TIME, YOU'VE FINALLY NOTICED AND ARE MAKING A HUGE FUSS ABOUT IT...
...WE'RE STILL GOING TO SUCCEED IN CREATING A WORLD **JUST FOR THE CHOSEN FEW.**

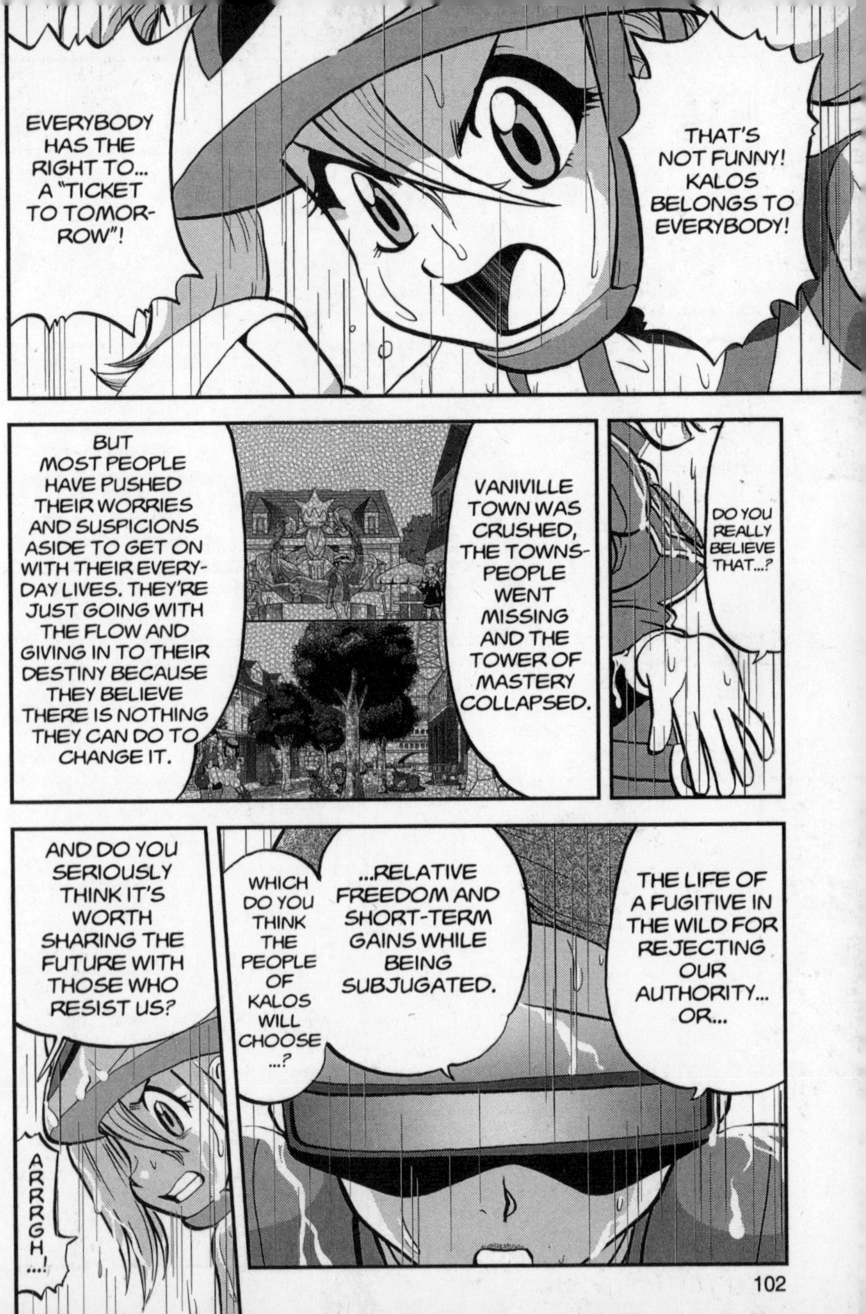
THAT'S NOT FUNNY! KALOS BELONGS TO EVERYBODY!
EVERYBODY HAS THE RIGHT TO... A "TICKET TO TOMORROW"!
DO YOU REALLY BELIEVE THAT...?
VANIVILLE TOWN WAS CRUSHED, THE TOWNSPEOPLE WENT MISSING AND THE TOWER OF MASTERY COLLAPSED.
BUT MOST PEOPLE HAVE PUSHED THEIR WORRIES AND SUSPICIONS ASIDE TO GET ON WITH THEIR EVERYDAY LIVES. THEY'RE JUST GOING WITH THE FLOW AND GIVING IN TO THEIR DESTINY BECAUSE THEY BELIEVE THERE IS NOTHING THEY CAN DO TO CHANGE IT.
THE LIFE OF A FUGITIVE IN THE WILD FOR REJECTING OUR AUTHORITY... OR...
...RELATIVE FREEDOM AND SHORT-TERM GAINS WHILE BEING SUBJUGATED.
WHICH DO YOU THINK THE PEOPLE OF KALOS WILL CHOOSE...?
AND DO YOU SERIOUSLY THINK IT'S WORTH SHARING THE FUTURE WITH THOSE WHO RESIST US?
ARRRGH...!

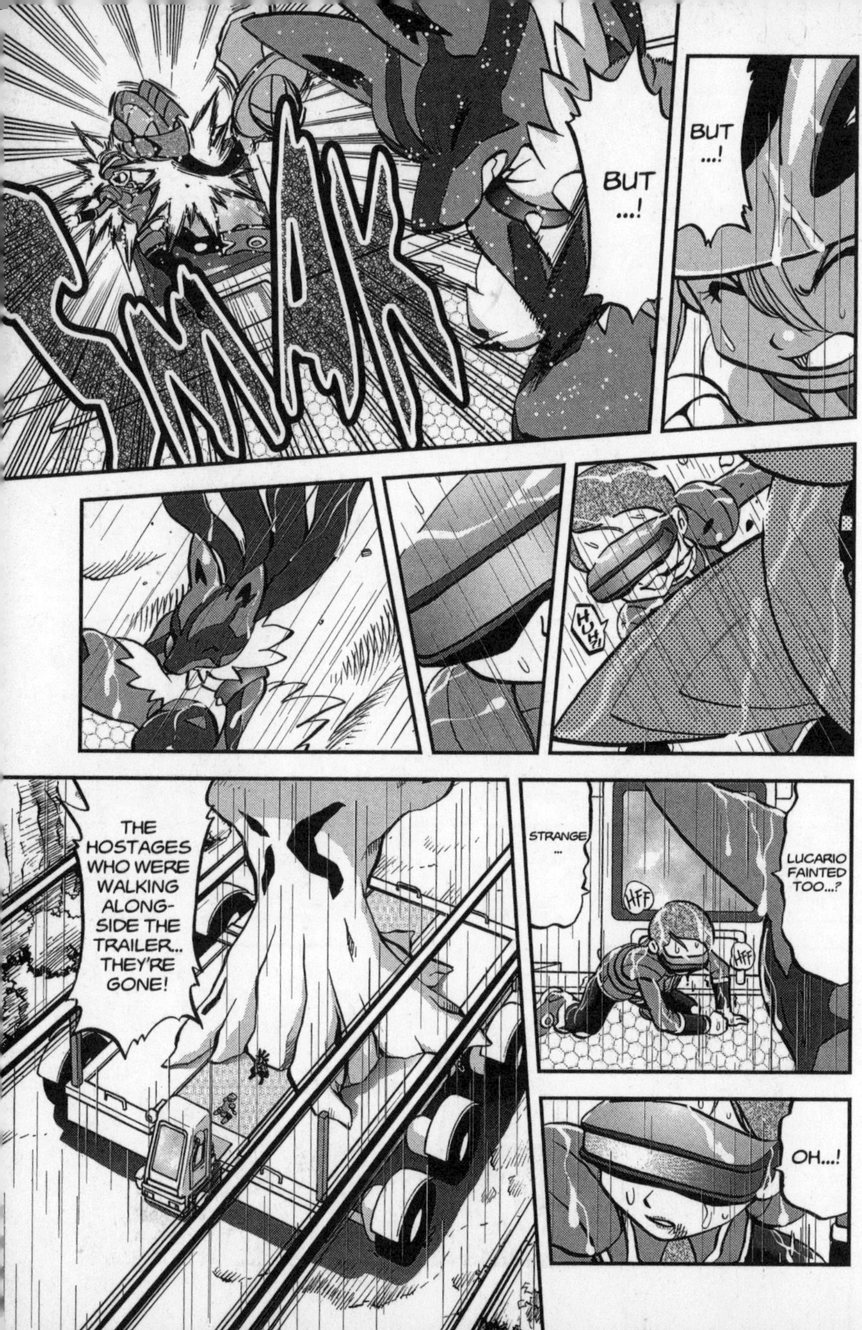
BUT ...!
BUT ...!
HUH!?
LUCARIO FAINTED TOO...?
STRANGE ...
HFF
HFF
OH...!
THE HOSTAGES WHO WERE WALKING ALONG-SIDE THE TRAILER.. THEY'RE GONE!

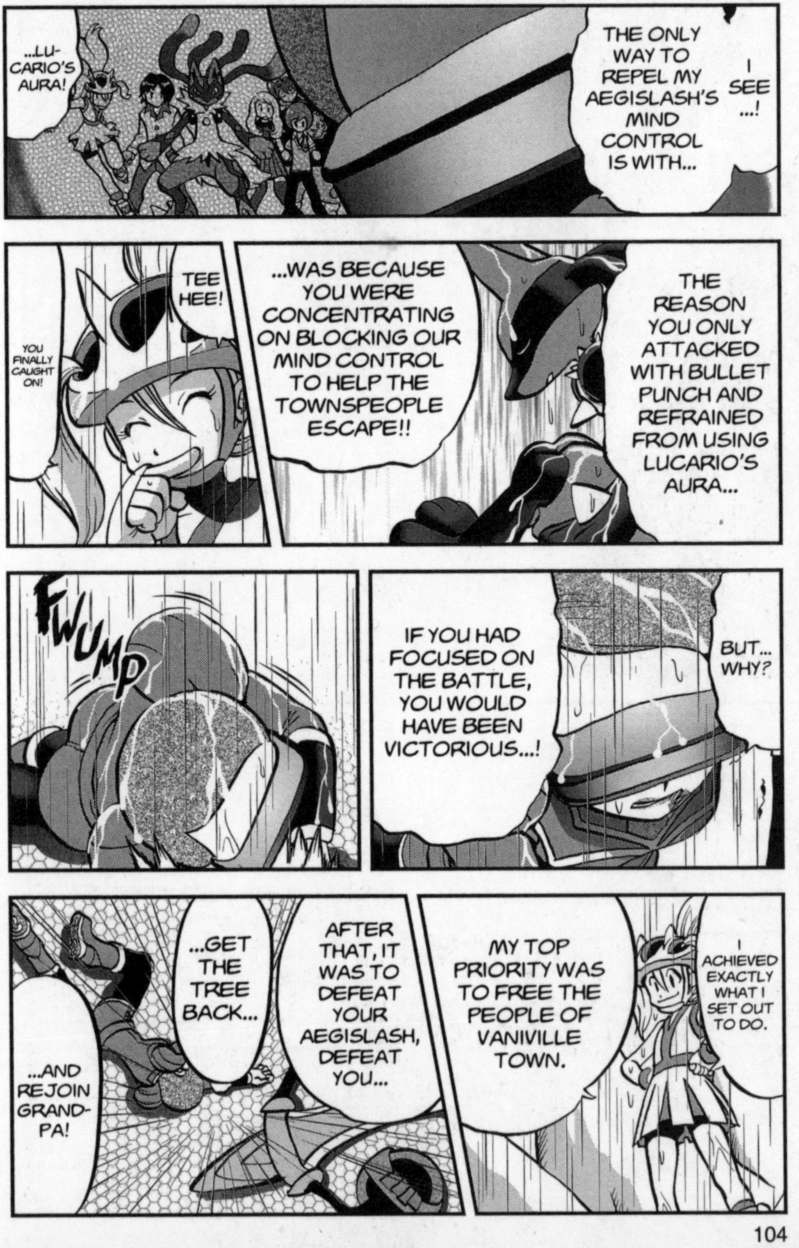
I SEE ...!
THE ONLY WAY TO REPEL MY AEGISLASH'S MIND CONTROL IS WITH...
...LUCARIO'S AURA!
THE REASON YOU ONLY ATTACKED WITH BULLET PUNCH AND REFRAINED FROM USING LUCARIO'S AURA...
...WAS BECAUSE YOU WERE CONCENTRATING ON BLOCKING OUR MIND CONTROL TO HELP THE TOWNSPEOPLE ESCAPE!!
TEE HEE!
YOU FINALLY CAUGHT ON!
BUT... WHY?
IF YOU HAD FOCUSED ON THE BATTLE, YOU WOULD HAVE BEEN VICTORIOUS...!
FWUMP
I ACHIEVED EXACTLY WHAT I SET OUT TO DO.
MY TOP PRIORITY WAS TO FREE THE PEOPLE OF VANIVILLE TOWN.
AFTER THAT, IT WAS TO DEFEAT YOUR AEGISLASH, DEFEAT YOU...
...GET THE TREE BACK...
...AND REJOIN GRAND-PA!

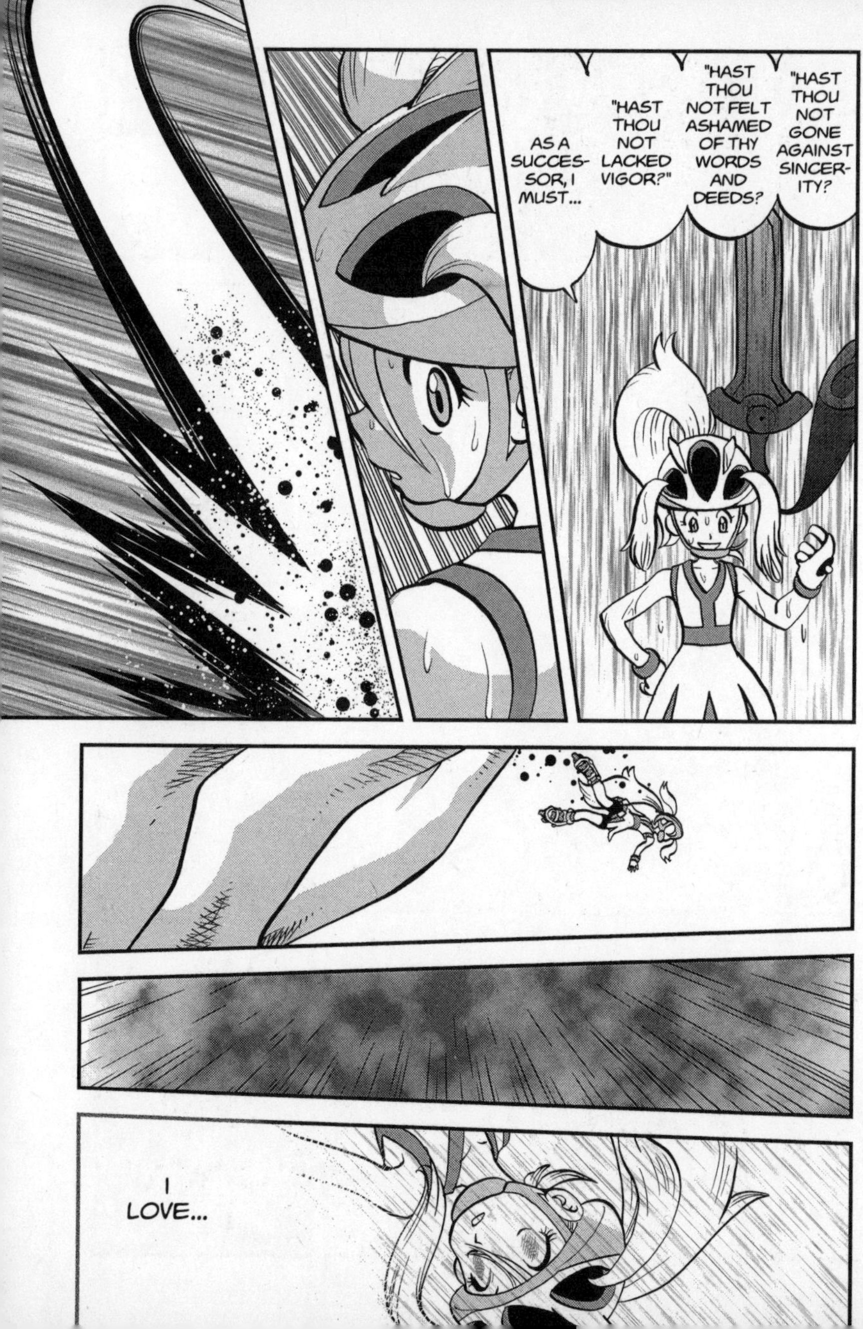
"HAST THOU NOT GONE AGAINST SINCERITY?
"HAST THOU NOT FELT ASHAMED OF THY WORDS AND DEEDS?
"HAST THOU NOT LACKED VIGOR?"
AS A SUCCESSOR, I MUST...
I LOVE...

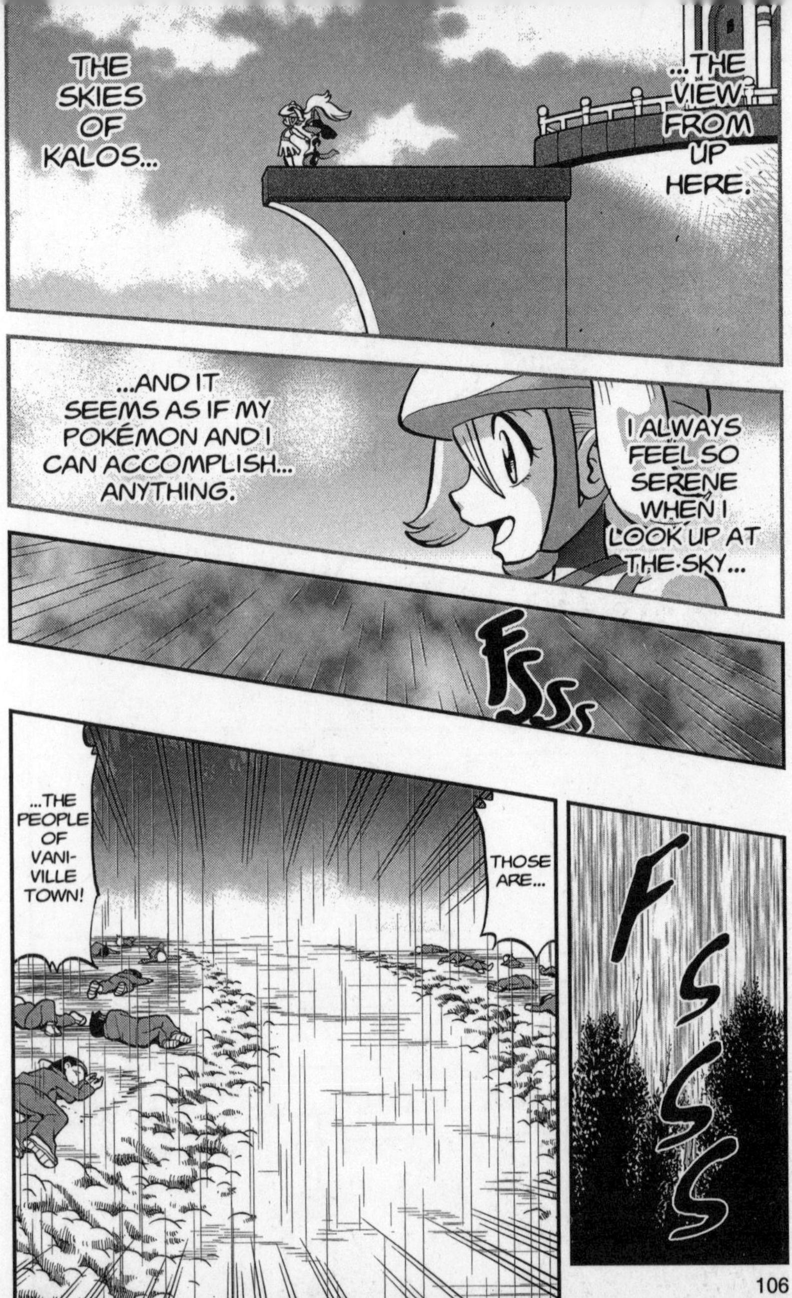
...THE VIEW FROM UP HERE.
THE SKIES OF KALOS...
I ALWAYS FEEL SO SERENE WHEN I LOOK UP AT THE SKY...
...AND IT SEEMS AS IF MY POKÉMON AND I CAN ACCOMPLISH... ANYTHING.
FSSS
FSSS
THOSE ARE...
...THE PEOPLE OF VANI-VILLE TOWN!

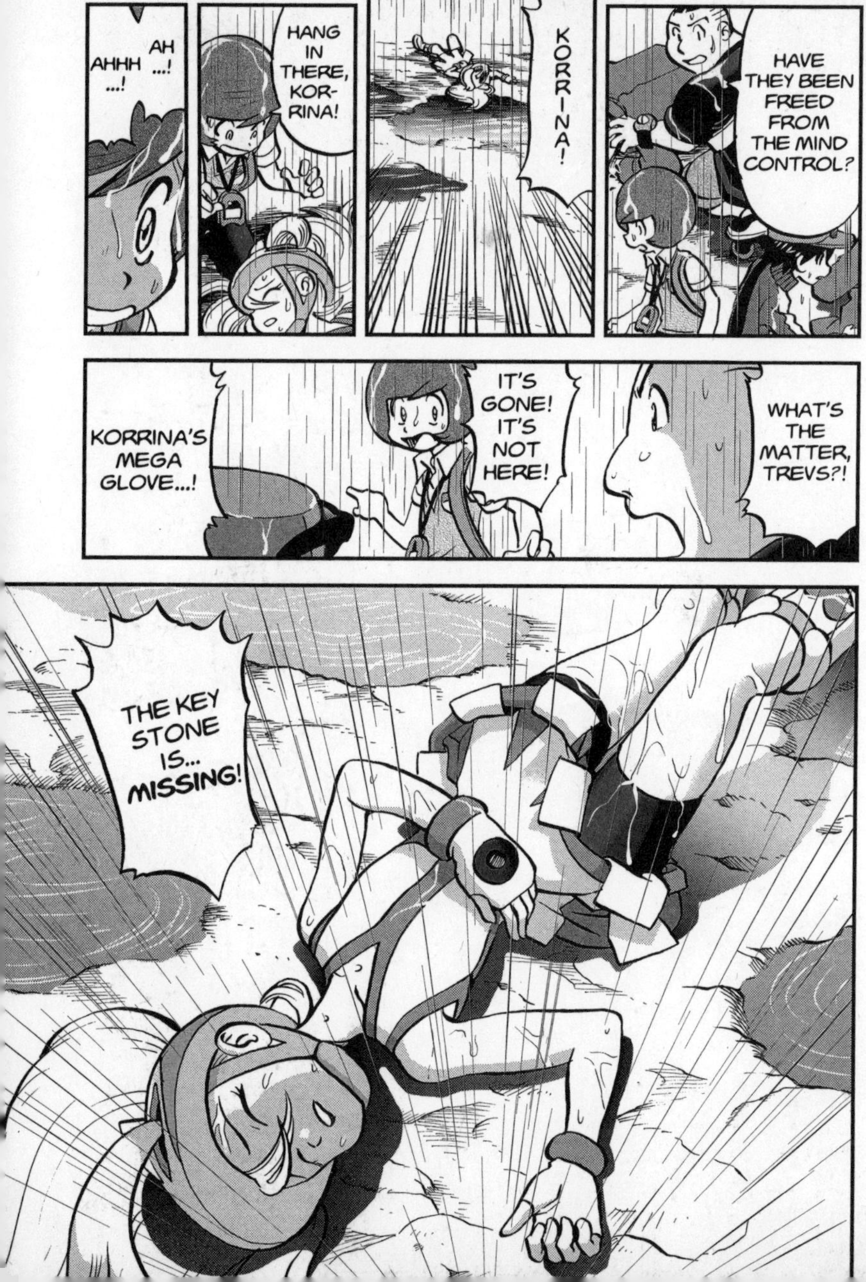
HAVE THEY BEEN FREED FROM THE MIND CONTROL?
KORRINA!
HANG IN THERE, KORRINA!
AH ...!
AHHH ...!
WHAT'S THE MATTER, TREVS?!
IT'S GONE! IT'S NOT HERE!
KORRINA'S MEGA GLOVE...!
THE KEY STONE IS... **MISSING!**

Current Location

Route 8
Muraille Coast

This is a road of great contrasts, from the harsh rock of the cliffs to the soft sands of the beach.

No.

Date

◆ CURRENT DATA ◆

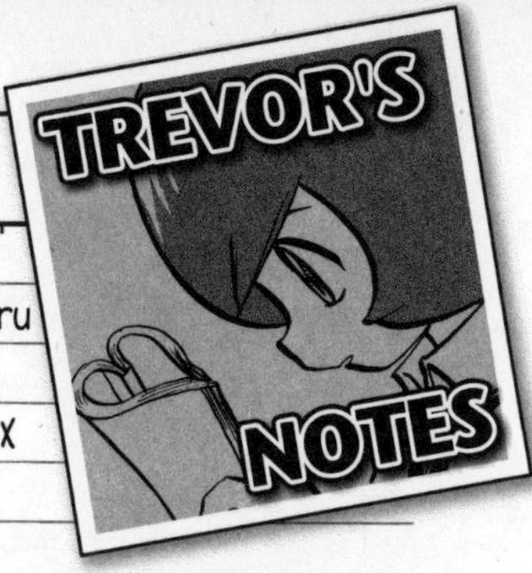
TREVOR'S
NOTES

- We met Mr. Gurkinn, known as the "Guru of Mega Evolution." He is Korrina's grandfather and the man who gave X the Mega Ring.

- X talked about how it felt the first time he wore the Mega Ring... "...my strength and my emotions...were all getting concentrated into the Ring—or the Key Stone embedded in the center of the Ring, to be exact. It was like I had another brain or heart...on my left arm."

- According to Mr. Gurkinn, that's the right way for a Mega Evolution successor to feel. But not everyone gets that feeling.

- Mega Evolution rule: Even if you have several Pokémon who can Mega Evolve, you can only Mega Evolve one of them at a time.

- Some Pokémon Abilities change after they Mega Evolve. For example, X's Pokémon...

  Kangaskhan (Scrappy) → Mega Kangaskhan (Parental Bond)

  Manectric (Lightning Rod) → Mega Manectric (Intimidate)

  Gengar (Levitate) → Mega Gengar (Shadow Tag)

- Also, some Pokémon types change after Mega Evolution, some Pokémon types **and** Abilities change, and some Pokémon types and Abilities **do not** change. And so on...!

Pokémon X • Y
Volume 6
Perfect Square Edition

Story by HIDENORI KUSAKA
Art by SATOSHI YAMAMOTO

©2016 Pokémon.
©1995-2016 Nintendo/Creatures Inc./GAME FREAK inc.
TM, ®, and character names are trademarks of Nintendo.
POCKET MONSTERS SPECIAL X•Y Vol. 3
by Hidenori KUSAKA, Satoshi YAMAMOTO
© 2014 Hidenori KUSAKA, Satoshi YAMAMOTO
All rights reserved.
Original Japanese edition published by SHOGAKUKAN.
English translation rights in the United States of America, Canada, the United
Kingdom, Ireland, Australia and New Zealand arranged with SHOGAKUKAN.

English Adaptation—Bryant Turnage
Translation—Tetsuichiro Miyaki
Touch-up & Lettering—Annaliese Christman
Design—Shawn Carrico
Editor—Annette Roman

Printed in the U.S.A.

Published by
VIZ Media, LLC
P.O. Box 77010
San Francisco, CA 94107

10 9 8 7 6 5 4 3 2 1
First printing, March 2016

www.perfectsquare.com

www.viz.com

PARENTAL ADVISORY
POKÉMON ADVENTURES
is rated A and is suitable
for readers of all ages.
ratings.viz.com

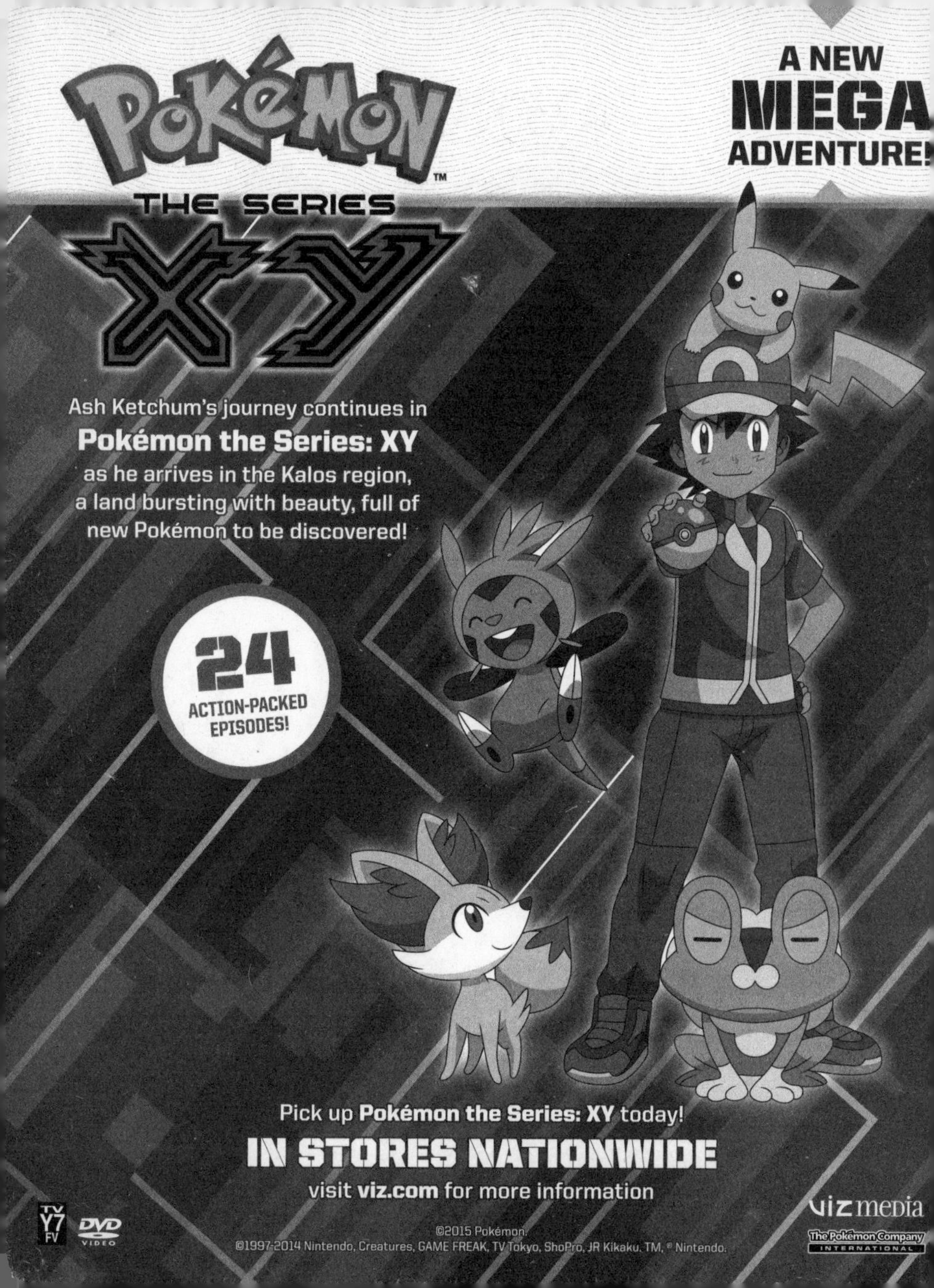
Pokémon™
THE SERIES
XY
A NEW
MEGA
ADVENTURE!
Ash Ketchum's journey continues in
Pokémon the Series: XY
as he arrives in the Kalos region, a land bursting with beauty, full of new Pokémon to be discovered!
24
ACTION-PACKED EPISODES!
Pick up Pokémon the Series: XY today!
IN STORES NATIONWIDE
visit viz.com for more information
TV Y7 FV
DVD VIDEO
©2015 Pokémon.
©1997-2014 Nintendo, Creatures, GAME FREAK, TV Tokyo, ShoPro, JR Kikaku. TM, ® Nintendo.
viz media
The Pokémon Company INTERNATIONAL

<<< READ THIS WAY!

THIS IS THE END OF THIS GRAPHIC NOVEL!

To properly enjoy this VIZ
Media gra~~~
turn it aro~~~
reading fr~~~

This book~~~
in the orig~~~
format in order to preserve
the orientatio~~~
artwork. Have~~~

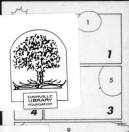

Follow the action this way.